To Tempt the Devil

Also in C. J. Archer's Lord Hawkesbury Series

Her Secret Desire

Scandal's Mistress

To Tempt the Devil

A NOVEL OF LORD HAWKESBURY'S PLAYERS

C. J. ARCHER

Montlake
Romance

Published by Montlake Romance
P.O. Box 400818
Las Vegas, NV 89140

ISBN-13: 9781612187150
ISBN-10: 1612187153

To Joe, Samantha, and Declan.

With all my love and gratitude.

CHAPTER I

London: 1598

"I'm going to prison," James said.

Rafe Fletcher thought few things could shock him anymore, but it took him a moment to gather his wits. After a seven-year absence, they were not the words of welcome he expected upon his return to the family home.

"Why?" he asked.

James groaned and buried his head in his hands, but didn't offer any more information. Rafe stretched out his legs and regarded his brother sitting across from him in the small parlor. James was seven years younger, but it might as well have been more. He seemed so childlike with his thin frame and innocent eyes, it was difficult to imagine him doing anything wrong. Assuming he hadn't broken any laws, there was only one reason why he could end up in jail.

"You're in debt, aren't you?"

James looked up. "How did you know?"

Rafe waved a hand, taking in the bare parlor. It was like an empty tomb with only two chairs and one small table. There was nothing in the way of comforts, not even a fire despite the chilly autumn air. It was vastly different from how their mother had kept it. Her embroidered cushions had adorned at least four chairs, a tapestry had hung on one wall, and the rushes had always been clean. James kept no rushes on his floor.

"I don't suppose you have any money saved to loan me?" James fixed Rafe with a wild-eyed stare. "I would pay you back as soon as possible."

"Not yet. I'm sorry." Rafe wished he'd saved the money from his missions and not given it all away in Cambridge.

But then he remembered why he'd given it away, and to whom, and he didn't regret it at all.

"I'll be starting a new job in a week and whatever I earn will go to your creditors, as long as I can stay here."

"Of course!" Relief flooded James's face. "Thank you. I'm sorry to do this to you. I didn't want to ask you for money…"

"Why not? We're family."

"Barely."

Rafe sucked in air through his teeth. He deserved that. They were half brothers, their mothers the same but their fathers different, and Rafe had been absent for a long time. He should have come home earlier, as soon as he heard about old Pritchard's death a year ago. James had been alone since then, struggling to survive on an apprentice's wage, and before that he'd had only the heavy-fisted Pritchard for company for six years. Without their mother to soothe the old man's tempers, and without Rafe to protect him, James must have lived on a knife's edge. It was no wonder he sometimes hated Rafe for escaping.

"What happened to your job?" Rafe asked. "Your last letter said nothing of problems with your apprenticeship."

James sighed again. "I lost it. Cuxcomb went into debt himself and had to close the shop. Tailoring apprenticeships are hard to come by. Times are difficult. And some consider me unlucky, having lost both my previous masters one way or another."

Rafe shook his head. Some people were ignorant, superstitious fools. Losing the apprenticeships wasn't James's fault. His father's death, while welcomed by almost everyone who knew him, meant James had needed to find another master, and Cuxcomb's debts couldn't be blamed on him.

"I put off my creditors for a while," James said. "But then they all called in the debts at the same time and I couldn't pay. I've been ordered to go to the Marshalsea prison until the debts are dissolved."

"It'll only be for a week."

"That'll feel like forever."

"I know," Rafe said heavily.

James rubbed his hands through his overlong hair, messing it up. "Is your new job a certainty?"

Rafe hesitated. "Almost."

"Almost?" James winced. "And how will you pay my debts off immediately upon starting? Your new master would have to be very generous to pay you in advance."

"I can only ask. And if Lord Liddicoat doesn't want to advance me some of my wages, then perhaps your creditors will agree to me paying off your debts in installments if I can prove I have secure employment. I won't let you starve."

"It's not the starving I'm worried about, it's the other prisoners. And the filth, the lice, and sickness. Have you ever been to a prison, Rafe? Have you seen the kind of base people housed in them?"

"They're not all base," he said. James didn't seem to notice his offended tone, which was just as well. Rafe didn't want his brother asking why he'd been in jail, because that would lead to questions about his activities over the last seven years. He'd told James he was a mercenary, and while that had been true at first, in more recent times he'd taken on a new role with a new master. Innocents like his brother didn't need to know what that employment entailed, especially now it had ended. Returning to London was the start of a new phase of his life, a fresh beginning. The past was better left buried.

Besides, he'd only been in jail twice and he'd escaped both times after a short stint. It hardly counted.

But his brother had a point. If the prison's conditions didn't get to him, the other prisoners might.

"Do you have any friends you could ask for a loan?" Rafe asked.

"One or two," James mumbled. "Well, just one."

"That's better than none. Who?"

"John Croft."

"The neighbor?" Rafe remembered the Crofts. They were good, respectable people, but Rafe had not had much to do with them in years past, distracted as he was with his own problems. "They have three daughters, don't they? The eldest married a lord a year or two before I left."

"Lord Warhurst. Jane, the youngest, is living up in North-umberland with them in the hopes of bettering herself. Lizzy still lives at home." His voice softened when he said her name and there was a ghost of a smile on his lips.

So Lizzy Croft meant more to James than merely being his neighbor. "I hardly remember her. A shy little thing, wasn't she? I don't think she spoke two words to me her entire life."

"She's changed. She's still a sweet-natured girl. Very good and kind. You'll adore her, Rafe. Everyone does."

Such a glowing recommendation. James clearly cared for the girl. "You're going to marry her, then."

"One day. There's an understanding between us. I can't afford to marry her until my apprenticeship finishes and that's some years off. If ever," he added gloomily.

"Then ask her father for a loan to pay your debts."

"I can't."

"Why not?"

"He's an old man now and doesn't work. He's still the tiring house manager for Lord Hawkesbury's Players, but in name only. Lizzy does all the work as his assistant. Her wages support both her parents."

"But surely the eldest daughter sends them money."

James shrugged. "I don't think Lord and Lady Warhurst have much either, what with their own family and their miners to take care of. The Crofts live as I do. If they have money, there is little to show for it."

Rafe struck Croft off his list, but not his daughter. "Why not see if there is work for you at the players' tired house?"

"Tiring house."

"If you can show you're working, your creditors might give you longer to pay them back."

"Perhaps."

"Perhaps? What do you have against the idea?"

James sighed. "I don't want to tell Lizzy what's happened. She might...think less of me as a man. I couldn't face her pity."

Bloody hell. Rafe hadn't expected his brother's pride to be larger than his fear of prison. "If she loves you, she wouldn't think less of you for a situation that isn't your fault." Love. What did Rafe know about love? It wasn't a sentiment men like him had the luxury of experiencing.

"Her company is prosperous but I wouldn't earn much as her assistant."

"It would be more than what you're earning now."

James's shoulders slumped and he lowered his head. "True."

"If you want to avoid the Marshalsea, brother, you need to ask her. And believe me, you want to avoid the Marshalsea."

He straightened. "You're right, I will, just as soon as she gets home from the playhouse."

"Glad to see you've still got some sense in that head of yours."

James gave him a withering glare. Rafe rose and clapped him on the shoulder. "I'm hungry. Got anything in your pantry?"

"There's bread, but that's it I'm afraid."

Rafe left him to inspect the provisions. He got as far as the kitchen when someone knocked loudly on the front door.

"Lizzy!" he heard James say upon opening it. Rafe smiled. He was curious to meet the middle Croft girl again after all this time. For the life of him, he couldn't recall what she looked like. It was shameful, really. He'd lived next to the Crofts for twenty-two years before leaving London, but Lizzy was faceless in his memory. He'd not even recalled her name until James mentioned it. Granted she would have been young when he left and he'd been an angry youth with burdens to bear, yet he felt some regret all the same now that she was to be his sister-in-law.

But first he'd leave the lovers alone for a few moments. It would give James a chance to ask her for work, then he'd join them to discuss what to do next.

At least, that was his plan. He abandoned it when Lizzy's voice rose above James's. "You *have* to marry me!" she cried. "And soon."

Rafe frowned when James didn't respond immediately. Then he sat down on the stool near the hearth. He wasn't going in there. His brother needed to sort this out on his own.

"James?" Lizzy prompted when he didn't answer her. "Did you hear me?"

"I...I..." James stared at her through dull, shadowed eyes that were usually a vibrant blue. "You look tired," was all he said.

This was his response? "I've been rushing about," she said, touching her hair and wishing she'd taken time to repin it beneath her hat before she left the Rose's tiring house. She wasn't sure how proposals of marriage should be given, but perhaps she would have received a better reaction if she'd taken extra care of her appearance.

James had not seemed to care upon seeing her in disarray before, except for the one time a chamber pot had been emptied from a third-floor window onto her head. He'd laughed. She'd been humiliated and stormed home in tears. His laughter had rung in her ears for hours afterward, until he redeemed himself by giving her a square of crisp white lawn to make herself a new pair of cuffs. They'd been thirteen, and he'd probably stolen the fabric from his father's shop, but she didn't care. She was just so happy to not be mad at her closest friend anymore.

She stopped fidgeting with her hair and said, "I'm aware women do not usually do the proposing, but time is running out. I'm desperate, James." She pushed past him and stood in the parlor, waiting for his sudden grin to light up the room and lift her heart.

It did not.

He glanced past her to the door leading to the kitchen area. She turned. There was no one there. Of course there wouldn't be. James lived alone.

"Lizzy, I'm glad you're here. I wanted to speak to you about something."

"One thing at a time. First we discuss marriage. Well? What say you?"

"I say why the sudden urgency?"

"Sudden? There has been an understanding between us for *years*."

"Yes, but you've never pounded on my door until it almost shattered, then demanded I marry you. So what has changed?" A lock of brown hair tumbled over one eye, making him look younger than his twenty-two years. A flash of dimples would have completed the effect of youth, but he wasn't smiling.

Lizzy offered up a weak one in the hope he would return it but he merely stared at her from behind the curtain of hair and waited. She drew a deep breath. "Very well. Let me explain. I could lose my position with Lord Hawkesbury's Players. We all could. The new Master of Revels, Walter Gripp, is going to shut us down. He's already banned one play and has promised to continue until we are ruined. And if the troupe is ruined, what will I do? Who will employ me at such good wages?

What will all my friends do? There isn't enough work for them here in London." She was rambling but couldn't stop herself. She felt hopeless, and Lizzy had not felt hopeless in a long time. Not since she'd grown out of her crippling shyness. "I can do nothing for them, but I can do something for myself. Marry you."

"I...ah..." He turned away and lowered his head. A few deep breaths later and he looked at her once more. "Lizzy, you're in a state." He took her by the elbow and steered her farther into the parlor. "Sit." He indicated the chair nearest the fireplace, the best position in the house reserved for favored guests. She felt honored, even though the fire wasn't lit. Perhaps his hesitation was because *he* wanted to do the proposing. She sat with her hands in her lap in case he wanted to get down on his knees and clasp them.

He didn't clasp them or get down on his knees. He sat too, not in the nearest chair, but on another far away. Indeed, he didn't even look her in the eyes at all, but looked again to the door that led to the kitchen, buttery, and pantry, then settled his gaze on the small ruff at her throat.

"Now, explain it again," he said. "Calmly."

She bit back the tears pricking her eyes. If she allowed herself to give into them, she could not be the calm woman he wanted. It wasn't James's fault that he wasn't reacting with the appropriate amount of sympathy. He didn't understand the seriousness of the situation. Very well, she must make him understand.

"Walter Gripp is the new Master of Revels and he hates Roger Style. Not a mild, passing hatred, but a vicious loathing that's grown deeper over the years."

James shrugged. "I can see how someone would dislike a pompous prig like Style, but *hate* is a rather strong word."

Lizzy spread her fingers in her lap and tried again. "Style stole Gripp's wife."

"*Roger* Style? Not his brother?"

She nodded. "Apparently they were secretly…you know… while they were both married. When Style's first wife died, Mistress Gripp left her husband to live with Roger."

"How did she get a divorce?"

"They didn't divorce." Despite old King Henry's precedent, one had to have a great deal of money and influence to obtain a divorce. "She lived with Roger for a few months, then left him too. Left London altogether apparently. He wed the current Mistress Style a year or so later. But Walter Gripp never forgave him. As far as he's concerned, his wife was a good woman until Roger corrupted her. He claims Roger seduced her with his *wicked theatre ways* as he calls it."

If it wasn't so awful, she'd laugh. It was impossible to think of Roger as a seducer, let alone the troupe being wicked. They were all respectable men from good families. Most of them anyway.

"Walter Gripp adored his wife by all accounts," she said. "He's been trying to hurt Roger ever since. He's threatened him with lawsuits and even placed his friends in our audiences from time to time to throw rotten fruit and jeer. Once he stormed in and announced he would ruin Roger by destroying the company. He was so angry he was foaming at the mouth and shouting like a madman. It was horrible."

"I'm sure it was. But if Gripp hates Style so, why doesn't he just challenge him to a duel?"

"Roger's too cowardly to agree to one."

"Run him through with his rapier in a dark laneway then."

"And be hanged for it? He's no fool. This way Gripp can ruin the troupe quite legally. Now that he's the Master of Revels, he *can* ruin us too." All new plays had to be read and passed by the Master of Revels before they could be performed. If he deemed a play too offensive or seditious, he could shut a production down. Doing that to every play submitted from Lord

Hawkesbury's Players would cause the company to lose money like a cracked barrel loses wine. They couldn't keep rerunning old plays—the London theatre crowd demands fresh stories and would quickly grow weary of repeats. "It's awful. I'm going to lose my job and the only solution I can come up with is to wed you."

"Thank you," he said, wryly.

"Oh, James, I'm sorry, that came out wrong. I do *want* to marry you."

"Lizzy..." He rubbed his eyes and blew out a breath. "Getting married isn't a good idea. Not now."

"Are you worried your wages can't support all of us?"

"Yes. Yes, of course. That's it." He looked relieved. "So you see the need to wait?"

"No, I don't. I have a solution. You can come and live with us and let this house to boarders. Or if you prefer, we could live here and let out Papa's house." It was only next door. Her parents could move easily enough, frail as they were. "The extra income will stretch if we live frugally until your apprenticeship is complete."

"You really have thought of everything." He sounded as if his doom was imminent.

"I'm sorry," she muttered. "Forget I said anything." She dropped her head into her hands and tried to suppress the sense of hopelessness welling within her.

"Now listen to me." He knelt in front of her and patted her arm. "Your company's plays are tame. With Lady Blakewell writing most of them, she's much too smart to put in even a veiled reference to dried-up old virgin queens who failed to put their country first and get an heir."

Lizzy glanced around out of habit although there was no one to overhear them. The royal succession was a sensitive issue. Any plays alluding to it never found an audience beyond the Master of Revels.

"It doesn't matter what our plays allude to, subtly or otherwise. If Gripp wants to hurt Roger, he will."

"Can't Style ask the Lord Chamberlain to intervene?"

She snorted softly. "Don't be a fool."

He sighed again. "I suppose not."

The Master of Revels came under the jurisdiction of the Lord Chamberlain's office, but the Lord Chamberlain was patron of a rival troupe. He had every reason to keep out of the matter.

"What about Lord Hawkesbury himself?" James asked.

"He won't want to interfere either." Lord Hawkesbury was rarely drawn into politics, even the politics of the theatre, unless the queen commanded it. If the troupe of players who bore his name ceased to exist, he would simply become patron of another.

Lizzy groaned. It was all so awful, so uncertain and terrifying! She'd grown up with Lord Hawkesbury's Players. The tiring house was as much her home as the house she lived in with her parents. She knew every costume in the storage room, every wig, every pin. She'd made friends with many actors and stagehands including some who'd become famous. She felt comfortable with them, not tongue-tied and awkward the way she often did around people. The players spoke the same around her as they did around each other. And that was how she liked it.

Yet it could all be destroyed by Gripp.

Her friends would scatter and there would be no wage to support herself and her aged parents. Without it, they would be destitute or have to survive on the charity of her sister's husband all the way up in Northumberland. So far from London and the people she loved. She would not burden Alice and Leo unless absolutely necessary. They had enough financial difficulty with a growing family and mines still in their infancy and not yet fully profitable.

No, Lizzy *had* to marry James to secure her future and remain in the city. There was no one else and besides, everybody knew they would one day wed. It was inevitable, so why not go through with it now to solve her problems?

James had sold his father's tailoring workshop after the old man's death, but creditors had pounced on the money from the sale, leaving nothing. He had found another master tailor to oversee the last years of his apprenticeship, but apprentices earned little since they usually boarded free of charge with their masters. James had insisted on remaining in his family home, but his wage had not been raised accordingly.

"I think you're overreacting," he said. "Gripp is hardly going to abuse his position because of an old feud."

She blinked at him. "Overreacting? James!" How could he say such a thing to her? "When have you ever known me to overreact?"

His gaze shifted sideways. "Well, there was that one time a chamber pot was accidentally emptied on your head."

"I was a child!"

He shushed her and glanced past her to the kitchen again. He stood and took both her hands in his. It had been what she'd wanted him to do earlier. So why did it turn her blood cold now? "You have such a temper," he said with half a smile. "But you only show it to me."

"That's because you're my best friend—the only person with whom I can truly be myself." Except that wasn't entirely true. She was herself around most of the troupe, she just found no need to get angry with them. None of them would ever accuse her of overreacting. Their very definition of it was probably vastly different from James's.

He bent and kissed her forehead. "You're right and I'm sorry. You rarely overreact." He sounded very serious all of a sudden. "So Gripp truly presents a problem?"

"If he decides to punish Roger, then the entire company will suffer. Including me."

He squeezed her hands and massaged the knuckles with his thumb. It was a soothing motion but there was nothing reassuring in his grave expression. He'd gone quite gray in the face. "You'll find work as a seamstress elsewhere. Your stitching is very fine."

"I wouldn't earn a tenth of what I earn now." The only way a seamstress could make a good income was to open her own shop and Lizzy didn't have enough money to do that, nor did she want to be a shopkeeper. The thought of conversing regularly with strangers made her gut churn.

No, the only way she could earn enough to support her parents and herself was to stay with one of the good theatre troupes and neither of the other two main London ones needed new tiring house assistants.

"I'll be without work soon," she said.

"When you say soon…how long do you think? Would you need an assistant in the meantime?"

"Of course not. Roger Style hasn't hired an assistant for my father before, why would he now when everything is so uncertain?"

"Yes. I see. I thought I'd ask anyway," he muttered, bowing his head again.

"Why? Do you need work?"

"A little extra would be nice."

No wonder he hadn't agreed to her marriage proposal. His lack of money must be playing on his mind. Perhaps he was poorer than he let on. She'd noticed that his fire was rarely lit of late, despite the cooler weather, and that the house seemed barer, yet she hadn't put the pieces together. Now that she looked, she could see his jerkin had more patches than original fabric, although it was difficult to pick them out, so good was the work. Lizzy felt terrible. She should have seen the signs earlier. Oh, James. Why hadn't he said something?

"You believe Gripp will force the company's closure?" he asked.

"Walter Gripp is a vindictive man and he has the power to do it. There is nothing and no one standing in his way."

"Want me to kill him for you?" The voice came from behind her. It was deep and low, quiet yet commanding. The sort of voice that belonged to men in control, respected men who didn't need to shout to get attention.

She recognized it although she hadn't heard it in many years. She felt cold through to her bones even as a warm flush crept up her neck.

"He's jesting," James said.

Lizzy didn't turn around but she could feel Rafe's presence the way an anvil feels a hammer's blow.

"Lizzy, you remember my brother," James went on. "Rafe. Rafe Fletcher," he added, perhaps to remind her that the brothers had different fathers. He'd left London suddenly on that terrible day when their mother died. Lizzy had no idea where he'd gone or what he'd been doing, because she'd never asked James and he'd never offered the information. Indeed, he rarely mentioned his brother at all and never discussed the incident that had led to his departure. But Lizzy hadn't forgotten him. Rafe Fletcher was not the sort of man a girl, or indeed anyone, could forget.

And now he was back.

She forced herself to turn, but she couldn't bring herself to look up at Rafe's face. She stared at his boots instead. They were good boots. Sturdy with scuff marks on the toes and... was that a bloodstain?

She suppressed a gasp but not a shiver.

"Light the fire," Rafe said. "She's cold."

James hesitated, then did his brother's bidding. Lizzy clasped her hands in front of her and kept her gaze down. Her insides roiled and surely her face must be the color of burning coals. It felt hot enough. She tightened her grip on her fingers.

"I doubt you remember me," Rafe said above her. Far, far above her. "You were still a child when I left."

Seven years ago, she'd been fourteen, hardly a child. She wished she could tell him that, but she just nodded instead. She'd tried so hard to leave the shy, speechless girl behind, yet here she was again with her flushed cheeks and twisted tongue. So much for all the practice she'd put in over the years. While the actors worked on remembering their lines, she'd studied them: the way they spoke to one another, what they said, when they laughed or teased or offered a sympathetic frown. She'd forced herself to imitate them when she'd rather have sat in the corner and hidden behind her sewing. Eventually she'd felt confident enough to put her observations into practice. Tentatively at first, then more often and with more people. It had worked. Old acquaintances commented on how she'd emerged from her shell, and new ones were none the wiser. None suspected the amount of effort and time she'd put into remaking herself.

But Rafe Fletcher had stripped all that hard work away as if it were merely a layer of the thinnest silk. And she hadn't even looked at him yet.

"So do you?" he asked. "Want me to kill this Gripp for you?"

"Rafe," James warned. "Stop teasing her."

"Who said I was teasing?"

Out of the corner of her eye, Lizzy saw a lit taper flutter into the fireplace and James's booted feet turn at the same time.

"Pay him no mind," James said. "He's not going to kill anyone."

"It's early yet."

From his light tone, she doubted Rafe was being serious, yet the thought of him killing someone wasn't a stretch.

He'd also nearly killed his own stepfather. And Lizzy had seen the whole thing from the first spray of blood to the moment Rafe walked away.

"Lizzy, sit down," James said, taking her elbow and steering her back to the chair. It was much warmer with the fire blazing but not cozy with Rafe in the same room. Not in the least. "There's something I need to tell you now that my brother is here."

She hazarded a quick glance from one to the other. James seemed distracted, his brow lined with concern, and he kept giving his brother what she could only describe as warning glares. Rafe, however, didn't seem to notice. He met her gaze with a mixture of concern and curiosity.

She blushed harder and stared down at her lap. Rafe Fletcher was as handsome as ever. He never had been boyish like James. There were no dimples, no big brown eyes, or errant locks. Rafe was all hard lines, dark shadows, and severely cropped black hair. If it wasn't for the friendly eyes, she would have frozen in fear.

That at least was different. The last time she'd seen him he'd been wound up like a tightly coiled rope, full of tension and threatening to snap. But he hadn't snapped back then, not entirely. He'd gone into his house and come out a few moments later with a pack slung over his shoulder. He'd sported a black eye, a bloody nose, and a distant, detached expression. His stepfather, James's father, had lain half-dead in the street.

That memory was going to be hard to shake loose, no matter how friendly he seemed now. Yet she could pretend, for James's sake.

She leaned forward slightly so that she looked interested and eager to speak to him. "Where have you been, Mr. Fletcher?" she asked in a strong voice.

"Call me Rafe like you used to."

She'd never called him anything. Indeed, this was the first time she'd ever spoken to him. "Rafe," she repeated dully. Then she attempted a smile. Smiles were a good way to make the other person feel comfortable. Not that Rafe looked uncomfortable. He looked remarkably at ease lounging against the mantelpiece, arms crossed over his chest, feet crossed at the ankles. Like he was the master and he was home.

"I've been abroad," he said, curt.

"How interesting. Abroad where?"

He lifted one big shoulder. "Here and there."

"How interesting." She winced. *You've already said that, fool.* "I mean, what did you do abroad?"

"This and that."

Right. So he didn't want to tell her. Indeed, why would he want to chat with *her*? He probably just wanted her to hurry up and leave so he could talk to his brother or get on with whatever business he'd returned to London to do.

"I think I should go," she said to James.

"Not yet." He put out a hand to stay her. "I still have something important to say. I have to go away for a while."

She frowned. "Where to?"

"Out of London."

He must have taken avoidance lessons from his brother. "Why?"

He looked down at his knee, jigging up and down. He pressed his hand to it and breathed in. "I have business to conduct."

"Where?"

"A small village. In Dorset. You won't know it."

"I might."

"Doebridge," Rafe said.

James glanced at him and then at Lizzy before staring down at his jigging knee once more. "Yes, Doebridge."

"Is that far?" she asked.

"Far enough."

"Is Cuxcomb sending you?" And why was he sending his apprentice all the way to Dorset? Lizzy had once traveled through that county with her family to visit Alice and Leo. It had taken two days in good weather by wagon. With the recent rain, the roads that weren't too muddy would be full of potholes. James could be gone awhile.

"How will you get there?" she continued. "Is he making you walk?"

"It really doesn't matter," James said. His leg stopped jigging and he finally fixed his gaze on her. She chewed her lip, unnerved. James was worried. Not quite afraid, but certainly apprehensive. "The important thing is, I won't be back for some time."

"How long?"

James stood and strode to the fireplace to stand beside his brother. He was slender next to Rafe's broad-shouldered frame although they were of a height. Perhaps that explained why he looked the more approachable of the two, like someone you would stop to have a conversation with. Rafe looked liked someone you crossed the street to avoid.

"A week," James muttered. "Maybe more."

"That's not too long. When you get back we can discuss the future." She watched Rafe furtively as she said it but he showed no curiosity over her words which meant he must have heard her earlier. Wonderful. She'd had her marriage proposal rejected by her best friend as well as overheard by his brother.

"I've asked Rafe to take care of you and your parents while I'm away," James said.

He wanted his brother to take care of them? A man who'd almost murdered his own kin? Lizzy made a sound of protest except it came out a whimper.

Amusement shone in Rafe's pitch-black eyes. "So it seems you'll need to speak to me after all."

CHAPTER 2

Rafe had never seen anyone blush so much. It didn't matter what he said or how he said it, Lizzy Croft's face lit up like a bonfire. It didn't alter her prettiness, only enhanced it and made her large doe-like eyes stand out more.

Doe. Doebridge. So *that's* why he'd come up with such a ridiculous name for the village. He'd been looking at the skittish woman with eyes so big they took up half her face and couldn't get the creature out of his head. The four-legged variety, not the two-legged. When James had hesitated in answering her, Rafe had said the first thing that came to mind and slapped "bridge" on the end. That part was thanks to Cambridge, the last place he'd been.

Where everything changed.

But he had the rest of his life to forget about Cambridge and what he'd done there. Perhaps he would forget, in time.

"I don't understand." Lizzy's voice was soft, but got James's attention. Whatever his brother's intentions were with the girl, he was attentive to her at least. He obviously cared for her and her family. Why else would he ask Rafe to look after them? "Why is Cuxcomb sending you to Dorset?" she persisted.

Rafe turned a raised brow on James. *Answer that, little brother.* James had come up with the lie in haste and although it was a good one, if he didn't follow through with equally good answers, it could all unravel.

James waved his hand dismissively. "It's a business matter. Something to do with one of his suppliers. You wouldn't understand."

Rafe turned both raised brows on Lizzy. Her face was red again but he suspected it was due to anger, not embarrassment or shyness. He'd be angry too if someone spoke to him like that. He might have only spent a few minutes in her company, but Rafe could see Lizzy was a clever woman and she most likely *would* understand, if only James stopped feeding her lies. So far she had pushed James with her questions, stood up to him. She wasn't afraid of him.

Not like she was afraid of Rafe.

He uncrossed his arms and sat on a chair nearby so they were the same, unthreatening height. Her eyes widened and she pressed herself flat against her chair's back. So the doe wouldn't be won over by that trick.

He silently willed her to challenge James and ask more questions, but she didn't. She seemed too flustered. As if she had lost her place in the conversation.

Rafe sighed. If Lizzy shied away from him every time they were near each other, it was going to make James's absence seem interminable.

"So you agree to come to my brother if you need anything while I'm gone?" James asked.

"Uh..." She blinked rapidly. "I suppose so." Her gaze flicked to Rafe then away. "When do you leave?"

"Tomorrow morning."

"So soon? Do you have everything you need?"

"Yes, Lizzy, don't worry." James smiled but it looked like it took a lot of effort. Rafe remembered a boy who smiled all the time despite having a prick for a father. The sight of this thin, empty lad had taken him by surprise. Thank God Rafe had returned when he did. Not that he could do much for James, yet, but he could at least take the burden of Lizzy and her parents off his hands.

"Your good coat needed patching last time I saw it," Lizzy said, frowning. "Did you repair it? And what about boots? You'll need sturdy boots."

"Lizzy," James said. "Stop fretting, I have everything I need." He sounded edgy, irritated. Rafe could have thumped him. Did he know how lucky he was to have someone like Lizzy? Someone to care enough to ask if he had the right clothing despite the burden of her own problems?

"You'd better go," James said. "Your parents will be getting worried. When I return, we'll discuss what to do next. You'll know how long the troupe will be able to continue by then."

She rose and gave Rafe a brief nod.

He stood and nodded back. "Let me know if the Gripp fellow causes you any problems."

"Please, don't concern yourself with Walter Gripp," she said in a soft voice. "Style will take care of everything."

His offer to kill Gripp had been meant as a jest but she must have taken him seriously. Yet she didn't know what he used to do for a living right up until a few days ago. She couldn't know. He hadn't even told James.

Rafe left them alone as his brother walked her to the door. He couldn't imagine James kissing her good-bye or whispering lovers' words in her ear. Indeed, they displayed none of the symptoms of a young couple in love. There were no longing gazes, no stolen touches, no intimacy at all.

"That was some very fast thinking you did just now," Rafe said when James returned. "She seemed to believe you."

James flopped onto the chair where Lizzy had been sitting. "I hate lying to her."

"Then you shouldn't do it. A lie's not a good base to build a friendship on, let alone a marriage."

"We're not getting married yet! Anyway, what would you know?" He sighed. "Lizzy can't get me a job at the tiring house. You heard her. I'm going to prison, after all, so I had to think of something to explain my absence. You don't mind looking after her while I'm away, do you?"

"Of course not. I'll need something to do."

"Thank you. That's one less burden at least."

"Come now, we need to eat," Rafe said. "Is that cookshop still down in Thames Street, the one with the good pies?"

"I can't afford a pie. I can't even afford the crust."

"I'm buying." He held up his hand when James protested. "I have enough money."

"Save it. You'll need it to live on until your new job starts."

"If you think I don't know how to feed myself without money, then you don't know me at all."

James looked up at him from behind the ragged strands of his hair. "You'd steal?"

"If the alternative was to starve, yes." He slapped James on the shoulder. "If I'd been around these last few years, you wouldn't have gotten yourself into this mess. The least I can do is buy you a pie so you can enjoy your last meal as a free man."

James buried his face in his hands and groaned loudly. "I can't believe it's come to this. You will get me out, Rafe, won't you?"

"I will. I promise. If I can't get an advance from Lord Liddicoat, I'll ask your creditors to accept an arrangement for when I do get paid. They'd be fools not to accept it."

James's smile was grim. "Thank you, Rafe. I mean it. I'll pay you back when I can."

"I know you will." He gripped his brother's arm and hoisted him out of the chair. "Let's go get that pie before I die of hunger."

On busy Gracechurch Street, shops were shutting for the day and people hurried home or into the nearby Swan Inn. Years ago Rafe had been to a performance put on in the inn's yard by Lizzy's theatre company back before they moved to the Rose. He'd enjoyed it. Perhaps he'd go see another of their productions in the big playhouse across the river when he could afford the entry fee.

That's if Lizzy's company was still operating.

"Why does this Gripp fellow have so much power over Lizzy's theatre company?" he asked.

"It's not *her* company."

They dodged the carts and wagons rolling along Gracechurch Street, and made their way down to Thames Street where the cookshops did brisk trade with dockworkers and sailors hungry for pies and fruit tarts. Rafe followed the smell of smoke and roasting meat to his favorite cookshop, paid the keeper, and handed a capon pie to his brother. They ate outside in silence as London passed them by and the sun sank lower.

Rafe had forgotten how alive the city could be, even at dusk. It throbbed with enterprise from the docks right up to its heart at the junction of Three Needle, Cornhill, and Lombard Streets. Years ago, he'd wanted to get out. The constant hum of tens of thousands of people living almost on top of each other had felt suffocating, especially trapped as he was with his stepfather. The house had been a dead, cold heart in a city that was too busy to notice.

But now London felt alive and free, not cloying, and the house was full of memories of James and their mother and few of his stepfather.

"Thank you," James said, wiping his mouth on the back of his sleeve.

Rafe nodded. "It was a good pie. I haven't eaten one like that since I left London."

"I don't mean just the pie." James stared off down the street, his eyes unfocused. "I mean for taking care of the Crofts. They need me." His voice caught and he cleared his throat. "She needs me. Lizzy's parents aren't good company for her these days. Poor old Croft can hardly see and his wife's feeble. Perhaps I should have agreed to marry Lizzy."

"It wouldn't be right with the debts hanging over your head. You did the most honorable thing in delaying her, although you should have told her why you couldn't wed yet."

James's only reaction was to sigh.

"I'm not sure what I can do to help her," Rafe said, steering the conversation away from marriage. "How am I supposed to look after her when she won't even talk to me?"

"She will. Give her time. She just needs to get to know you. It can take her a while to feel comfortable around strangers."

"I'm not a stranger."

"You might as well be. What do you think of her, anyway?"

"I liked her." She seemed gentle and good, just as James had described her. What he hadn't described were her big eyes and tiny waist which emphasized the curves of hip and breast. Nor had he mentioned her lips. They were made for—

Whoa. She was his brother's intended. Lizzy Croft was not available to fulfill Rafe's fantasies.

Fortunately there were many other women who were. London was full of curvy young women. He watched one of them walk past, her swaying walk emphasizing those curves.

"You're lucky to be betrothed to such a girl as that," Rafe said. "I mean, such a girl as Lizzy." He glanced at James but his brother didn't seem to have noticed the woman or Rafe's distraction.

"We're not betrothed," he said absently, almost as if he'd said it so many times it just slipped out.

"But you have an understanding."

"She's my very great friend. We're meant to be together."

Rafe watched his brother closely. He was wrong. James's head might be turned to Rafe but his gaze, half-hidden beneath lowered lids, followed the woman down the street. "I see," Rafe said slowly. "Glad to hear it."

James frowned. "Oh? Why?"

"She's a nice girl, not the sort you can dangle your wick into then leave."

"Don't be such a barbarian. Of course she's not like that. Anyway, what would you know? You're nearly thirty. You should be settled by now with your own nice girl."

"I've been busy earning a living."

"Huh. Some way to earn it. A mercenary for hire, offering your services to the highest bidder, whoever that might be. No allegiance to any man or country."

Lucky he didn't know that Rafe had been working with a more elite group, a far more dangerous and less reputable band than the mercenaries he'd first joined seven years ago. There was already enough disdain in James's tone, there was no need to fuel it by telling him he was an assassin.

"I'll wager you killed people too," James said, looking at Rafe sideways.

"Never Englishmen." He tried to make it sound like a joke. It wasn't. He was, however, lying about the Englishmen. He'd killed one only a week ago.

James threw up his hands. "Then don't go around offering to do it!"

"Do you think this Gripp fellow will cause her any problems?"

"I don't know." James threw up his hands. "If she says he will then he will. But I can't think about her problems right now. I have enough of my own." He stalked off across the road, not looking left or right. The traffic had lessened and he made it safely to the other side of Thames Street but Rafe still caught him roughly by the arm and pulled him to a stop. James winced. "Leave me alone."

Rafe let go. "I'm going for a walk."

He strode down a lane so narrow, the upper levels of the buildings lining both sides jutted out so far they almost met overhead. Reach through the window on the third story of one and a man could shake the hand of someone standing at the window of the opposite house. The canopy blocked out what little daylight remained and darkness swallowed Rafe. He stilled, waited for his eyes to adjust, then walked off.

Someone followed him. Not James, the footsteps were too heavy. It could be a stranger with business in the street but he braced himself anyway and felt for the rapier hilt at his hip.

"No need for that," came a light, familiar voice behind him, "unless you want me to run you through in self-defense."

Rafe laughed and let go of the sword. "I'd like to see you try." He turned and gripped his patron's arm in a sturdy, friendly shake. No, not his patron. Not anymore.

"Ho, ho! Sounds like a challenge I'd like to take you up on. Shall we make a wager?" Lord Oxley asked. His white teeth flashed in the dark. "I win and you come back to us. You win and you still come back."

Rafe grinned, shook his head. "Not today."

"Coward."

"I'm not returning, Hughe."

Hughe St. Alban, the earl of Oxley, gripped Rafe's shoulder and urged him to walk on. Rafe had no choice but to move forward. Despite appearances, Hughe was not a man easily shaken off. He was as tall and broad in the shoulders as Rafe and every part of him was packed with muscle, but he hid his physique well beneath a bombasted and heavily brocaded silk doublet. When at court or entertaining at his estate, he was a ridiculous sight, singing drunkenly late at night or shouting poetry from the landing.

To anyone who didn't know him, he was an affected, gallant courtier. To anyone who truly did know him—and their number could be counted on one hand—he was a ruthless and highly capable killer. If Rafe wanted to get away from him, he would have a fight on his hands.

"What the devil are you doing strolling down a narrow, dark lane on your own?" Hughe asked with a click of his tongue. "Have you lost your wits already?"

"No one's after me now," Rafe said. "I'm not part of the guild anymore."

"Doesn't mean you should forget your training." His grip tightened, halting Rafe. "Doesn't mean people don't want you dead."

"No one alive knows I was part of your band except you and the others," he said, voice low. "Barker is gone. I got to him before he could sell our names."

Hughe's grip became bruising. "We need to talk. But not here." His ominous tone put Rafe on edge.

He nodded and Hughe let go. They walked side by side in silence until they reached the Old Swan waterstairs in the shadow of the bridge. The river was quiet, most of the watermen having tied up their wherries for the evening and gone home or to a tavern. On the other side of the bridge the larger ocean ships crowded together near the legal quays like giant swans keeping each other company.

Water lapped gently against the jetty's posts beneath where they sat. From there they could see in all directions and could escape into the river if necessary.

It wouldn't be necessary. As far as the world knew, they were simply a nobleman and a journeyman having a conversation in the fading light. Why Hughe had insisted on such a spot, Rafe didn't know. But Hughe was like that. Despite outward appearances, he was always alert, always careful, always thinking like the leader of a band of assassins.

But something was wrong. Perhaps more than anyone alive, Rafe knew Hughe well enough to know that. After leaving England and joining a mercenary force on the Continent, Rafe had spiraled down a destructive path of needless violence. Hughe had pulled him out of it. He retrained Rafe, taught him control, showed him friendship until Rafe learned to focus his anger on others more deserving than his stepfather. In time, he had come to appreciate life again. The irony of it wasn't lost on him—he was employed to end the lives of others.

"How's your new beginning?" Hughe asked, voice light once more.

So he wanted to play it like that—find out the lay of the land before stating his business. Rafe could wait. It was all part of the game with Hughe.

Rafe stretched out his legs. "Slightly less dangerous, but not without intrigues of its own."

"For example?"

"For example, I forgot I retired and offered to kill someone today."

Hughe chuckled. He stretched his legs alongside Rafe's and massaged his knee. "Should I be worried about your operating a rival band here in our fair city?"

"No. She turned me down."

"She? That does sound intriguing. Care to elaborate?"

The image of Lizzy looking up at him with big, scared doe eyes lodged in his mind and he couldn't shake it off. "There's nothing to tell. She's my brother's...close friend."

Hughe arched a brow. "A female friend?" he scoffed. "An impossibility."

"Perhaps. I admit I don't understand why he hasn't secured her. He has lettuce leaves for brains."

"Speaking of your brother, was that him with you outside the cookshop?"

"You've been following me that long?" Rafe shouldn't be surprised. Hughe had a way of going unseen in a crowd, even with such an excessive ruff. "That was James," he said. "He's a tailor's apprentice. Or was." He sighed. "Got himself into some money problems and he's off to the Marshalsea tomorrow morning until I can pay off the debts."

That imperial brow forked higher. "What about your savings?"

Rafe caught his friend's gaze and held it. "Who said I had savings?"

"You were paid excessively well and never spent more than you needed to. You obviously weren't sending it back here or your brother wouldn't have gotten himself into debt, so... where is it?"

Rafe said nothing.

"You gave it away, didn't you?"

Several beats passed. Neither man so much as twitched a finger.

"To his sister?"

There was no need to mention a name. Rafe knew who he meant. His stomach rolled and his chest tightened like it always did when he thought of John Barker, of what he'd almost done. And of what Rafe had been forced to do to stop him. With Barker dead, his only kin, a young sister, was alone. Rafe had to give her all his savings. He couldn't live with himself if he'd left her with nothing.

"I don't regret giving it to her," Rafe said. "She no longer has anyone to support her. Will you lend me the money to pay off James's debts? It'll be better than relying on Liddicoat to advance my wages."

"I'll give you the money. On one condition."

"Ah. Of course. You want me to return to the guild."

"Just for one last commission."

"I don't know."

"You are my trusted friend, Rafe. You never let any of us down. Ever," Hughe said. "Don't start now."

Their gazes connected, held. The moment grew long, stretched, and thin. Hughe hadn't understood why Rafe wanted to leave the guild, hadn't understood that Rafe couldn't follow orders anymore, not the sort that forced him to eliminate men he'd once called friend. Yet to save James quickly...

Hell.

"Who's the target?"

"Barker. He's still alive."

CHAPTER 3

"What!" Rafe exploded. "How?"

"Quiet." Hughe glanced around but there was no one nearby. Night had crept over the city. Lamplight flickered in the windows of the lodgings above the shops on the bridge and on board some of the ships beyond, but their immediate surroundings were dark, still. They would hear someone approaching.

Rafe's heart felt dead in his chest. "I killed Barker in Cambridge. I can assure you, he's not alive."

"I can assure you he is," Hughe said. "He's been in contact, making the same old threats to expose us unless we pay him. Did you see the body?"

How could he? Barker had fallen into the Cam River during their fight. Rafe had waited for several minutes, but Barker didn't come up for air. He'd drowned. Must have.

Unless he'd swum underwater to safety…

Rafe felt like he'd been punched in the throat. He stood and gripped the post until his fingers hurt. "No," he finally said through his hard breathing. "I didn't see his body."

"You have to finish him," Hughe said flatly.

Rafe could just make out his patron's silhouette in the darkness. He still sat on the jetty, legs outstretched as if he were lounging in the sunshine without a care in the world. "Do you know where he is?"

"I traced him here to London."

"London? Why? His sister lives in Cambridge."

"I think he's here because of you."

Rafe frowned. "Me? But he wants to sell our names to the highest bidder. How will getting revenge on me achieve that?"

"He could have sold them already if that was indeed his intention." Hughe got lightly to his feet. "But he hasn't. I wonder if perhaps he never meant to follow through on his threat. He just wanted me to pay the blackmail money."

Then Rafe had killed him for nothing. Or tried to. And failed. "Then why not pay him now and let the matter rest?"

Hughe shook his head slowly as if it was too heavy for more vigorous movement. "Because the fact that he's here looking for you and not following me around the country means it's no longer about money. Rafe, I think he's going to try to kill you."

"Then let him try," Rafe snarled.

"I don't want any of you to be harmed," Hughe went on. His voice sounded far away, not at all like he was an arm's length from Rafe. "You're the brothers I never had. You, Orlando, Cole."

"And John Barker?" It was unfair and Rafe wished he could take it back.

"Barker was never one of us and you know it."

True. The other members of their group were the best of friends, brothers like Hughe said. If one was ever caught, he could be relied upon to keep his silence no matter what incentives were heaped on him, or how much torture inflicted.

Barker was the last to join and had never quite fit in. He set himself apart from the beginning, choosing to eat alone, drink alone, work alone. He'd wanted to kill indiscriminately and grew angry when Hughe turned a job down.

"It'll be like a regular contract," Hughe said. "Only I'll be the one hiring you, not a stranger." When Rafe said nothing, he added, "The payment will be substantial. More than enough to pay off your brother's debts and set him up when he finishes his apprenticeship. There'll be enough left over for you too."

Rafe breathed deeply, drawing the briny scent of the river into his body.

"You have to do this, Rafe. You know what Barker's like. He'll stop at nothing to bring all of us down, one by one, starting with you. And he won't care who he uses to do it."

"James." He'd be an easy target in the Marshalsea.

"And his woman you spoke of. Barker *will* learn of her existence. It's only a matter of when."

Rafe felt sick. Hughe was right. Barker had no morals, which was why he'd been cut loose from the guild. He might go after James and Lizzy to make Rafe suffer.

"Very well," he said. His mouth felt dry, his body cold. "I'll do it. And this time I'll make sure he's dead."

Hughe removed a leather pouch from his belt. The coin inside clinked. "Take this for now. It's only enough for a meal or two, I'm afraid."

Rafe accepted it. "Do you know where I can find Barker?"

"No. You'll need to draw him into the open. Let him find you."

"Let him find out who I care about, you mean."

"It's the only way to make him show his face. He's too good to get caught any other way." Hughe clasped Rafe's arm in farewell. "I'm going away for a few days. I'll check in before I leave. Stay alert."

"Just have the rest of my money ready on your return."

~~~

Lizzy watched James leave from her bedchamber window early the next morning. His steps were slow and he looked woefully unprepared for a long journey in the damp autumn weather. He wore his good coat and his sturdiest boots but the pack he carried was too small to contain more than a single change of clothing. Where was his food, a wineskin? She went to open the window to shout down to him, but then she saw Rafe striding up to join his brother. His gaze locked with hers. He smiled, a curiously tentative half smile as if he were wondering about something—something about her. As usual, her face heated and she silently thanked the lord she was too far away to be seen properly.

Then Rafe's smile broadened as if he'd seen anyway. She dropped down on the rushes out of sight. Why did he make her feel like she needed to hide?

A knock at the door sent her heart leaping, but it was only James. Rafe stood a little behind, glancing up and down the street as if looking for someone.

"I came to say farewell," James said.

"Oh," she said. "Farewell. Be careful."

He shuffled his feet and she thought he might kiss her but he didn't. Of course not. He'd only ever kissed her on the lips once and that was because she'd surprised him last summer at St. Bartholomew's Fair behind the puppet show stand. He'd quickly pulled away and admonished her for her forwardness.

"I'm glad Rafe's back in time to take care of you in my absence," he said.

She hazarded a glance past him to his brother, but Rafe was still standing out of earshot. Nevertheless, she lowered her voice. "I'm not sure having Rafe take care of us was a good idea."

"Why not?"

"In truth, we're a little fearful of him."

He paused. "Oh. I see. But there's no need. Rafe is very good at protecting people. There's none better."

"But that day. He—"

"Don't. Don't speak of it." He winced as if in pain and half-turned to leave. "Don't dredge up the past."

Lizzy wasn't so sure avoiding the discussion was a good idea, but James had always found it a difficult topic and she couldn't blame him for wanting to bury it.

He gave her a quick smile. "Let him take care of you. It will ease my conscience."

She nodded and watched him rejoin Rafe, then shut the door. She ate a breakfast of cold beef and bread alone in the kitchen then carried in two trenchers to her parents, still abed.

"What is it, Child?" her mother asked, patting the mattress beside her.

Lizzy sat. "Rafe Fletcher is back."

Her father paused in his task of tearing the bread apart. "Aye, we know. The vicar was here yesterday and gave us the news. We should have told you last night."

"I saw him when I visited James. I didn't mention it then because I didn't want to worry you, but now...you probably should know."

"So how did he look?" her mother asked.

"The same but...different somehow. Not as...angry."

Her father reached across and took her hand. "Do not let that deceive you. Best to stay away from Fletcher. He's unpredictable."

"You think he's still dangerous?" She'd hoped her parents would reassure her, tell her she had nothing to fear from Rafe seven years after his violent outburst.

"I don't know," her father said, transferring his hand from his daughter to his wife. Lizzy's parents exchanged grim glances. "In my experience, men don't change dramatically, and it would require a dramatic change for him to become an accepted member of our community."

"Everyone still remembers that day," her mother said. "Nothing can change that."

"Do you know what led to Rafe to do it?" Lizzy shivered. It was still so vivid. She doubted she could ever forget. But she'd not known what caused Rafe to lose control like he did. James had never discussed it with her and he'd always dismissed her questions when she'd posed them.

"No one knows," her mother said. "Pritchard was no saint himself, but to warrant such a beating from his own stepson! It's quite unthinkable."

"Rafe was a wastrel," her father added. "He didn't work. Just fought and got drunk in alehouses."

"He frightened the entire neighborhood. We kept our distance when we saw the type of man he'd become."

"We had to." Her father stroked his long white beard. "With three daughters to protect, the likes of Rafe Fletcher were not welcome to our door. Stay away from him, Lizzy. He'll leave again soon enough."

She didn't tell them James had asked Rafe to take care of her in his absence. There was no point troubling her parents with something they couldn't control. Hopefully James would be back before they ever discovered she'd kept the truth from them.

"I'd better go to work," she said.

"Tell us as soon as the situation with Gripp changes," her mother said.

"I will."

"That Gripp..." Her father's beard stroking became faster. "I'd like to wring his neck."

"John!"

"Father, hush." Lizzy leaned over and pecked his forehead. "He hasn't shut us down."

"Yet."

Lizzy left them to their peaceful day and walked down Gracechurch Street and across the bridge, already choked with farmers driving geese and pigs to market in the city. The Bankside thoroughfare running along the south side of the river was quiet by comparison. It wasn't the sort of area people wandered into unless they sought out the pleasures of the playhouses, bearbaiting pits, or whorehouses, and it was too early for any of those entertainments.

She entered the Rose's tiring house through the rear door that led directly out to the street and not through the theatre itself. Edward Style looked up from the prompt book, nodded, and returned to studying his lines. Henry Wells came down the stairs, gave her a bleak smile, and sat on a stool opposite Freddie Putney, slumped in a chair in the corner and apparently fast asleep, although it was difficult to tell since he wasn't snoring like usual. Indeed, the room was silent.

"Lizzy!" Antony Carew waved from the stairs. "Watch this and tell me what you think. I've been practicing." He lifted his velvet gown and at least two cotton underskirts and descended the stairs with his head high, flat chest out, and as much grace as any noblewoman. Once on the floor, he dropped the skirts and twirled toward Lizzy, miraculously avoiding props and furniture. The hem of the costume settled around his bare feet with a delicious *swish*. Antony was short enough that most of his costumes didn't need lengthening with an extra band of cheaper fabric. It meant his velvet, silk, and satin gowns had a much more satisfyingly rich sound than those she needed to alter.

"You look very elegant," she said, accepting his kiss on her cheek. "You would look more elegant if the hair on your legs was a little less...hairy."

He flicked his long red-gold curls off his shoulder and finished the flourish with a graceful twist of his hand. It was his signature action, one he'd perfected on stage for the female roles he played. "I've been told my legs are the shapeliest in all of England." He lifted his skirts to study them and pulled a face. "I'll wear stockings on stage."

"I have some in the storeroom which go nicely with that gown. The staircase scene will be a triumph."

If they ever got to perform it.

No one said it, but the air in the room seemed to tighten, stretch, and the four members of Lord Hawkesbury's Players who were awake exchanged grim glances. They were all thinking the same thing: the play they were practicing might never get approved by the Master of Revels.

"What shall we do now?" Antony asked. "How dire *is* our situation?" He had joined the company only a few months earlier after the previous actor's voice deepened too much to play women. While Antony was a man and not a boy, he sounded, looked, and often dressed like a woman on and off stage. Style liked him for that reason—less training for new boy-actors meant more profit in his pocket.

"Dire enough," Edward said. As the manager's brother, he was well placed to know how desperate the situation was. "Roger is trying to reason with him now."

"He's gone to the Revels office this early?" Lizzy asked.

"Aye."

"Is that wise?" said Henry Wells, the big handsome actor who played most of the lead roles. He'd proved to be very popular with the females in the audience over the years to the point where Roger Style had capitulated and given him the roles he used to keep for himself.

Edward shrugged. "Is anything Roger does wise?"

The four of them thought about that for a moment. "He commissions Lady Blakewell to write most of the plays," Lizzy finally offered.

"Aye, but only because he still thinks her husband really writes them. He refuses to accept that *she* is the playwright."

With a sigh, Lizzy picked up the pair of wings she'd left on the table overnight and sat at the high stool. She threaded a needle and carefully pierced the delicate holland fabric near a tear. It was an activity that required her concentration so as not to ruin the wing altogether—a blessing since it meant she thought less about Walter Gripp bringing the company to an end.

As the morning wore on, more players and stagehands arrived. Usually a crowded tiring house meant laughter and chatter in between preparing sets and learning lines. But not this time. They brought nothing but more gloom with them and a silence that crept into every corner and festered like an open wound.

It was almost a relief when Roger Style finally burst in and shouted, "We're doomed!" He had a flair for making dramatic entries. As manager and actor for Lord Hawkesbury's Players, he'd perfected the art of attention seeking in a trade full of attention seekers. But his explosive statement, complete with door slamming and a well-timed pause, was excessive even for him.

Ordinarily such histrionics would produce eye rolls from the others or a snigger, but this time Roger had everyone's attention. Everyone except Freddie. He let out a loud, nasally snore. Roger cut a swath through the tiring house and kicked Freddie's feet off the stool. The actor snorted and snuffled awake.

"Bloody hell! Who fu—?" He swallowed the rest of the sentence when he saw Roger standing over him, hands on hips. "Oh, it's you." Once upon a time Freddie would not have curtailed his language for anyone, including his employer. *Especially* him. Freddie had grown up with the company, first acting in the female roles then moving on to the male ones when his voice deepened.

He'd changed in the nine years since Lizzy had joined Lord Hawkesbury's Players. So had she, but in an entirely different way. Freddie may have learned to temper his more outlandish behavior, whereas she had shed her inhibitions and stepped out from behind her father's shadow. In the tiring house at least. These days she and Freddie alike valued their positions within the company and neither could afford to leave.

"We *are* doomed," said Freddie to no one in particular.

"Well?" Edward asked Roger. "What happened?"

"What do you think happened?" said Freddie. "He's not going to come in here and announce 'we're doomed' if everything has been smoothed over."

Edward shot him a glare. "Shut it, Putney."

"He's right for once," Roger said.

"Gripp's rejected the next play too?" Henry asked.

Roger had supplied the Revels office with another play the day before. Gripp had promised to have an answer for them that morning. "He said nothing about the play. All he did was tell me he thinks I'm a scourge." He snatched the prompt book off Henry and held it up as if it were a bible blessed by the archbishop himself. The pages flipped back and forth as he waved it about above his head. "If the Master of Revels gets his way, this is the last new play we'll be performing in London. Ever."

The Master of Revels *would* get his way, of course. There was no one to stop him.

"How long before our audiences grow bored with our current stock?" Henry asked. "Another season?"

"A week or two is my guess," Edward said.

"I wonder if Burbage is hiring," Freddie muttered.

"I'll not go to that pompous ass if he begs me," Roger said.

"He doesn't have any work," Henry said. He shrugged. "I already asked."

"We could travel," Edward said. "Until Gripp forgets and becomes reasonable again." But he didn't sound convincing and no one agreed. Gripp's feud with Style had gone on for nearly a decade, it was likely to last as long or longer and none of them wished to traipse across the country forever. Besides, though he might not have any authority outside of London, a man in his position would have powerful friends who did.

"Perhaps he'll die," Freddie said.

"Freddie!" Lizzy chided. "That's a terrible thing to say."

"Not unreasonable though," he said with a shrug. "He's aged. Aged people die."

"He's not aged," Roger said. "He's younger than me."

Freddie snorted. Roger stalked over to him and dropped the collection of bound pages that acted as the prompt book into his lap. Freddie yelped but picked up the only complete version of the play and began reading.

The tiring house settled once more into uneasy silence. "Lizzy?" Antony whispered, leaning closer. He flicked his curls over his shoulder, but not with the self-conscious flourish of earlier. He rarely bothered with the artifice around Lizzy. "Did you speak to your betrothed? Did he agree to an earlier wedding when you explained your predicament?"

She winced as the sharp reminder of her conversation with James came back to her. "No. He hasn't agreed. Not to bring it forward and not to marry me."

"But…you said…"

She shook her head and looked down at the wings. They were so fine, so pretty, but terribly damaged. They were a central part of the play, worn by the fairy king, and she had to fix them or the performance would be ruined. "I know what I said." She fingered the wings. "James and I were never *actually* betrothed. There was a general sort of agreement between us, a long-standing acknowledgment that we would one day wed. There still is," she hastened to add. "He had to leave London for a few days, but we'll discuss it upon his return."

Antony kissed the top of her head. "Good. I'm glad you'll be secure."

Lizzy finished mending the wings and left them on the table. They were too big to take upstairs then bring down again when the performance was only a few hours away. "I'll be in the storage room if anyone needs me," she said, rising.

"Those wings repaired yet?" Roger called out when she was halfway up the stairs.

"Yes."

"And the devil's tail? We need it for today."

"I'm going to do it now. Won't take long."

She worked steadily in the storage room alone for the rest of the morning, listening to the sounds of the actors rehearsing downstairs. The first one to come up and see her sometime later was Freddie, surprisingly.

"God's balls, it's like somebody died down there," he said, throwing himself onto a stool and almost toppling off the other side. He belched and wiped the back of his hand across his mouth.

"You'll need to visit the barber before you go onstage," Lizzy said.

Freddie rubbed his chin where a reddish growth had sprung up. Ever since he'd stopped playing the female roles, he'd tried to grow a beard but the hair sprouted in clumpy, uneven patches and Roger usually made him shave it off. Sometimes Freddie even complied.

He belched again. "Care to do it for me, Liz?"

"There isn't enough incentive in the world to induce me to touch you, Freddie."

He managed to pull a face and, thankfully, left. She picked up a fan and waved it in the direction of the stool until the smell of him dispersed.

"Ugh," said Antony, holding his nose as he came through the door. "That man is disgraceful. To think he used to perform the female roles."

"He was good," she said, "but not as good as you."

He blew her a kiss and sat on the stool. "It's awful down there. Everyone's so worried."

She handed him a mess of twine and directed him to untangle it while she finished sewing the tail back on the devil's costume. Henry Wells had stood on it during the previous performance and torn it off, leaving a large hole in the rear. The audience had erupted in laughter but Roger, playing the role of the devil, had been furious when he gotten off stage. He'd blamed Henry for his clumsiness and Lizzy for her poor workmanship. Henry had apologized later for making her look bad. She told him not to worry. Ever since she could recall, Roger had blown up over the slightest matter, especially when he was made to look the fool in front of an audience. When she'd been younger, his tantrums used to frighten her, but as she grew up she saw that he was all bluster and no one paid him much attention.

"Has there been any more talk about Gripp and his ill intentions?" she asked.

Antony's long, nimble fingers worked deftly on the knotted twine. "They're discussing how long before Lady Blakewell could get a new play to us and whether Gripp would dare ban it."

Minerva Blakewell had been writing plays for the company for years, but not as many as she used to thanks to her growing brood of children. She and Blake—now Sir Robert Blakewell—had three at last count and another on the way. Unfortunately, the play currently being read by the Master of Revels wasn't one of Min's but Ben Jonson's.

Jonson had been jailed the year before for cowriting a lewd and seditious comedy, *The Isle of Dogs*. Gripp's predecessor had not only banned it but reported it to the Privy Council. The noblemen, usually favorable toward the players, had been outraged at the way the play treated the queen and ordered the writers to be jailed. Jonson had found himself in the Marshalsea for two months. Although the incident had blown over, Jonson's name was a tainted one. It wouldn't take much for the new Master of Revels to claim Jonson's latest play unfit for an audience and everyone would believe him.

"So we wait," she said.

"Aye. We wait."

They conversed on less serious matters until it was almost time to take the costumes downstairs for the players to change into. "Try the fairy queen's wings on," she said to Antony. "I adjusted them a little so hopefully they're more comfortable."

The enormous pair of wings complete with long ribbons attached to the lower edge was as large as the door when turned sideways. She stood on the stool to assist him into the straps.

"Walk over there," she said.

He did but didn't judge the distance to the table well and the wings skimmed across its surface, sweeping off the spools of thread. "Sorry." He bent to pick them up and knocked three hats and a Roman centurion's helmet off their wall hooks. Antony cursed and Lizzy giggled.

"At least we know they're not likely to break easily like the fairy king's pair," she said.

"I was going to perform a spin but I think I'd better just take them downstairs." He headed for the door.

"Antony! Remove them first!"

He winked. "I was only teasing you. Of course I was going to take them off."

She scowled. "Very amusing. No, stay there. I'll come to you. Another step and you might completely wreck my storage room." She jumped off the stool, picked it up, and carried it to where he stood near the open doorway. She climbed back up and gently untied the first strap. "Hold this side while I do the other," she said.

Antony didn't move. "Good lord," he said on a breath. "Who is *that*?" He leaned forward, pulling the wings with him.

"Stay still," she snapped. "Now hold this side please."

"He's coming up here," he whispered.

"Antony!" she barked. "Concentrate or you'll break them."

"Can I help?" She heard the deep, familiar voice before she saw him. Then the tall, broad-shouldered frame of Rafe Fletcher filled the doorway. He looked imposing with the stern set of his jaw and his fierce black eyes scanning the storeroom. There was no friendly twinkle in their depths today.

Distracted, Lizzy almost toppled off the stool, but Rafe reached past Antony's wingless side and steadied her with a hand to her elbow. Her heart pounded wildly in her chest.

"You can help in any way you want," Antony said, his face all but buried in Rafe's chest.

Rafe let Lizzy go and held the wings while she undid the other strap and slipped them off Antony's shoulders. The player didn't move out of the way.

She pinched his arm. He yelped and stepped aside to allow Rafe in. With the wings in one hand, held high so they didn't scrape on the floor, he helped her down from the stool. His gloveless fingers were surprisingly warm. And big. Very big.

She gulped and turned away, cursing her pale complexion that had grown hot upon his arrival and hotter still when he touched her.

"Where do you want these?" he asked.

"I'll take them," Antony said.

She turned back when she could hear no movement. Rafe held out the wings to Antony but Antony hadn't moved. He simply stared at Rafe, a delicate blush infusing his cheeks too. Rafe frowned and shook the wings. Antony smiled.

"I'm Antony," he said. "And you are?"

"Getting tired of holding these for you."

Antony giggled and took the wings.

"My name's Rafe Fletcher. I live next door to Lizzy."

Antony's eyes widened. "James's brother?"

"You've met him?"

"Of course. He's Lizzy's..." He glanced at her. "...friend."

"He's gone away for a while. I'm looking after her in his absence."

I'm right here, she wanted to say but couldn't. Her tongue had tied itself into a knot.

Antony glanced at her, frowned, no doubt waiting for her to speak and wondering why she didn't. He turned back to Rafe. "She's very good at looking after herself."

Rafe smiled and Antony loudly sucked in a breath. Lizzy had to admit the effect of the large, imposing man with perfect teeth in a perfect smile was quite a sight to behold. It was entirely unexpected too. She thought he'd frown and stomp about and perhaps curse like he used to when he was younger. She didn't know he had a sense of humor.

She smiled too. Rafe glanced at her and it shriveled up.

"Then it seems I'm in for an easy time ahead," he said and clapped Antony on the shoulder.

Antony stumbled to the side and would have dropped the wings if Rafe hadn't steadied him in the same manner he'd steadied Lizzy, by catching his elbow.

"Will you be able to take those downstairs on your own?" he asked Antony.

"I'm sure one of them will help me."

Rafe and Lizzy followed Antony's gaze to the doorway. Henry, Roger, Edward, Freddie, and one of the hirelings stood in a huddle like naughty children.

Henry was the first to speak. "Everything all right?" he asked Lizzy with a glance at Rafe.

She nodded. "Yes, thank you."

The tall, blond actor tilted his square chin at Rafe. "This fellow came in and asked after you. Freddie told him you were upstairs before any of us could find out what he wanted."

Freddie barked out a laugh. "Like any of us could stop him."

Edward elbowed Freddie and he yelped.

"I'm looking for a...friend who may have stopped by," Rafe said. "Has anyone been here this morning? Any strangers?"

"No," Edward said. "Why would your friend come here?"

"In search of me. If he learns my neighbor works at the Rose, he may want to ask her if she's seen me. If he does come and I'm not here, send him on his way. Don't let him inside the tiring house. My friend's touched with madness, see, and—"

Lizzy gasped and whatever else Rafe had been going to say died on his lips.

He swallowed. "I'm sorry. I didn't mean to frighten you."

Roger cleared his throat. "I don't suppose you can act, sir?"

"Depends."

Freddie screwed up his nose and scratched his nether region. "On what?"

"You don't want to know."

Roger came into the room slowly, hesitantly, as if he approached an untethered bull. "It's just that you'd make a great Thor," he said.

"*I* play Thor," Freddie protested.

"You need to wear blocks of wood under your shoes to give you height," Edward said.

"And padding," the hireling said with a snicker.

"It's not a great speaking part," Roger went on. "Any fool can learn the lines."

The hireling laughed and Freddie shoved him in the chest. Henry caught him before he toppled down the staircase. "I need a drink," Freddie said and stomped down the steps. Nobody stopped him.

"You just stride about onstage," Roger said to Rafe. "Look menacing and...big." He poked Rafe's upper arm where the jerkin stretched taut over his chest. "I think you can manage that."

"Thanks for the offer," Rafe said. "But I wouldn't make a good player. I'll stay back here and help Lizzy instead."

Everyone turned to look at Lizzy. Antony winked at her. "Then let's leave them to tidy up," he said. With the wings in hand, he moved fast, not giving anyone a chance to get past him. With the limited space on the landing, they all had to file down the stairs or be swept off like the spools on the table.

Lizzy was left alone with Rafe.

Well. So be it. She would be all right. There was no need to be afraid anymore. He'd changed. She blew out a breath and picked up the stool.

"Let me help you." He grabbed it and they performed a short tug-of-war until she let go. There was no way she could win. "Where do you want it?"

"Over there."

He set the stool down where she indicated, and looked around at the stacked trunks, the crammed shelves, and the props hanging from the walls and beams. "You take care of all this?"

"Yes."

He fingered a crown of dried leaves used for both Roman emperors and fairy royalty. "James would choose to be a tailor in a shop over this?" He shook his head. "I don't understand that boy." His pitch-black eyes searched her face. "Don't understand him at all."

She busied herself repacking one of the trunks but could still feel his gaze on her. She didn't dare look up at him.

"What can I do to help?" he asked.

"I don't need help."

"I know but I need to do something."

She bit her lip. Why couldn't he leave her alone? Did he enjoy making her feel like an awkward fool?

He came up beside her, a looming tower of solidness. She edged away and he suddenly dropped to his haunches. "Is that better?"

"Is what better?"

"Me at this height."

He thought she was afraid of him because he was tall? She pressed her lips together and lifted one shoulder.

He sighed and sat on the floor, leaning back against the table leg. "So tell me how it goes with that man Gripp?"

An intensity she'd never noticed before swam in those deep, dark eyes, like he was trying to see into her. Like he *could* see into her, right into her heart, her hopes and fears. Definitely her fears. It was unnerving, terrifying, and yet somehow thrilling. To be the focus of such a dangerous, mysterious man as Rafe was not something she was used to.

Why did he have to look at her like that? Why was he asking about Gripp? So he could kill him?

No. Of course not. That would be sheer foolishness. Whatever Rafe might be, he was not a fool. So what did the welfare of the company matter to him?

She opened the trunk and rummaged through the shirts inside, searching for something, anything, to keep herself busy so she didn't have to look at him.

"Our future is still uncertain," she said.

"Gripp has that much power over you?"

"The Master of Revels can ban our new plays and stop us performing at court, but he also has other means of ruining us. He can put pressure on Henslowe to have us removed from this theatre, for example. I doubt any other managers or landlords would lease their playhouses to us if they knew Gripp is against us."

Out of the corner of her eye she could see him nod thoughtfully. "That was quite a long speech you made."

She smothered a laugh and tightened her grip on whatever object she held. It was her anchor while her head suddenly felt light and giddy.

"Lizzy…" he began, his voice melodious, thick, and without a hint of humor. He paused for several beats as if considering his next words carefully. "Is there a reason you don't like looking at me?"

She dared a glance. He half-smiled as if he was unsure what reaction his question would receive. It was almost laughable that *he* was unsure of *her*. She who was predictable and reliable to the point of being dull.

She returned to studying the trunk's contents.

"Have I done something to offend you?"

"No," she blurted out without thinking. "I mean, I've hardly spoken to you so...no."

"Not even years ago, before I left London?"

"We've rarely spoken, ever, especially before you left," she said crisply. "You were a great deal older than me."

"Not a *great* deal."

"Almost eight years."

He whistled. "I'm an old man."

He was making fun of her. A pox on him. She didn't need to listen to such rudeness in her tiring house.

Except how could she get rid of him? Well, she *could* ask.

She gripped the hard object in the bottom of the trunk tighter for courage and stood. His brows shot up, surprised. He raised his hands in surrender.

"You really don't like me that much?" he asked, standing.

She looked down and saw that she gripped the handle of a Roman-style sword. "I'm sorry! I wasn't going to use it," she said with a wave of her hand.

"Whoa." He dodged out of the way of the blade. "That's not how it looks from here."

She winced. It got worse and worse. "I'm sorry, I didn't mean to..." *Keep your mouth shut, Liz, and nothing foolish will fall out of it.*

"Is it real?"

She hefted it up so he could see but almost sliced him through the chin as he leaned forward. "Sorry!"

His lips quirked up in amusement. "Stop apologizing. There's little chance you'll do any real damage holding it like that."

She frowned at the sword hilt. "How am I holding it?"

"Like a girl."

"I am a girl."

"Not anymore."

Her insides flipped. He looked at her again with that intense stare, the one that made her scalp prickle and her heart swell to thrice its size.

"Here," he said. "I'll show you." He moved behind her and gently placed his right hand over hers on the sword hilt. His skin was warm but callused. The long fingers wrapped around hers, trapping them. He was so close she imagined she could feel his heart beating at her back, but she must have been mistaken because there were many layers of clothing between them.

Her heartbeat on the other hand was like a rampaging warrior, smashing against bone with violent blows. Surely he could feel its vibrations through her body. If not then perhaps he could feel the heat sweeping over her with just as much force. Her reaction to him coupled with the melody of his rumbling voice made it impossible to concentrate on his words. He was saying something about her grip...or was it hip?

His thumb stroked hers for no discernible reason she could determine but it felt...wonderful. Comforting. Her heart slowed to a steadier rate but each *thump* was just as violent, just as bone-jarring.

His other hand rested on her waist and she adjusted her stance to better fit against him. Or did he do the adjusting somehow? It didn't matter. Nothing mattered except those hands, the solidity of him, the feeling of being cocooned by a powerful man.

"Good," he murmured into her hair above her ear. "Very, very good."

His words sent a jolt through her. What was she doing? Rafe was dangerous and almost a stranger to her.

He was also James's brother.

She pulled away and dropped the sword onto the rushes. "I'm sorry," she said although she had no idea what she was sorry for. What had happened was entirely his fault. Most definitely all his fault.

She bent to pick up the sword but he caught her wrist. "Lizzy." His eyes were half-closed like he was just waking up.

Then all of a sudden he shook his head and let go of her. His chest rose and fell like he'd been laboring long and hard. "I should go," he said gruffly, turning away.

Oh. Well. Good.

Except there were some tasks she could set him doing, tasks that required strength and an extra pair of hands. Big, capable hands...

Like showing her how to hold a broadsword.

She cleared her throat. "Rafe, would—"

"You!" shouted Roger Style from below. "Bloody pig's pizzle! Get out of my theatre!"

The sound of wood shattering sent Lizzy running for the stairs. Rafe was a step ahead of her.

CHAPTER 4

"I said, get out of my theatre!" Roger stood with hands on hips, feet apart, and chin thrust forward in the classic hero pose for which he was famous. An audience of mostly groundlings paying a penny for entry would have gasped or cheered, but an audience of players who knew him well simply shook their heads.

"He's not the only pizzle in this room," Freddie muttered.

Roger ignored him. The short, flat-faced man he confronted laughed so hard it became a snort. He must be Gripp. The only other man Roger would order to leave was the lead actor and cosharer of the Lord Chamberlain's Men, Richard Burbage, and the newcomer wasn't he.

"It's not *your* theatre," Gripp said, smiling beneath a long, drooping moustache. "It's Henslowe's."

It was true. Lord Hawkesbury's Players leased the Rose off the Admiral's Men and their manager, Philip Henslowe. Both companies performed there several times per week, often one after the other. It made for a crowded tiring house at times.

Roger took a step toward Gripp and kicked aside the pieces of a stool which had suffered most from his tirade. "If you don't get out," he snarled, "I'll kill you."

Lizzy exchanged a worried glance with Antony on the other side of the room until Rafe gently drew her behind him. If it had been anyone else she would have dug her elbow into his ribs and chastised him, but since it was Rafe she simply stepped out from his shadow.

"Steady, Roger," Edward said to his brother. "We don't want a scene here. The audience will be arriving soon."

"I don't give a toss about the audience," Roger said without moving his jaw or lips. "I want this man gone from my presence. He's poisoning the air of this hallowed theatre."

"You're an arse," Gripp said. "And you couldn't kill a bee if it stung you on that beak of a nose." He rocked on his heels, looking pleased with himself. "Now, care to know why I'm here?"

"No," Roger, Edward, and Henry said at once.

"I'm here to tell you *The Spoils of War* has been banned."

"Banned!" Roger bellowed.

"Why?" asked Henry.

"It's a vile piece of work," Gripp said.

"Vile!" Roger huffed and snorted and wagged a finger at his nemesis. "How is it any different from any other play put on by this company or indeed Lord Chamberlain's Men?"

"You speak of yourselves in the same breath as that illustrious troupe! You're a fool as well as an arse, Style."

Teeth bared, Roger took a step forward but was held back by Edward and Henry. Rafe made no move to assist them. He simply crossed his arms and watched the proceedings with interest.

"You…you vindictive *swine*!" Roger shouted. "Selfish, ox-brained…pizzle!"

Gripp laughed. "That's all you can come up with? Maybe Jonson could pen better insults for you. He certainly has a knack for them if *The Spoils of War* is an indication."

"There's nothing wrong with that play," Roger snapped. "It contains nothing of a treasonous nature."

"I didn't say it was treasonous."

"Then what's wrong with it?" Edward asked.

Gripp smoothed down his moustache with his finger and thumb, drawing out the dramatic pause as expertly as any master actor. "I don't need to answer to any of you."

Lizzy held her breath as Roger exploded with a series of curses that made even Freddie's eyes pop.

"I think we get the idea," Rafe said in that calm but commanding voice of his. It got everyone's attention, even Roger's midtirade.

"Exactly what I was going to say," Gripp said, triumphant.

But Roger would not be silenced. "All this hatred because Margaret chose me over you," he said with a sneer.

That seemed to put a prick into Gripp and deflate him.

"It's no surprise to anyone that she did," Roger went on. "Look at you with your sour face and your dreary clothes. You are a dull, small man with an inflated opinion of himself. Leaving you was the best thing she ever did."

Gripp's cheeks reddened above his magnificent whiskers. "You *stole* her," he hissed. "You seduced her with your swaggering hips and your lewd ways." His gaze swept around the room, taking in each of the onlookers. "You're all vile creatures, acting in your crude plays for a barbaric audience. At least the Lord Chamberlain's Men are a refined lot." Someone—Henry?—snorted. "They're the only company fit to perform in front of the queen. The only ones I'll *allow* to perform for her. You and your *men*"—he jerked his head at Antony—"will never grace her audience chamber again with your filthy ways."

"Filthy!" Antony cried. "I am certainly *not* filthy, unlike some others I could mention." He gave Freddie a pointed glare. Freddie merely shrugged.

Lizzy edged closer to Antony and squeezed his hand. "Pay him no mind," she whispered.

"I don't care about court," Roger said to Gripp. His lips stretched into a white, flat line. "This is where the money is, where the audience truly appreciates our art."

He was lying. Roger cared more about performing at court than he did about his own children. He idolized the queen and adored staging plays for her. It appealed to his snobbish nature.

"I *will* ruin you," Gripp went on. "I'll make sure your audiences grow bored of you, and when they grow bored, they'll maul you out there. They'll make you wish you'd never become an actor, make you want to crawl back in here. I'll ruin you, Roger Style, and your troupe."

With a frenzied cry, Roger ran at him again. Once more Henry and Edward had to hold him back. Rafe shifted closer but didn't interfere. He seemed more interested than a stranger should be.

"You destroy my company and I *will* kill you," Roger spat.

Gripp laughed and teased his moustache. "Of course you will."

"You might not think me capable." Roger's gaze switched to Rafe and lingered before focusing once more on Gripp. "But I know someone who is."

Rafe straightened to his full, formidable height and his face became strangely blank, not empty but masked. A chill crept down Lizzy's spine. He was once more the youth she remembered from her childhood—cold, detached, ruthless.

"I think it's time for Mr. Gripp to leave," he said.

Gripp cleared his throat and nodded as he backed through the tiring house curtain and out onto the stage beyond. "Ah, yes, well, good day to you, sir." He doffed his hat without taking his eyes off Rafe.

"Good riddance," Roger shouted after him.

No one else spoke. The rest of the troupe, including Lizzy, watched Rafe. She didn't know what she expected him to do or say but she did expect some sort of reaction.

But there was no reaction of any kind in those deep, black eyes. Rafe simply stared at Roger, who took no notice of him.

"Where's that devil's costume?" he roared. "Elizabeth! I need it now!" He snapped his fingers at Lizzy.

In a move so fast it was a blur, Rafe caught Roger's fingers, silencing the snaps. "Do not shout at her," he said evenly.

"The costume is upstairs. Go and get it yourself." There was no menace in his voice. It wasn't necessary. He had a way of sounding threatening without so much as a change of tone.

Roger's face drained and he made a squeaking noise. "I...I will. I mean I was. Just needed to check with her first."

Rafe let go and Roger tucked his hand under his armpit. He scampered up the stairs without looking back.

The rest of the troupe exchanged glances then dispersed to prepare for the performance. More than one kept a wary eye on Rafe. Antony winked at Lizzy then went upstairs in search of his costume.

Lizzy picked up the prompt book and hugged the bound pages to her chest. She was all too aware of Rafe nearby, watching her. She didn't need to see him to know; she could feel his gaze on her. Why didn't he say something? Why didn't he leave?

Did she want him to leave?

"Lizzy—"

"You don't have to stay," she said. "I'm sure you would rather be anywhere else but here after..."

"No."

"I'm sorry about Roger."

"Don't be. It doesn't concern me. I'm worried about you. This fight between Style and Gripp looks like it might turn nastier."

"Don't concern yourself. It'll probably all blow over." She bit her lip. She didn't believe that at all. If Gripp had banned *The Spoils of War* for no apparent reason, what would he do next? She hazarded a glance at Rafe, just a brief one, and saw that he was indeed still watching her. "I'm sorry Roger implied what he did about you."

He laughed softly. "Worse things have been implied about me. Some of them were even true."

Like what Roger said—Rafe was capable of killing.

"Lizzy? What's wrong?" He frowned and stepped toward her.

She moved quickly away. Her skirts brushed against a stool, pushing it over, and she bent to pick it up. It gave her an excuse to not look at him, to not see the confusion in those endlessly dark eyes.

"I better go," he muttered. "Do you remember why I came—about my friend who's a little mad?" She nodded. "He's tall, like me, with longish brown hair. Don't let him in."

By the time she'd digested that order and looked up, he was gone.

~ ~ ~

The Marshalsea prison was crowded, damp, and stank worse than a pair of old boots. Hughe's money had bought James a clean cell with only three others and a sackful of food. There was no more coin left.

James sat in the corner on a pallet, his forehead resting on his drawn-up knees. He looked up long enough to see the warden let Rafe in, then lowered his head with a groan.

"Unless you've paid off my debts you can go away," he said.

"That's no way to greet your only kin." Rafe dropped the sack at his brother's feet and sat down. "I brought bread, cheese, and apples. Don't eat them all at once." He eyed James's cell mates, who all watched him back, one openly and two surreptitiously. None looked to be starving but the big one, the one who didn't hide his interest, had a cockiness about him that could be dangerous if he decided to prove his superior strength. "There'll be enough to share around if need be."

James peered inside the sack. "Did you steal all this?"

"No, little brother. I sold an old sword I don't use anymore." The lie rolled off his tongue easily enough and James accepted it with a shrug and bit into an apple.

"Everything well here?" Rafe asked, keeping one eye on the big prisoner. Their gazes met and the other man's held steady. That alone set him apart. Usually the cocky sort saw the warning and backed down. Even the big ones. Either this oaf was too stupid or he was throwing out a challenge.

"Everything's perfect here," James said with obvious sarcasm. "I only got bitten two hundred times last night by whatever is living in this pallet and I'm fortunate to be able to see the feet of passersby through that window. Sometimes they even throw us little presents through the bars, like mud or rotten fruit."

He was lucky that's all they threw in.

"Has anyone been to visit you?" He considered telling James about Barker but decided against it. James had enough troubles of his own.

"No. Nobody but you knows I'm in here."

"Good. And don't worry. I'll get you out."

James sighed and rubbed a hand through hair not yet as dirty as that of his fellow inmates. In another few days it would become greasy and itch like the devil. "Thank you, Rafe, you're a good brother. Always have been." He offered up a weak smile then looked quickly away, but not before Rafe saw the tears in his eyes. There was no need to ask what they were for. They both knew.

"I could have been better." *Should* have been better. "I could have been here more."

"You think I wouldn't be in prison if you were around?" All trace of sentimentality was gone. Defiance flashed in James's eyes where before they'd swum with despair. "I am not a child, Rafe."

"I never said—"

"You didn't have to. I know what you meant. You think I'm not capable of taking care of my own affairs."

It was no use arguing with him. James was a young man, angry at himself and the world. More than anyone, he knew that a few days in prison wouldn't be long enough to knock that out of him. It would take time and perhaps a few life-threatening events. Or a woman. Lizzy could do it. She'd be good for James. A sensible, leveling influence.

He rested his head back against the wall with his eyes closed—a bad idea because it brought memories of the way Lizzy had felt against him when he'd shown her how to hold the sword. She'd been soft, her skin smooth, and she smelled of honey. Even now, amid all the filth of the prison, he could conjure up the scent of her.

"Rafe? Are you all right?"

He opened his eyes to see James frowning at him and guilt swamped Rafe. For God's sake, she was his brother's intended! "Yes."

"You seem a little unwell."

"Don't worry about me." Rafe tried to force every last thought of Lizzy away but his efforts failed. He worried about her. The situation between Gripp and Style looked volatile and the company's ruin at the hands of Gripp seemed inevitable.

Rafe couldn't believe two grown men could be so antagonistic and not actually fight each other. Perhaps if the players had let Style attack Gripp, they could have gotten it out of their systems and it would all blow over. Then again, perhaps not. Neither looked like they'd give up on their feud so easily. Which brought up the question—would Style kill Gripp?

Rafe didn't think so, but he *might* hire someone as he'd implied. It was that suggestion that had turned his blood cold. Not the fact that he'd thought Rafe was the type capable of killing, but more the reactions of everyone in the room. The sharp intake of breaths. The tension stretching tighter and tighter as they waited for Rafe to explode in anger.

The fear in Lizzy's eyes.

She'd backed away from him like she would a vicious dog. The frightened doe had returned and he didn't like it. He wanted to see the woman who'd blossomed beneath his touch up in the storeroom. The one who pressed herself into him and shuddered when he whispered in her ear, and not with fear. That woman trusted him enough to let him close.

He liked that woman.

"Everything's well with her," he mumbled.

"Lizzy?" James asked.

"Uh...yes. We were talking about Lizzy." Weren't they?

"No, but I'm glad to hear she's in good health."

At least Barker hadn't tried to get to her and use her against Rafe. Perhaps he didn't know about the connection between Lizzy and James. Perhaps James was the more likely target. Even so, Rafe felt better having warned her.

"Has anything happened with the Master of Revels?" James asked.

Rafe almost told him about the confrontation at the Rose but instead said, "No." It was yet another worry his brother didn't need.

"Perhaps it will all amount to nothing," James said. "I hope so. The Crofts are good people, the best, and Lizzy's a sweet girl. Losing her job at the tiring house will be a terrible blow."

Rafe winced. His brother loved Lizzy. They would be wed in a few years' time. He certainly should not be thinking about her soft curves. They were *not* his to think about. Never would be.

"Take good care of her," James said.

Rafe cleared his throat. "I'll treat her like a sister." He could do that. "It would be easier if I didn't have to lie to her about your whereabouts. Why won't you trust her and let me tell her you're here?"

"No!"

"Why not? I don't understand."

"Of course you bloody don't," James snapped. "Look at you."

Rafe looked down at himself and shrugged.

"You're big and strong and capable. You always have been."

Cold fingers of ice gripped Rafe's heart and squeezed. "Not always."

"I don't need Lizzy thinking I'm a failure too."

"Too? Why, who else thinks you're a failure?"

James sighed and lowered his forehead to his knees again. "I knew you wouldn't understand."

True. Rafe didn't. If he had a woman like Lizzy in his life he'd tell her all his troubles. He'd wager she had a sympathetic ear and practical suggestions.

"I should go. I'll return tomorrow." He slapped James on the back and leaned closer. "Keep an eye on that prisoner, the big one. Offer him some cheese and an apple."

"What if he doesn't like cheese or apples?" James mumbled into his knees.

"Dig your fingers into his eyes."

James groaned loudly. Rafe slapped him again and stood, but the big prisoner blocked his path to the door. He was huge, with a trunk shaped like a barrel and a boulder of a head on top of a thick neck.

"I haven't got time for this," Rafe said. "Tell me what you want so I can tell you that you can't have it, then we can get to the part where I make you wish you'd picked on someone else."

The big oaf screwed up his face, thinking hard. Rafe waited until he'd caught up.

"I want what he's got," the man said.

"You mean you want his charm and wit and good looks? Sorry, I can't do that. Would you like an apple instead?"

The bulging brow crinkled again then cleared as the big man realized he'd been insulted.

"Rafe," James warned from the corner. "Don't kill him. Not here."

The ogre grunted. "Him kill me? Ha!"

Rafe sighed. "Just move aside so I can leave."

The prisoner puffed out his chest, stretching his jerkin to its limits. "You get past me and I'll open the door for you."

Rafe didn't want to be the one to swing first. He usually liked to wait and let his opponent take the initiative. It was a good way to get him off balance immediately so that Rafe needed only one well-placed blow to finish the fight before it got out of hand. But the man wouldn't budge unless Rafe made him.

He stepped forward and grinned. As the prisoner thought about whether to grin back or not, Rafe landed a punch just below the ribs. He didn't pull back and it must have hurt, but the man merely grunted.

"That all you got?" he snarled.

Rafe shrugged one shoulder and half-turned, but kept the ogre in his sights. The big man rolled up his sleeves to reveal thickly muscled forearms.

"What are you doing?" James yelled. "Fight him!"

"How can I?" Rafe said. "He's bigger than me."

"You're giving up? I thought you were a mercenary." His voice turned shrill. "I thought fighting is what you did best. I thought it was the only thing you were good at."

"Now, that's not fair. I haven't got a weapon on me. Mercenaries don't fight without weapons." The disbelief on James's face almost made Rafe laugh. His poor little brother was working himself into a panic. Time to put him out of his misery. "Oh, wait, I *do* have a weapon," Rafe said.

James sank to the floor with relief. "Thank God," he murmured.

"You're gonna need more than a knife," the prisoner said. Out of the corner of his eye, Rafe saw him cracking his knuckles as he advanced.

"I haven't got a knife," Rafe said. "No blades, no hammer, not even a pin." Confused, the oaf paused and his eyes narrowed at Rafe. "But I do have this."

Rafe swung round and landed a punch on the man's jaw that sent him stumbling back into the door. He recovered and with a roar of anger, ran at Rafe. Rafe ducked and, as the giant lumbered past, tripped him. The prisoner tumbled to the dirty rushes like a felled tree, landing with a *thump* that shook the floorboards. It all happened without Rafe really thinking. In moments of combat, his mind seemed to empty and switch to another level. The motions were effortless, instinctive, and he could see his opponent's weaknesses as clearly as he could see the shape of him.

Perhaps James was right and fighting was the thing Rafe did best.

He pressed his boot to the back of the man's neck, not hard enough to crush anything vital, but hard enough to induce fear. The trunk-like arms flailed about trying to grasp Rafe's leg and his feet kicked aimlessly. It looked comical, but no one laughed. James and the other prisoners had to live with him once Rafe was gone and weren't stupid enough to make an enemy of the giant.

Rafe removed his foot and held out his hand. The oaf glared at it for a long moment, then he took it and heaved himself to his feet.

"Help yourself to an apple," Rafe said. He still held the man's arm in a grip that would leave bruises. "But that's all. I'm not an almshouse. I can't afford to feed everyone in here."

He stepped up to the prisoner and lowered his voice. "Touch my brother and I'll kill you."

The ogre said nothing but he didn't seem as cocksure as before. It wasn't a promise, but it would have to do. Rafe let him go.

James edged around the cell to avoid the big man and sidled up to Rafe. "You're mad," he said.

Perhaps he was. Rafe sometimes felt he wasn't in complete control of his mind and body when he fought. A kind of shadow passed through him, sucking out his essence, leaving behind all the things that made him a good assassin—ruthless efficiency, a heightened awareness of his surroundings, and instinct.

He opened the unlocked door and stepped out with a nod at the nearby guard. In the cell, the ogre was busy demolishing an apple from James's pack. Perhaps he was simply hungry. It must take a lot to fill up that big body and hunger can do terrible things to a man.

The two smaller prisoners moved past them and headed for the central courtyard that all the prisoners were free to use during the day.

"I'll bring more food tomorrow," Rafe said to James.

"Thanks." James clasped Rafe's forearm. "I do appreciate it."

"I know."

He followed the guard through the warren of tunnels past the other cells to the front office and out into daylight. London was bathed in autumn sunshine. He turned his face to the blue sky and breathed deeply. It was good to be a free man in a free city. Except he wasn't completely free. Not while his brother was locked away in that hell, and not while Barker was alive, biding his time until he'd learned the best way to make Rafe suffer.

He set off on the long walk to Lord Liddicoat's house on the Strand on the other side of the river. With Hughe's initial payment all gone and most of Rafe's money too, an advance payment from Lord Liddicoat was increasingly necessary, especially if he needed to feed James's dangerous cell mate too. At the bridge, he almost detoured to the Rose to see Lizzy but decided against it. He liked it there and had enjoyed helping her in the storage room above the tiring house. If he visited again he might not want to leave. Right now he had business to conduct.

He was almost at the bridge when he realized he was being followed.

CHAPTER 5

Rafe studied his surroundings. A mixture of shops and lodgings, coaching inns and brothels lined Borough High Street, the street leading up to the bridge. It was as busy as always with late-morning traffic heading into and out of the city proper on the other side of the river. The figure blended into the crowd with his simple, dark clothing, but Rafe saw him—first in the doorway of the saddler's shop and again exchanging words with a leather seller farther along the street.

Once Rafe was over the bridge, he took the smaller, quieter lanes instead of the main thoroughfares in the hope of drawing Barker out. But no one approached him or tried to kill him despite the many opportunities. By the time the city wall was behind him and the grand estates of the Strand ahead, he began to wonder if he'd been mistaken and it hadn't been Barker. Perhaps no one followed him.

But he couldn't be wrong. As with fights, his instincts in such moments were sharp and never failed him. It must have been Barker. And drawing him into the open for a confrontation was not going to be as easy as Rafe thought.

~ ~ ~

Lizzy left the tiring house soon after the performances. Most of the players went to the Two Ducks Inn but their mood was somber and their conversation filled with dire predictions. She couldn't stay at the Rose because the Admiral's Men needed the tiring house for their late afternoon performance, so she took some mending home with her. She was about to turn into her street when she met Rafe coming from the opposite direction.

"Let me carry the sack for you," he said.

"That's not necessary."

"I know." He held his hand out and she gave him the sack. "I need to be of some use or I'll go mad." At her quizzical frown, he added, "Don't mind me. I wanted to begin my new job early but was refused. Lord Liddicoat doesn't return to London until next week, so there'll be no work until he's back."

What would someone like Rafe do for that illustrious nobleman? Work in the stables or grounds of Liddicoat Hall? Perhaps, but the lord himself didn't need to be in London for Rafe to begin those kinds of duties. Surely a steward would direct him. Same with working in the house, unless he was groom of the chamber for Liddicoat himself. No. She couldn't see Rafe dressing anyone, no matter how much they paid him. She stifled a giggle but a little snort escaped.

Rafe cocked his head to the side and a half smile tugged at his mouth. "What's so funny?"

"Nothing."

"Were you laughing at me?"

"No!" She hurried ahead but he easily caught up to her. The man had a stride twice as long as hers.

"You were," he said.

She dared to glance at him and was relieved to see he was still smiling. They arrived at her house and he didn't give the sack back, which meant she'd have to invite him in. The neighborly thing to do would be to ask him to stay for supper, since he was on his own.

Before she could dig up the courage, the front door opened and her father squinted out at them. "Lizzy, I've been…Oh. You brought company."

"Papa, you recall Rafe Fletcher."

"Yes."

Rafe cleared his throat. "I have Lizzy's mending. May we come in?"

"Uh…well…" Somewhat reluctantly he opened the door. It seemed his manners were stronger than his uncertainty of Rafe.

"Do you mind, Lizzy?" Rafe asked.

She shook her head. What else could she do? At least her parents would do most of the talking so she wouldn't have to think of something to say. No, that wasn't quite right. She could *think* of many things to say to him, she just didn't know *how* to say them. Most of the time when he was near her throat went dry and her tongue grew fat. Speaking had become torture.

"Why is no one coming in?" Croft asked, sticking his head forward and screwing up his poor eyes more. "You'll catch your death out there."

"It's not cold, Papa."

He grunted. "It is when you're my age." He kept his wary gaze on Rafe as he entered. Lizzy shrugged and mouthed an apology when she passed him, but he didn't seem to see it. Up ahead in the kitchen, Lizzy's mother gasped.

"Mr. Fletcher!"

"Sorry to startle you, Mistress Croft. And please, call me Rafe."

"Of course. Whatever you wish. Lizzy?" Her mother lifted her face to receive Lizzy's peck on her cheek.

"Be calm," Lizzy whispered in her ear. "Treat him like a regular neighbor."

Rafe set the sack down in the corner then gave her mother a respectful bow.

"I can't help you with the mending tonight, my girl," her father said with a wave at the sack. "My eyes are tired."

"It's all right, Papa, I don't need help," she said, stirring the beef stew warming in the pot over the fire.

"That's it, make an old man feel useless."

"That's not what I meant."

"Ignore your father," her mother said. "Will Shakespeare came by today and told him about Mr. Gripp banning *The Spoils of War*."

"Selfish little toad." Her father lowered himself carefully to the bench seat running the length of the table. "Worse than Style. If I were younger I'd knock him flat, make him—" He glanced at Rafe. "I'd talk to him," he muttered into his beard.

"I'm not sure talking would work," Rafe said. If he felt uncomfortable, he showed no sign of it.

"Let's speak of other things," Lizzy's mother said with false cheerfulness. "So James has gone away?" she said to Rafe.

"Ah, yes. Just a word on that," Croft said before Rafe could answer. "Shakespeare asked me for the name of a good tailor, so I directed him to Cuxcomb, but he told me a most curious thing. He said Cuxcomb has gone out of business, shut up shop."

"That's not right," Lizzy said. "James works there. Will must have been mistaken."

They all looked at Rafe. He shrugged. "Supper smells delicious. I remember the wonderful cooking smells coming out of this house in my youth. My stomach growled every time I passed."

Lizzy's mother's smile turned genuine. Complimenting her cooking was always an effective way to get into her good graces. "Shall we go into the parlor to sup?"

"No, please, no need to trouble yourselves on my account," Rafe said. "It's more comfortable in here. Warmer."

Lizzy spooned stew from the pot into four bowls and handed them to Rafe, who placed them on the table. When they got to the last bowl, he suddenly smiled at her but it was the oddest smile, sweet. It was very disarming coming from such a rough man and her stomach did a little somersault.

She turned back to the pot and stirred vigorously.

"Come sit with us, Lizzy," her mother gently chided. But the only spare stool was next to Rafe.

She sat. No one spoke as they ate, and the awkward silence was made heavier by the furtive glances Lizzy's parents shot Rafe when he wasn't looking. They didn't seem to know what to make of him eating at their table. When her father mopped up the last of the juices with a slice of bread, he patted his belly. "Time for you to retire, my dear," he said to his wife.

"I'll just clean up first," she said, hauling herself to her feet with some difficulty.

"No, Mama, I can do it."

"I'll help," Rafe said and began collecting bowls. "Do you have any water?"

"Out the back," Lizzy said.

Once he was out of earshot, Croft said, "You should've refused his help."

"I didn't want to be ungracious," Lizzy said.

"Don't worry about manners."

"Now, Husband, that's enough," his wife said. "He's been polite all evening and he certainly doesn't seem bitter and resentful anymore. I wonder what happened to bring about the change."

"He grew up."

"Perhaps. Or fell in love."

Croft scoffed. "You women think falling in love solves everything. It doesn't change all men."

"It changed you," she said. "And it's only when a man meets the *right* woman that he becomes a better man."

"Off to bed with you, Wife. I'll stay here until he goes."

She shuffled off just as Rafe returned carrying a pot of water. He hooked it onto the iron rod over the fireplace.

"Thank you," Lizzy said.

"It's the least I can do in exchange for supper." He found a cloth and began wiping the table.

"You don't need to do that," Croft said, settling back down on a stool in the corner. "Lizzy can."

Rafe shook his head when she put her hand out to take the cloth. "I don't mind. I'll clean, you mend, Lizzy. That sack was very full."

It *would* take her some time to work through it all, and Rafe didn't look like he was going anywhere. With the cloth slung over his shoulder, he moved about the kitchen with purpose, as if he cleaned up all the time. That went some way to disproving her mother's theory that a woman had changed him. Clearly he was used to taking care of himself.

Why wasn't he wed yet? And where had he been and what did he do? Did he keep house for just himself or a group of other men? The questions burned in her brain and she even formed the right way to ask, but just couldn't do it. What if he got offended? What if he thought she was accusing him of being womanly?

A bubble of laughter burst out before she could control it, not loud enough to disturb her father, snoring softly into his beard, but Rafe noticed.

He straightened, that curious half smile playing on his lips again. "You *are* laughing at me," he said. "I knew it."

Her laughter shriveled up and she shook her head. "No! I would never laugh at you."

Still smiling, he edged closer. She backed up and plopped down on the bench seat near the sack of mending. "Not even when I make a joke?" he asked with mock offense. "I tell the funniest stories. They'd have you rolling on the floor, crying with laughter."

"Er..." Should she laugh again? That might make him stop teasing her. He was teasing. Wasn't he? Or perhaps he truly was offended but was pretending not to be...Her stomach twisted itself into a painful knot.

"But I won't tell you any jokes since you don't find me in the least amusing," he said.

"I do! Only when you're pretending to be amusing." She winced. That came out all wrong. "I don't mean *pretending*, I mean when you *are* amusing. Deliberately, that is. When you're not, then I don't. Find you amusing." *Tongue, be still!*

No problem there. Rafe had come even closer and her tongue suddenly refused to work at all. He leaned down and his merry eyes met hers. But slowly, slowly, the merriment died away and his smile disappeared and everything shifted. He kept looking at her but now it was with heavy-lidded curiosity. And then even the curiosity became something else. Desire. She recognized it deep in the pit of her stomach. His gaze lowered to her mouth and he sucked in a long, measured breath.

Her heart skipped wildly and her skin grew hot and tight. He was going to kiss her. On the lips.

God help her, she wanted him to.

Her eyelids fluttered closed and a kind of madness welled up inside her. How else to explain why she leaned forward?

But nothing happened. She opened her eyes to see Rafe standing, the sack of mending in hand. He dumped it on the table then began wiping down the surface around it with vigorous strokes as if he could polish the aged oak to a high sheen.

"So were there any more problems with Gripp today?" he asked, turning to the fire and the pot of water.

It took several heartbeats for Lizzy to begin to think clearly again and realize Rafe had not only *not* kissed her, but he'd probably never intended to. She must have misread him. What sort of man would kiss his brother's intended?

What sort of woman would want him to?

Poor James, he didn't deserve such a fickle girl as his future bride.

"Lizzy?" He glanced at her over his shoulder but quickly turned away again. The water seemed to be the most interesting thing in the room.

"Uh, no. No problems with Gripp today." She removed a Roman tunic from the sack and her mending kit from a basket tucked under the table. It was growing dark and she needed to light some candles to see the fine stitches required on the garment, but the candles were all near the fire. Near Rafe. She would just have to dispense with them until he left.

"Has Style made any more public threats toward him?" he asked.

"No."

"Private ones to you or any of the players?"

"Not that I'm aware." It was almost impossible to thread the needle in the waning light but she managed it.

Rafe plunged the cloth into the pot of water and squeezed the excess out of it before wiping one of the bowls. "Gripp seemed furious yesterday. Furious to the point of irrational. They both did, he and Style. I've seen men like that before, men who want revenge no matter the cost."

Lizzy paused and watched his back. She'd seen men behave like that too. One man in particular. A young man, intent on doing harm and not caring about the consequences.

"People like that are dangerous," Rafe went on.

She concentrated on her mending, lifting the tunic so that the window was behind it and she could use as much of the fading daylight as possible.

"You're worried, aren't you?" Rafe said, glancing at her over his shoulder again. He frowned, shook his head. "Economizing is one thing, Lizzy, but you shouldn't work in this light. Your eyes will suffer." He used the low flames in the fireplace to light the candles and set the candelabra on the table near her.

"Thank you," she said. She wanted to add that he was being very kind, not at all like he used to be, but she bit her tongue and bent to the mending.

"I'll pay Gripp a visit in the morning," he said.

"What?" She missed the stitch and stabbed her finger. A drop of blood bubbled out of the skin. She sucked on it.

Rafe pressed his lips together and swallowed hard. "I... uh..." He rubbed the back of his neck. "The sooner the better."

She removed her finger. "No, Rafe. Thank you but don't trouble yourself. Please."

"It's no trouble. Don't worry, it'll just be for a talk. I'll make sure Gripp understands that he can't ruin the company and get away with it."

How would Rafe make him understand? With fists? A blade? "It'll sort itself out," she said.

"It might but I doubt it'll be in a way that will be good for the troupe and your job."

Her job. Yes, she needed it.

"I'll come." It was out before she'd thought it through. Perhaps that was a good thing. If she had thought about it, she wouldn't have spoken at all. She should go with him. She *needed* to go with him—at least Rafe might not be inclined to use his unique powers of persuasion if she was there.

"Very well," he said cautiously. "But don't be alarmed if you hear me say some...threatening things."

Too late for that. She was already very alarmed.

~ ~ ~

They had just set out for the long walk to Gripp's home and office in Clerkenwell when a rider on the back of a magnificent white horse trotted proudly down the street toward them. Lizzy hadn't seen such a fine animal since Leo had courted her sister nine years ago, although Leo's horse had never been so pristine. It was like something out of the tales the older playwrights told over their ales, minus the shining armor. If the gentleman rider wasn't at least a knight in rank, she would be surprised.

"'Lo!" the horseman shouted. "Fletcher! I need to speak to you."

Rafe held the horse's bridle and patted its nose. "Can't keep away from me, eh?"

"Is that any way to speak to your superior?" the man said, sliding off the horse and landing lightly on his feet. He wore a black doublet with gold thread and gold buttons and a large lace ruff high up under his chin. Lizzy had seen gentlemen wear similar elaborate garments to the playhouse. "In front of a lovely young lady too." He flashed a smile at her. It was dazzling. She smiled back, and then she flushed, of course.

"My superior?" Rafe grunted. "Have you forgotten I bettered you the last time we fought?"

They fought? Was this man an enemy of Rafe's? Neither seemed on guard. In fact, Rafe looked pleased to see the newcomer.

"That was hardly a fair fight," the gentleman said. "My left arm was in a sling and I wasn't trying very hard. I didn't want to hurt you."

"How considerate."

The gentleman bowed to Lizzy. "My apologies, dear lady, for this ruffian talk. Rafe, are you going to introduce us?"

"If you'll let me get a word in, gladly. Elizabeth Croft, this is the earl of Oxley."

An earl! Good lord. She curtsied and the earl bowed low. She should say something, but what does one say to an earl? In the end, her face grew hotter and she said nothing.

"Honored," Lord Oxley said. "Tell me, what is a delightful lady such as yourself doing with a savage like Rafe?" He leaned forward, conspiratorial. "He's not leading you astray, is he?"

She bit back a grin and felt herself relax. "He's my neighbor."

"Ah. And a better neighbor you'll never find, I'm sure. However." His blue eyes twinkled with boyish mischief. "I do hear he's living alone while his brother is away. And you know what that means?"

"What?" Lizzy and Rafe both said.

"It means he'll do anything for a hearty meal. You haven't invited him to supper, have you?"

"None of your business, Hughe."

Rafe called him by his first name? She'd never known any ordinary man to be so disrespectful to a nobleman's face.

"It is my business." Lord Oxley patted the neck of his restless horse. "It's my duty as a gentleman to protect this lady."

"You're not protecting her, you're turning her against me. She was just beginning to like me."

"Were you?" Lord Oxley said with mock disbelief.

"I confess he supped with us last night," she said. Clearly the earl was teasing Rafe and she was going to enjoy every moment of it. For some reason she didn't feel nearly as uncomfortable around Rafe in the earl's presence.

Lord Oxley clicked his tongue. "You'll never be rid of him now. He's like a stray dog that way. Feed him and he's yours forever."

"So I'm a dog now?" Rafe growled.

"What do you think, Mistress Croft?" He winked at her.

"I...uh..." *Don't think you should insult him.* Who was this man who spoke to Rafe like a friend? Surely he wasn't a mercenary too. For one thing, lords did not risk their lives unless the queen ordered it, and secondly, he looked incapable of wielding a sword, let alone defeating anyone. He was just as tall and broad across the shoulders as Rafe, but he wasn't in the least aggressive or imposing. Indeed, he was quite foppish.

Rafe clapped Lord Oxley on the back and said, "I doubt you came here just to insult me."

The earl's smile faded and he cocked his head to the side. "I apologize, dear lady. It's just that Rafe is so easy to tease that I couldn't resist."

Just like that, her shyness vanished once more. The earl made her feel comfortable without seeming to try. He reminded her of some of the actors. They knew how to read an audience and adapt accordingly. Lord Oxley would fit right into the troupe, absurd though that thought was.

"No apology necessary, my lord. I can see that you and he are great companions."

Rafe huffed. "So great that he doesn't mind it when I tell him to state his business then go away."

"I think that's a hint," Lord Oxley said. "I'd better not be here when he decides to stop hinting and become persuasive. I've seen how he persuades people."

So had she. Lizzy rubbed her arms as a chill wind blew up the street.

"Get. On. With. It," Rafe ground out.

The earl glanced over his shoulder down the street. When he turned back, his face was suddenly serious. "Any news on that mutual friend of ours?" Was he talking about the madman Rafe had warned her about in the tiring house?

"Not yet," Rafe said.

"I hoped it would be closer to being resolved by the time I had to leave this afternoon."

"I'm afraid it isn't."

The look of concern that passed from one to the other made the hair on the back of Lizzy's neck stand up. Then Lord

Oxley suddenly smiled again. "All jokes aside, can I ask you to take care of Rafe in my absence, dear lady?"

"I'll do my best," she said.

"I can take care of myself," Rafe grumbled. "Been doing it a long time."

"Perhaps too long," Lord Oxley said with quiet sincerity. He clasped Rafe's arm. "Be careful, my friend."

Rafe clapped him on the shoulder. "You too. Don't get that pretty doublet of yours dirty."

Lord Oxley chuckled. "I'll come and see you as soon as I return."

Rafe held the bridle as his friend remounted. They followed Lord Oxley down the street and parted at the corner. He waved at them from the saddle and gave them a final, dazzling smile.

"Peacock," Rafe muttered.

"I liked him," she said before she could check herself.

"So I noticed." He strode off and she trotted to catch up to him.

~ ~ ~

With the office of the Master of Revels came the ample accommodations provided by the old Priory of St. John buildings northwest of the city proper. Walter Gripp didn't have the space all to himself, however. He had to share with his vast staff as well as the props, costumes, and even the stage used for the courtly entertainments he managed.

A few inquiries within the priory gate led Rafe and Lizzy to Gripp conducting a rehearsal within the vast hall. The play looked to be some sort of grand re-creation of the Armada defeat complete with a quarter-size reproduction of the *Golden Hind*. Two carpenters hammered at the replica ship's hull and another hung from a sling attached to the main mast. Rafe was impressed with the detail, right down to the complicated web of rigging. It would be quite a sight once it was completed, but difficult to transport it to wherever it needed to go.

"I'm not so sure this is a good idea," Lizzy said. "What if I say the wrong thing? What if we make the situation worse?"

"Could it be any worse?" Rafe asked.

"I suppose not. But Rafe, let me talk to him first."

Did she expect him to threaten Gripp without first talking to him? Perhaps she did.

They walked up to Gripp where he stood in a huddle with two other men inspecting a sheet of parchment. He paled when he saw Rafe but gathered himself quickly.

"What do you want?" he snapped.

"I want you to listen to my friend, Elizabeth Croft. She has something to say to you."

Beside him, Lizzy seemed to shrink away. He touched her hand to give her courage and she curled her fingers around his. But then she let go, like a released trap, and took a step away from him.

"Is there somewhere we can talk in private?" she asked.

"No." Gripp sniffed. "Now be gone, wench, I have business to tend to." He looked down at the parchment.

Rafe snatched it out of his hand. "Listen to her."

Gripp's companions backed away and his bravado faded along with them. "We can talk in my private office."

Lizzy and Rafe followed him out of the hall into a small building near the great southern gate. The first room was filled with piles of papers, some bound, stacked on one of the two large desks. A plan of a ship was spread out on the other desk. Gripp didn't offer them a seat. He stood in the center of the room, arms crossed.

"Go on," he said to Lizzy. "State your business."

"I want you to leave our company alone," she said. "The unfortunate matter between yourself and Mr. Style needs to be set aside or you'll make us all suffer."

"Your suffering will make Style's suffering so much sweeter." Gripp smirked. Rafe closed his fist at his side. He could wipe that smirk off the prick's face with one punch.

"Please, Mr. Gripp." Lizzy clasped her hands together in front of her, begging.

Rafe hated seeing her like that, pleading with the little turd. Gripp didn't deserve it. Nor did Style.

"Style should not have taken your wife," she said in a soothing voice he'd never heard before. Not that he'd heard her speak often. Not nearly often enough. "We all acknowledge that he behaved very ill toward you." Her conciliatory words and gentle tone seemed to calm Gripp. "Style himself is sorry—"

"Ha!"

"He *is* sorry," Lizzy insisted, "but he's too proud to admit it. You know what he's like."

Gripp nodded. "He's a coward and an arse—"

"Language," Rafe cut in.

Gripp pouted. "I won't release *The Spoils of War*." Of course he wouldn't; that would make him look weak after so vehemently banning it.

"We don't want you to," Lizzy said. "But perhaps you could allow the next play through. It's by Lady Blakewell and won't contain anything of a crude or dangerous nature in it. Her husband, Sir Robert, is very well connected."

"I know that." Gripp twisted the ends of his long moustache. Clearly he was pondering the dilemma. He didn't want to appear to back down from his threats to Style, but Minerva Blakewell's husband was indeed influential. He was a favorite at court and was said to have played an important role in the Armada's defeat a decade ago.

"Please, Mr. Gripp. I promise you shall not have to see or hear from Mr. Style again. We will all do what we can to keep him from your presence."

If Gripp didn't capitulate after that plea, Rafe really would give him a bloody nose to remember them by.

But Gripp nodded and said, "If Mistress Blakewell's play is as clean as you claim, I will not stand in its way. Sir Robert would have my head if I did."

Lizzy rocked on her heels and gaped at Gripp. "Thank you, Mr. Gripp, I appreciate you listening to me."

Rafe followed her out of the office, leaving Gripp behind. "The Crown should employ you in a diplomatic role," he said as they walked beneath the gate's arch. "England might become the most powerful nation in the world if you were let loose on our enemies."

She bit her lip, suppressing what he assumed was a smile, but it didn't suppress the light in her eyes. They danced with happiness.

"You shouldn't do that," he said.

"What?"

"Stop yourself smiling or laughing."

Her eyes shadowed. "Oh."

Bollocks. He'd said something wrong. Again. It seemed he couldn't say the right thing around Lizzy. She must think him a thug compared to the actors, and beside Hughe he certainly must seem dull. It had been obvious that she'd liked Hughe, but then women usually did. It had never bothered Rafe before, however.

Perhaps it was because her shyness had only lasted a few minutes in Hughe's company, whereas Rafe had been with her for hours and she'd hardly spoken a word to him directly.

He paused at the gatehouse and scanned the vicinity. Dozens of people walked past, going about their business. Only one was the same height and size as Barker, but the cloaked and hooded figure disappeared around a corner before he could be certain. Rafe kept close to Lizzy and checked and rechecked their surroundings. He spotted the man again when they reached Newgate. He kept to the shadows, walked with the crowd, and used all the same techniques to look inconspicuous as Rafe would.

Definitely Barker.

Time to flush him out.

Rafe told Lizzy to go ahead without him. He couldn't pretend that her obvious relief didn't deflate him somewhat. It seemed she didn't want his company nearly as much as he wanted hers.

"Thank you for accompanying me," she said.

"No need to thank me. You did all the hard work yourself."

"Perhaps. Or perhaps your presence was sufficient to convince him I was right."

Great. Wonderful. So he was useful when it came to frightening people, just not interesting enough to have a conversation with.

He watched her until she was through Newgate's arch, then he wandered into a nearby alley and waited. And waited. Barker didn't join him.

Strange. Barker never slunk away from a confrontation. He liked to state his case and fight. The fact he didn't only confirmed what Hughe had said—Barker would find a way to hurt Rafe using those he cared about. Thank God Lizzy was gone. Even so, Rafe would follow her, keeping his distance until she reached the tiring house safely.

But the question remained: Had Barker followed them all the way out to the priory without Rafe noticing? Possible, since he'd been distracted by the way Lizzy responded to Hughe's flirting. Rafe should have told him she was almost engaged to wed James, only he hadn't thought about it at the time.

He seemed to be losing his wits. Ever since Lizzy's mouth had beckoned him for a kiss over her kitchen table, he couldn't think clearly. There'd been a smokiness in those big doe eyes, and for a brief moment he almost believed she desired him more than she feared him. But that was—

Bloody hell. She was doing it again and she wasn't even there.

He was a terrible brother.

~~~

"Walter Gripp isn't going to hold up any more of our plays!" Lizzy announced upon entering the tiring house.

Edward looked up from the prompt book. "What do you mean?"

"I mean I just went to see him and told him Sir Robert Blakewell would be most unhappy to have Min's plays banned, and he agreed to allow hers through. I don't believe he'll allow Jonson's, however."

"Lizzy!" Antony hugged her. "You're a marvel."

"God's blood!" Freddie whooped. "*You* got him to back down?"

"I did." She grinned. She could hardly believe it herself. *She'd* convinced Gripp to back down. Not Edward, Henry, or one of the players, not even Rafe, but *her*.

"In that case," Henry said, crouching down to rummage through a trunk, "we all have new lines to learn." He pulled out a stack of pages tied together with ribbon. The other players crowded around him, but not before Antony gave her another hug and Edward kissed her forehead. Even Freddie congratulated her on her achievement. Lizzy couldn't wait to tell Roger. He'd be so pleased. Perhaps he would give her a bonus this month.

She sat down at the table, picked up the toga that needed mending, and tuned out the players' voices as they went through their lines. It was easy to do, distracted as she was.

And she wasn't only distracted by her achievement. Her wits had been addled ever since supper the day before. Ever since Rafe had almost kissed her. Indeed, she was so distracted, she stabbed herself twice with the needle and sewed the toga to her own skirt.

"You are a disaster today," Antony said, pulling up a stool and sitting beside her.

"I am?"

He nodded and held up a bright marigold wig she'd forgotten to arrange. Antony was supposed to play a Roman empress that afternoon. She had so much to do before then.

"I'll fix it after I finish this," she said, unstitching the toga from her skirt.

Antony giggled. "Never mind, I can manage. You keep working on the toga. So, this strangeness of yours doesn't have anything to do with that mysterious Rafe Fletcher, does it?"

"No! Of course not. Rafe is simply a neighbor, nothing more."

"Not even the brother of the man you're going to marry?"

"That too, of course."

Dear James. She hadn't thought much about him since his departure, something she must rectify now everything was returning to normal. What was he doing now? Wherever he was, she hoped he was warm and dry.

"So if it's not the devilish Rafe, you must be deliriously happy that Gripp is no longer a threat to us."

"He certainly isn't a threat anymore," said Roger Style, standing in the curtained exit leading out to the stage. "He's dead."

"What?" came a chorus of voices from the tiring house.

"Are you sure?" Edward asked.

"Best bloody news I've heard all year," Freddie said.

"He can't be," Lizzy said. "I just saw him not long ago."

Style came slowly inside. His gaze settled on her, cautious and...nervous?

Cold fingers of ice gripped her heart and squeezed. It beat once then stopped.

"How did he die?" asked Antony slowly, his gaze sliding back and forth between them.

"Murdered," Roger said without taking his eyes off her.

"It wasn't me," she whispered. They all looked at her.

"The authorities don't think so. They have a witness who says you did it."

"A witness! That's impossible."

"You and that ruffian friend of yours. I hear they're going to arrest you both."

CHAPTER 6

Rafe! She had to tell Rafe. Had to warn him.

Antony gasped. "You've got to get away!" He dragged her to her feet but she was already halfway up. "Now! Go!"

She threw her sewing on the table, scattering pins. Some fell onto the rushes.

"Leave them," Henry said when she bent to pick them up. He shoved her toward the back door.

"My parents!"

"We'll take care of them," Edward said. "Now go!"

She ran.

"But who will get the props ready?" Roger wailed behind her. "We have a performance in less than three hours!"

"We'll do it," someone yelled at him.

She opened the door and barreled straight into Rafe. He held her and for one brief moment she leaned into those big, capable arms and nestled against his solid chest and felt safe. His heart beat ferociously against her cheek. They hadn't arrested him.

Thank God.

"You're here," she said between gasps.

"I wanted to check that my friend...What's wrong?" he asked, searching her face. "Lizzy, what is it?"

"Gripp's dead and they think we did it. They have a witness!"

He swore and glanced over his shoulder. "Then the constables will be here soon."

"We can tell them we're innocent," she said, tears stinging her eyes. She blinked them back. Now was not the time for hysterics.

"They won't believe us."

He was right. With a witness claiming to have seen them, their case was hopeless. It wouldn't matter if he was lying, there were many other witnesses at the Revels office who had indeed seen them speaking to Gripp that morning. No jury would think them innocent.

Rafe gripped her hand and pulled her down the steps to the street. She stumbled on the bottom one and he caught her around the waist. "I'm so sorry, Lizzy," he said, "but we need to be fast." He closed her hand in his and tugged her after him. "This way."

They ran down a thin alley wedged between two crooked buildings. The deep shadows swallowed them as footsteps came closer. Rafe's big arm flattened Lizzy against the wall and his body hid her from anyone passing. When the footsteps retreated, he took her hand again and ran. At the other end of the alley he paused, looked right and left, then turned right into another dark, narrow lane.

"Where will we go?" she asked, running alongside him. He had shortened his strides so she could keep up, something for which she was grateful.

He stopped abruptly near the alley's exit and pulled her hard up against his body. She pressed herself into him, a solid wall of strength, and felt the steady rhythm of his heartbeat against her cheek. He folded his arms around her, holding her there, and she reached around his waist and clung on. He kissed the top of her head and she lifted her face to look up at him. Heat smoldered in his half-closed eyes as they focused on her mouth.

Two men ran down the adjoining street and Rafe shifted, breaking contact. One of the pursuers pointed to the alley where Lizzy and Rafe hid in the shadows. Rafe tapped her on the shoulder and pointed back the way they'd come.

They hadn't gotten far when another two men blocked their exit. The original two advanced from behind.

Trapped.

"Stay here." Rafe let go of her hand and she wrapped her arms around herself. He touched her cheek. "It's all right. Don't be afraid. There's only four."

Only four!

He stepped into the middle of the alley with his hands in the air. "Let her go," he said. "She's innocent. I'll face the charges."

"Rafe!" she cried.

"Our orders are to take both of you," one of them said. "You're outnumbered. Don't put up a fight and it'll all be over with no one getting hurt."

He was right. They had no choice. Rafe nodded and she closed her eyes and sank to the ground. It was all over. They would have to face a court and argue their innocence somehow. But at least they were still alive and unharmed.

Hot tears slid down her cheeks. What would become of her parents? Who would look after them? And James? Poor James would return to London to find her in prison, or worse... hanged for a crime she didn't commit. His brother too.

"A good choice," one of the constables said. "Come with— *oomph.*"

Lizzy opened her eyes. One of the men clutched at his cheek and another charged at Rafe, fists swinging. Rafe ducked and the constable careened past, off balance. He landed facedown in the earth.

The other two constables drew out swords, the whine of the metal against the leather-covered scabbard loud in the alley. A scream caught in Lizzy's throat. She should look away but couldn't. There was too much happening and Rafe might need her.

He drew his rapier. "I don't want to harm you," he said to them. "You have a job to do, I understand that."

"Then put down your weapon," the biggest man said.

"Can't do that unless you promise to let her go."

"Our orders are—"

"I know what they are. I'm telling you to forget your orders and let her go. Tell your superiors she got away from you." As he spoke he moved in a slow circle toward them, but instead of staying still, they circled too until they were near their other two injured companions. Rafe stopped. "Well?"

"Our orders are to get both of you."

He shook his head. "Not employed for your brains, I see."

The big man bared his teeth, or what few he had, and lumbered toward Rafe, the other constable right behind him. Rafe parried the first strike then the second. His blade diced and jabbed in a rapid dance, forcing his opponents back into the wall. It was nothing like the choreographed fight scenes on the stage. This scene was brutal and fierce, yet with an elegance all its own in the way Rafe wielded his weapon. He was clearly a master swordsman, the rapier an extension of his arm, as natural to him as his own fingers.

He felled first one then the other constable, not fatally, only to have the first two recover and join in. Hats got crushed underfoot and the bigger of the constables was breathing hard and sweating like a fountain. Rafe didn't look in the least tired and his pace quickened.

"I'll give you one more chance," he said. "Take me, leave her, and I won't hurt you."

"Can't do that," said one and lunged.

Rafe stopped the man's blade with his own and forced it down to the ground. It became a battle of strength, which Rafe appeared to be winning until a second constable then a third came at him.

Lizzy screamed. Rafe turned, dragging his opponent with him by the front of his jerkin. He shoved him back into the two advancing constables. All three tumbled to the ground in a move that would have had the groundlings roaring with laughter if it had been performed onstage.

In the fray, they'd almost forgotten the fourth man. Cradling one arm to his chest, he lurched to his feet behind Rafe and rushed with his sword.

"Look out!" Lizzy shouted.

Rafe turned and parried the blow. Nearby, the other constables stirred. Two of their swords had been sent skittering across the ground when they fell, and landed near her. She blinked at them. Could she? No, let Rafe take care of it. Violence was his life, not hers.

One of the men groaned, stirred. He eyed her then the swords. When she didn't move, he inched closer. Closer. If he got to one, there would be no hope. Rafe couldn't fight them all at once. The man reached out.

Lizzy snatched the swords up and sliced through the man's shoulder then his companion's as he too stirred. Their shouts of pain bounced off the walls and throbbed between her ears. Her gut heaved at the sight of the oozing blood, but she quickly recovered.

She'd done it. Mousy Lizzy Croft had fought off two men.

She felt quite wild with relief. And powerful. Is that how Rafe felt after fighting off attackers? Did a kind of thrill rush through him when he performed his mercenary's duties?

"Witch!" cried one of the constables, backing up into Rafe. His wide, terrified eyes didn't leave hers. "No mere wench could wield a sword like that."

Rafe disposed of his opponent with a swift kick to the stomach then dealt with the young constable, who appeared more terrified of her than him.

"You need to meet more women," Rafe told him and punched him in the nose. The man crumpled to the ground and didn't get up.

None of the others advanced. They were all unarmed, breathing hard, and injured. Rafe grabbed Lizzy's forearm because she still held the swords in her hands, and together they ran out of the alley.

They wended their way through Southwark's streets and discarded the extra swords behind a stack of empty barrels near an inn. They ran on, not stopping until they reached the busy thoroughfare of Borough High Street. It was easy to blend into the passing traffic, but Rafe kept Lizzy tucked into his side. She didn't want to be anywhere else.

They passed the Tabard Inn's arched entrance and stopped at the door of a tiny two-story house with a distinct lean to the left. If it wasn't for the leather worker's shop propping it up, it would probably fall down. The walls were a patchwork of wooden beams and the occasional brick with the spaces in between filled by daub. He removed a loose brick near the bottom and removed a key from the cavity. He unlocked the door and hustled Lizzy into a large but mostly empty room then closed the door behind him.

She sagged against the wall and gulped in air, relief and fear making her legs weak and her body tremble. And there was still that strange thrilling sensation too. She had wielded a sword to save herself. How many women could claim to have done that?

"Wait here," he said and disappeared up the stairs. The boards creaked overhead and dust drifted down onto her bare head. She'd lost her cap some time ago and her hair tumbled around her shoulders in a tangled mess.

She'd almost caught her breath by the time he returned, and her blood had ceased pumping through her veins. Where before she'd felt light and alive, now her limbs weighed her down.

They were being hunted for murder. The authorities thought she and Rafe had killed Gripp. There was no escaping.

"We're alone," he said.

Alone. With Rafe. And she couldn't go home.

She sank to the floor, put her head on her knees, and burst into tears.

Rafe wanted to do something. He should hold her or say something reassuring or perhaps tell a joke. He did none of those things. They probably wouldn't be welcome and he could only think of crude jokes anyway. Being holed up in one of Hughe's properties after a fight brought them all to mind again.

He drew in a long, measured breath because his heart was still racing even though his body had stopped. It ached too, ached like the devil. That was new. It might have something to do with the scared, miserable woman sitting on the dusty floor. Her fear was palpable. He could feel it like an echo deep within him. Worse than that, there was nothing he could do to comfort her. She wouldn't welcome his efforts—she'd made that clear in their short reacquaintance.

So he sat next to her, close but not touching, and rested the back of his head against the wall. Hopefully it would be enough.

Her sobbing eased immediately and after a few more moments she stopped crying altogether.

"I'm sorry," she said, wiping her cheeks. "I'm all right now."

"There's no need to apologize."

She peered at him from behind a curtain of wavy hair the color of sun-bleached straw. There was so much of it. Why hadn't he noticed it before? "I don't ordinarily crumble like that, no matter what you might think," she said.

"I don't think anything." Except that she was pretty even when she'd been crying.

She gave him a wobbly smile. It was the most real one she'd given him yet. "Thank you, Rafe. For everything. If you hadn't been there those constables would have arrested me."

"And me. I was trying to save my own neck too."

"I was on my way to warn you."

He stared at her. "You were?" So she did give him more than a passing thought. Well. Of course she would. She was the kindest soul he'd ever met. She wouldn't think twice about putting her life in danger to save another's, even if it was the life of someone she hardly knew and didn't particularly like. "Thank you, Lizzy."

Her smile dimmed and she looked down at her shoes. It was difficult to tell if her face was red from embarrassment or crying. It would seem her brief moment of trusting him, of not being afraid, was over.

"What happens now?" she asked.

"Now we stay here until either the real murderer is found, or until we come up with a better plan."

"That's it?" She bit her lip as if she hadn't meant for the retort to slip out.

He laughed and God, it felt good. He needed to laugh. The day hadn't been a bad one compared to how they usually went when he was working for Hughe, but it felt far more draining. He was relieved to get Lizzy far away from those constables. Innocents like her shouldn't be embroiled in filthy business like murder. Whoever was behind it would feel the sharp end of Rafe's blade through his gut when he found him.

"I haven't had time to think of anything else yet," he said. "Maybe after I eat." He got to his feet and held out his hand.

She hesitated then took it. Her fingers were so small in his, so fine and delicate despite the callus on the middle one from using a needle for so many years.

"Is there food?" she asked, withdrawing her hand. She made her way through the hall to the kitchen. It was small, smaller than the one at his house, and contained only one stool, a table, and a few cooking utensils hanging from hooks. A tinderbox beside the fireplace at least had flint stones and dry tinder. They checked the adjoining storeroom but it was empty except for a grain sack with its contents oozing from a hole.

"Rats," he said.

She screwed up her nose and retreated to the kitchen. He left her lighting the fire and went to inspect the outbuildings. They looked like they hadn't been used in years. The door to what had once been a brewery came off in his hand. He propped it back up and picked some logs off a log pile then rejoined Lizzy in the kitchen. He placed one of the logs on top of the lit kindling in the fireplace. It popped and hissed then caught.

"Is there water?" she asked.

"No. I'll fetch some."

"You can't go out now! The street will be crawling with constables looking for us."

He smiled. He couldn't help it. Having someone worry about him was a new experience and he liked it. "After dark then. Don't worry, I'll provide for us."

She opened her mouth, took a breath, and for a moment he thought she would ask him some questions about how he would provide for them or about the house, but she said nothing and turned back to the fire.

"This place belongs to Hughe," he said.

"Lord Oxley?" Why did her face light up at the mention of his name? "Did he tell you where to find the key?"

"Yes."

She tossed her hair over her shoulder and inspected a pan. "Why doesn't he put tenants in it?"

Like the other properties Hughe owned, the house was used by his men during assignments. It provided shelter and anonymity but wasn't set up for lengthy stays. Rafe could tell her none of that. It was against Hughe's rules. It would also lead to many more questions, ones he couldn't answer without making her even more afraid of him. She was skittish enough knowing he'd been a mercenary, she'd be even worse if she knew he'd been an assassin. Recently.

"Who knows why Hughe does what he does?" he said.

She rubbed the pan with her sleeve. "Can he help us with the authorities? Talk to them or vouch for your character?"

If Hughe did that, he would draw attention to himself. The wrong attention. Another thing Rafe couldn't tell her. "He's not in London at present."

"Oh yes. I forgot. Do you think he could help when he returns?"

"No."

"But he must have some influence at court."

"No."

"Not even a little?"

"Not even."

"But he's an earl!"

For a shy little thing, she had a tenacity about her when she forgot she was afraid of him. "An earl with no influence."

With a shake of her head, she removed a gridiron from the hook where it hung and weighed it in her hand. "Is he married? I imagine a gentleman of Lord Oxley's station would have a wife or betrothed."

Or a mistress or several. "You're full of questions all of a sudden."

She colored and pretended the gridiron was the most interesting thing in the room. The topic of Hughe St. Alban, the earl of Oxley was laid to rest, thank God. Rafe didn't need reminding that his friend had a way of making sensible ladies lose their heads or shy ones find their voice.

He left her to her inspection of the kitchen utensils and made his way back to the main room. He peered out through the single window facing the street but could see little except the houses across the road. Upstairs, he stood next to the window of the front bedchamber and watched the street below for a long time. A group of five men walked by twice. None of them were the men he'd fought. All of them were alert and scanning their surroundings, but Rafe knew he couldn't be seen. The bedchamber was dark thanks to the thick layer of grime covering the windowpanes.

One of their number, a thin man wearing a tall black hat and short cloak, asked questions of the neighboring shopkeepers but he didn't visit the houses. If anyone had seen Rafe and Lizzy enter the building, they were keeping their mouths shut. The people of Southwark had no love for the authorities or for disruption to their daily lives.

Dusk crept up and calmly extinguished daylight and the activity that went with it. The constables didn't show their faces again and wouldn't until morning. Rafe went downstairs and found Lizzy sitting on a chair near the hearth, her back to him. The light from the fire edged her hair in gold and he had a sudden urge to touch it to see if it was as soft as it looked.

He curled his fingers and dug the nails into his palms. "Hungry?"

She jumped and he wished he'd made more noise coming down the stairs.

"Did I wake you?" he asked.

She shook her head and held up a leather-bound book. He laughed. Bloody Hughe and his books. He always had at least one stashed in a chest in each of his houses to stave off boredom, so he claimed. When Rafe or one of the others urged him to remove them to Oxley House on Hughe's estate for safekeeping, he merely shrugged and said it didn't matter if they were stolen, as he'd read them all anyway.

"I am a little," she said. "Hungry," she added, when he gave her a blank look.

"I'll fetch us something to eat."

"You have money?"

"Yes," he lied. No need to add to her troubles by telling her he would steal to feed them.

He stretched his hands out to the fire to warm them but her small, desperate voice beckoned his attention. "Rafe."

"Yes?" The word caught in his throat at the sight of those big eyes turned on him, despair trembling in their depths.

"What do we do now?"

He crouched at her feet and caught both her hands in his. He wanted to bring them to his lips, taste them, kiss them, press them to his heart. But instead he simply said, "Now I get us something to eat. When our stomachs are full, we talk."

~ ~ ~

Rafe took bread and a pie from the baker and in a nearby house he found a bottle of ale and a wedge of cheese in the untended kitchen. He followed the smell of cooking meat to a large house and waited a long time for the occupants to retire before he relieved them of bacon and pigeon. He packed everything into the sack he'd taken from the storeroom of Hughe's house, the bottom tied up to close the hole nibbled by the rats.

He spared a thought for James as he ate a slice of bacon. Rafe needed to see him and soon. The food he'd given him wouldn't last much longer. Then there was the danger of what the big ogre of a prisoner might do out of hunger, frustration, or boredom. *Hold on, brother.*

Rafe made his way back to the house and Lizzy. As he passed the Tabard, a drunk lurched out of the archway and pissed against the wall beneath a lit torch. A thin man followed him, his steps steadier. He wore a tall black hat and a short cloak. The leader of the constables. His blunt gaze connected with Rafe's and narrowed, sizing him up. He would have been given a description of his quarry, but had not seen him in person.

Rafe staggered off, just another drunkard on his way home. He'd almost left the inn behind when another man cradling his arm joined Tall Hat and the Pisser. A man Rafe recognized as one he'd fought in the alley.

"It's him!" he shouted.

"Arrest him!" yelled Tall Hat. "Sound the hue and cry, NOW!"

CHAPTER 7

Rafe hoisted the sack over his shoulder and set off at a run in the opposite direction of Lizzy and Hughe's house. Behind him, dozens of voices rose into the night air, some of them sounding excited but most of them drunkenly slurred. Those he lost at the first fence.

He leapt over it and into the yard of a house. A pig squealed and a hen clucked in indignation. Mud splattered over his boots and up his legs but didn't slow his progress. He jumped the next fence then the next. The shouts followed him, although most seemed farther away.

He dropped into another yard, startling a woman standing in the doorway of her house, a candle in hand. She wore nothing but a shift, the top unlaced to reveal an immodest amount of her extraordinarily large breasts.

"Get out!" she shouted and made a rude gesture.

"Gladly," Rafe said as he climbed over the back fence.

"Moll!" one of the leading pursuers called out. "Got a wench and an ale inside?"

"Sure do, Hal," she said with a welcome in her voice. "Which will it be first?"

Rafe scaled one more fence and found himself on a street outside another inn. Those that hadn't stopped at Moll's establishment might be inclined to stop for a drink. Southwark men weren't the sort to pursue a stranger to aid a constable once it grew too hard or the thrill of the hunt wore off. He glanced over his shoulder and was surprised to see the group's leader, minus his tall hat, closer than expected. His cloak billowed behind him as he ran. Five others followed, panting heavily.

They wouldn't last much longer. The leader, however, was a wiry fellow and fleet of foot. He would be difficult to shake.

Time to get creative.

Rafe hoisted the sack higher onto his shoulder and ran faster. Another glance back proved it was a good tactic—only two men had kept up, the leader and one other, a sprightly lad with long hair. Rafe liked those odds.

He slipped into an alley and found the perfect hiding spot. A few moments later his pursuers entered and stopped. Looked around.

"Where is he?" the lad asked between gasps of air.

Come closer. A few steps.

"Must have gone straight through," the leader said. He was breathing hard but not as much as the lad. "Where's this lane go?"

"To another street. He's fast for a big fellow, ain't he?" The lad sounded impressed. Rafe was beginning to like him.

"He's a murderer." As if that explained it. The leader drew his sword and nodded at the lad to go first.

The boy set off like an eager puppy on his first hunt.

Rafe timed the drop perfectly. The laden sack hit the boy on the head and he crumpled to the ground without a sound.

The leader glanced up. "What in—"

Rafe swung from the beam of the overhanging upper story and booted Tall Hat's sword out of his hand before he had time to wield it. He landed on the ground near the disarmed leader and got in a swift punch before the man had time to think.

"London is my favorite place for playing hide-and-seek," Rafe said, drawing his rapier. He lunged at the fellow but gave him only a minor cut to the chin, enough to scare him but not enough to do any grave injury. "Now, let's come to an agreement. You let me go and I won't kill either of you."

"I can't do that." It was too dark in the alley to see more than an outline, but Rafe could hear him clearly enough—he didn't sound in the least afraid. Nor was he cocky. Just very determined. "My job is to arrest you."

"Then you might die. But what about the lad? Is it his job to arrest me too?"

The man hesitated. Rafe flexed his fingers around his sword hilt. He didn't have time for this. He was hungry and he wanted to get back to Lizzy. She might be worried about him. He smiled into the darkness. He quite liked the thought of that.

"Sorry, my friend, I'm an innocent man. Innocent of Gripp's murder, at least. I'm also very busy." He sheathed his sword and saw the leader sag a little, relieved. Fool. Never relax in the presence of a threat. Ever.

He feinted a punch to Tall Hat's stomach, but when he moved to protect that area, Rafe hit him in the jaw instead. The crunch of bone on bone echoed through the silence. Another blow to the head saw his opponent fall to the ground, out cold.

Rafe set off but didn't get far. The lad jumped on his back and landed blow upon blow on Rafe's sides and head.

Rafe reached around and grabbed him by his jerkin and tossed him against the wall. The boy slid to the ground, his hair covering his face so Rafe couldn't tell if he was conscious or not.

"Good try," he said and picked up the sack. "Next time, use a blade, not your fists."

He set off down the alley. No one followed. He ran down streets, climbed more fences, zigged and zagged through Southwark. He snatched clothing off washing lines and just before he reached Hughe's house, he found two buckets full of water tied to either end of a pole. He settled the pole across his shoulders, picked up the bulging sack, and headed home.

~ ~ ~

Lizzy gasped with relief when Rafe came through the back door. He wasn't harmed. Thank God. She'd heard the hue and cry and had been worried sick ever since. When he didn't return she thought the worst. Yet here he was, unharmed and smiling, carrying provisions.

He set down the buckets of water and dumped the sack on the kitchen table before she could decide how best to react. "Miss me?"

Somehow she held back a sob and managed to smile despite her thundering heart. "Yes. My stomach has been reminding me how much."

He chuckled. "And here I thought you were growing to like me for me and not for what I could provide."

"I do like you for you," she said, feeling giddy and happy and so very, very relieved. "I like you for the way you can carry two buckets of water, a sack of food, and..." She peered into the sack and pulled out a woman's shift. "Clothes!"

"I hope it fits."

"You thought of everything." She blinked up at him and was granted another big, open smile.

He moved closer. It would be so easy to touch the tiny creases on either side of his mouth, caress those curving lips, and capture his happiness in her hands. She wanted to see him grinning forever, wanted *this* Rafe, the joyful, boyish Rafe. She could almost forget the other when he smiled at her like that.

But his smile slipped and his eyelids lowered, smothering the shining, dancing eyes. He stepped away and ran a hand through his hair.

"The fire in the hall will be visible through the front window," he said and moved off.

"I doused it as soon as I heard the hue and cry go up."

He nodded his approval. "We'll have to avoid that room except to access the stairs."

He poured a bucket of water into the pot over the fire while she unpacked the contents of the sack. There was enough food for two days if they were careful, and a spare set of clothes for each of them. There were actually two ladies' bodices, but one was built for a woman of extremely generous proportions. Lizzy could take it in and use the excess fabric for something. One of the trunks had contained a serviceable sewing kit along with the book and spare candles. She'd moved all the contents into the storeroom for easy access.

"I think the pie has split," she said, removing it from the sack. "It looks edible anyway."

They ate some of the pie cold and stored the rest in the bread box in the storeroom, wrapped in a cloth along with the bread, cheese, and meat. Rafe checked the water in the pot then fetched two bowls and two cloths from the storeroom. "For washing," he said. He set them down on the table and sat on a stool. She sat too and although she wasn't watching him, she could feel his gaze on her. It made her hot all over. Her skin prickled. She tucked her hands between her knees and stared down at the knotty wood of the table surface.

"Don't be afraid," he murmured.

Was she afraid? Yes, but not as much as she probably should be. Not since Rafe had returned. Having him with her was a comfort and not a cause for increasing her fears the way his presence usually did. That surprised her. Perhaps she could even speak to him without turning into a radish.

"I know you're worried about your parents," he said.

"I am, but Antony and the others will take care of them. Word will reach Blake and Min soon enough too, and they'll ensure Mama and Papa are not left alone, as well as write to my sisters." She passed a hand over her eyes and blew out a breath. "I'm only worried about them because they'll be so worried about me. Is there any way we can let them know we're safe?"

He shook his head. "I'm sorry, Lizzy, we can't risk it. For their sakes as well as our own." He reached for her hand but she withdrew it out of instinct.

His fingers closed on empty air and he let his hand fall. A small ache lodged in her chest. He'd only been trying to comfort her. She shouldn't treat him as if he really was the murderer. He'd been nothing but kind and helpful. Yet she couldn't bring herself to completely set aside her apprehension.

And she would be alone with him all night.

"What do we do now?" she asked, breaking the awkward silence.

He sighed. "Now we wait. Tomorrow they'll start looking for us. They spotted me outside the Tabard, so they'll likely concentrate their efforts near here. I expect them to search the houses and shops now that they have reason to believe we're close."

Search! Then they would be discovered! "So we have to leave tonight?" She was so tired from running and worrying, but if she had to go then she would. There was nothing else to be done.

"I have a better plan."

"Oh?"

He gave her that odd half smile, the one that made him look a little like James. "Have you ever wanted to perform on the stage alongside Antony and the others?"

He outlined his plan. By the time he was finished she was staring at him, awed by his deviousness. It obviously wasn't the first time he'd been pursued by the authorities.

"I'll wake you early to get ready," he said.

"And afterward? We may avoid our pursuers, but how will we prove our innocence?"

"Leave that up to me."

She pressed her lips together to bite back a retort. Did he think her useless? A hindrance? Perhaps she would be, but sitting around waiting for him while he sought the real murderer and worrying if Rafe was dead or injured was not how she wanted to spend her day. She would simply have to think of a way to be helpful. So helpful he had no option but to include her.

"The water should be warm now," he said, rising. He dipped a bowl into the pot and handed it to her then filled the other one for himself. "I'll go upstairs," he said.

"No, I will." She left, but realized she'd forgotten the cloth and returned to the kitchen.

Rafe, his back to her, was in the process of undoing his jerkin. She should look away or alert him to her presence but she didn't. She watched as he removed his shirt.

God's blood, *look* at him.

She'd never known the male back could be so magnificent. His skin was the color of warmed honey and looked just as smooth. It stretched taut over muscles, across wide shoulders, and down to his narrow waist. Scars of varying lengths and shapes marked his skin but only enhanced the magnificence, the way intricate carvings turned a plain piece of wood into a beautiful one. There was a curved scar on his left shoulder, a straight one on his right, and another ringing his upper arm.

Without either doublet or jerkin fastenings to hold them up, his hose began to slip off. And then they were completely off and he was entirely, utterly, gloriously naked.

Oh. My. Heavens.

She should leave. But how could a girl not look at all that hard, smooth flesh when it was put in front of her? And those buttocks…Was it sinful to want to sink her teeth into them? Probably. Anything that delicious had to be wicked. She would pray twice as long next Sunday to save her soul.

He picked up the cloth and she held her breath. If she had any sense she would turn away but it seemed sense had fled and her mind was empty of every thought except one—that many women, and perhaps some men, would pay dearly to have a front-row position at this performance.

He squeezed water out of the cloth and scrubbed it across one shoulder. Droplets slid over the undulations of muscle, down his back to one perfectly mounded buttock.

Lizzy licked her top lip and pressed her palm to her rapidly beating chest. She was suddenly thirsty. Parched. A few drops of water would rectify that. A lick here and there. Oh yes, *there* for certain. All over his—

He turned. Fully. A small, strangled sound gurgled up from her throat. She'd never seen one of *those* before. The actors never changed in front of her and without brothers, the male parts were somewhat of a mystery. Was it supposed to lean to the left like that? Or be so big and, well, dangly? And should it move of its own accord? Why was it growing all of a sudden?

A pair of big hands holding a damp cloth dropped in front of it.

Lizzy jumped, spilling water from the bowl onto the floor. Her face blazed fiercer than ever before. She couldn't look up. She'd rather die first. Indeed, death would be a welcome escape.

Please kill me.

She spun around. Tried to gather her wits and still her racing heart. "I...I...I'm sorry," she whispered. "I shouldn't have...I'm very sorry."

His low rumble of laughter cooled her heated face a little. "Don't be. I'm not embarrassed."

Then why cover up?

She heard the gentle *splash* of water followed by the *splish* of drips. He must have resumed washing. She closed her eyes, but that was no help. The image of the water sliding over his muscular back, down to his buttocks and thighs...

She tried to think of something to say but couldn't. Where had her mind gone? Ah yes, straight to his nether regions.

"You're quite the innocent, aren't you?"

An innocent. Well, she supposed she was, compared to him. Rafe must have lovers in cities and villages all over the world. How many *did* he have? Dozens? Hundreds?

It didn't matter. It wasn't her business. However many he'd had, it was more than she, virgin that she was, and more than James.

James. She groaned. Poor, dear James didn't deserve the sort of woman who desperately wanted to turn around and take another peek at his naked brother.

On the other hand, it would be a good thing if she wasn't such an innocent going into the marriage bed. What man would want a silly girl who couldn't stop staring at his manhood like it was an exotic creature? Best to get the staring out of the way before they married so the sight of him wasn't such a shock on their wedding night.

She glanced over her shoulder and her heart sank. Rafe was already dressed in a clean shirt and hose. He caught her looking. She expected him to laugh at her to ease the tension and her flaring embarrassment, but he didn't. His handsome features looked pinched, pained almost. He blinked once, slowly, and turned away.

She bit the inside of her lip. She must have offended him after all with her blatant staring.

"I'll go upstairs," he said. "You might as well stay here now and come up when you're finished. Can you find your way in the dark? We'd better not use candles."

She nodded and folded her arms against a shiver.

"Good night, Lizzy."

"Good night, Rafe."

He paused at the door, and she thought he would say something further but he didn't. She waited until she heard his footsteps reach the landing upstairs, then she removed her clothes and washed.

~ ~ ~

Rafe wasn't known for making poor decisions, so why in God's name did he undress while Lizzy watched? Why hadn't he checked she'd left? He must have lost his wits during the pursuit. No other explanation for it. Lizzy was an innocent. He shouldn't have subjected her to his nakedness. If he'd walked in on another man bathing in her presence he'd have thumped some sense into him.

Not that Lizzy seemed to mind. Her gaze had been firmly fixed on his cock. She hadn't looked appalled or repelled. Not in the least. Fascinated and thrilled if her flushed face was any indication. She'd been smiling too, just the hint of one on those full lips. Until he'd covered up. Then, and only then, had she been embarrassed.

Worse than that, he'd *liked* the way she'd watched him. The way her big curious eyes fixed entirely on him, the way her tongue had skimmed across her lips and her breathing quickened. He recognized desire and want, the aching need to touch and explore and *be* touched and explored. Recognized it in himself too. He grew hard again just picturing her face. She'd wanted him down there in the kitchen. God help him, he would have taken her too if he hadn't come to his senses just in time.

Because she hadn't wanted *him*, just his cock. There was a difference. She might be curious about the male body but that didn't mean she desired the man attached to it. Nor should she. She was James's intended. She loved James. James loved her, needed her.

Rafe rolled onto his side and punched the lumpy straw pallet. It was going to be a long, restless night.

He must have drifted off to sleep eventually because he awoke with a start. Someone was talking. It only took a moment to realize it was Lizzy's voice coming from the bed-chamber across the landing. He crept out of his room, his feet silent on the bare floor. Straining to hear, he could just make out Lizzy muttering quietly beyond her closed door.

Cold tentacles of fear wrapped around his insides. He reached for the door handle.

Lizzy screamed.

CHAPTER 8

The screaming woke Lizzy. The door crashing back on its hinges sent her scrambling to the end of the bed, clasping the blankets to her chest.

"Lizzy? Lizzy, are you all right?"

In the darkness she could just make out Rafe's big frame rushing into her room. She drew her knees up close to her chest, tried to make herself small and inconspicuous, but still a whimper escaped. That's when she realized the screaming had come from her.

She'd been dreaming. Rafe had been in the dream, coming for her. A menacing, powerful presence with madness in his eyes and teeth bared in a primal snarl.

It was the same expression, exactly the same, as that awful day years ago.

"Lizzy! Talk to me!" His voice was thready, desperate. He stood over her, so close she could reach out and touch him. She kept her hands inside the blanket, clutching it so tight her fingers cramped.

He checked under and around the bed, rattled the clasp on the casement window to see if it was still locked. Then he came back and sat down on the edge of the mattress. Very close. His breathing was loud in the silence, almost louder than her own.

He wrapped one arm around her and pulled her gently to his chest. She could feel his warm breath in her hair and his palm against the back of her neck. His body shuddered or perhaps hers did.

Her heart leapt into her throat. She closed her eyes, breathed in the scent of him, and forced herself to relax. *This* was the real Rafe Fletcher, not the monster from her dream. *That* Rafe, the nightmare one, had come at her with anger and hatred oozing from him like blood from an open wound. He was not like that anymore. Definitely not.

So why was she so frightened of him?

She shifted away and tugged the blanket high up under her chin. But it wouldn't work. No matter what he did, no matter how kindly he treated her, she would always remember the Rafe of his youth. The one who'd almost killed his own kin, then looked at her, a child of fourteen watching from the shadows, and smiled with satisfaction.

He must not remember seeing her there that day, but she did. She remembered every pound of his fist, every spray of blood, every sneer. Most of all she remembered the cold ruthlessness in those pitch-black eyes. Killer's eyes.

He'd almost murdered the man who'd raised him from infancy. She knew old man Pritchard hadn't been the warmest of fathers toward either of his sons, but surely he'd not warranted such a brutal beating on the street by his own stepchild. Her family and neighbors had been too shocked and too scared to stop him, and he'd left before any of them could summon the courage to confront him. They'd helped Pritchard inside and that's when his wife's body was discovered, with a tearful James cradling her. When asked if Rafe had somehow contributed to her death, he'd been adamant it wasn't his brother's doing. It was the last thing he'd ever said on the matter, to anyone.

"Lizzy?" Rafe moved closer. She moved back. It was too dark to see his expression but she could sense his confusion. "What's wrong?"

"N-n-nothing. A bad dream. Sorry I woke you."

"You didn't wake me." He blew out a breath. "I thought someone was in here. I thought...Never mind. I'm relieved it was only a dream."

It *was* only a dream, yet it was a memory too. While a dream could be dismissed with a laugh and a lit candle, a memory could not.

"Can I get you anything?" he asked. "I think there's some pie left."

"No, thank you."

"Cold bacon?"

"I'm not hungry." Especially for cold bacon.

"Spiced wine?"

"We don't have any."

"I could find some."

That was a jest, wasn't it? His teeth flashed white in the darkness. Yes, it was. The remaining shackles of her dream fell away and she lowered the blanket to her waist.

"What if I said yes?" she asked.

"Then I would set off and find some. But that would present a problem because it means leaving you here alone and vulnerable."

"You could leave me your sword."

"You would have me go out unarmed?" he asked with mock horror.

"No, you would still have the twin weapons of wit and charm in your arsenal."

He laughed softly. "Then I really would be in trouble. I am not Hughe. Wit and charm are not two of my God-given talents."

No, but he made up for the lack in so many other ways. His sheer size and brute strength for one, and a way with his fists. A brutal way. She hugged herself. His admirable attempt to make her forget her nightmare with jokes suddenly fell flat.

"Thank you for your kindness," she said.

"Ah. You're dismissing me." He made no move to go. "Care to tell me what happened in this dream?"

She shook her head. "It was just a dream."

"But one that clearly haunts you still. Lizzy." He touched her cheek with the back of his hand. She flinched and jerked back. "Lizzy," he whispered, his hand dropping to the mattress. "What scares you? What are you afraid of?"

"Nothing." She blinked back hot tears. Why was he doing this, being so considerate and kind? Why couldn't he just leave her alone?

A long silence stretched painfully. Several times he drew a breath as if he would speak. Finally, he whispered, "Is it me?"

Her throat hurt. She couldn't swallow, couldn't speak.

"Lizzy." His hand swept her hair off her shoulder. She stayed very still. Even her heart stopped. "Why are you afraid of me?"

All she could offer was a shrug and a mumbled, "I'm not."

"You never look at me directly. You cower when I'm near and bite your tongue rather than say what's on your mind." He paused, perhaps waiting for her to speak but she said nothing. There was nothing to say. He was right but she couldn't even acknowledge that. "I'd never hurt you."

He sounded so convincing. And yet she couldn't reassure him that she wasn't afraid. Not when she didn't believe him.

"I-I'm worried about James," she lied.

"James. Yes. Of course you are. I'm worried about him too." He sighed and pressed his fingers into his eyes. "I hope nothing's happened."

She frowned. Why did he sound so worried? James was sensible; he would travel only during the day and he didn't look wealthy enough to be carrying anything of value, simply because he owned nothing of value. No outlaw would bother with him.

The mention of James brought Rafe's visit to an end. He bid her good night and returned to his bedchamber. Lizzy lay awake, trying not to think about her nightmare, or the vulnerability in Rafe's voice when he asked her if she was afraid of him. And she tried very hard not to think about the way Rafe touched her.

She failed on all counts.

~ ~ ~

The hammering on the front door was too loud to be a fist. Lizzy swallowed, counted to three, and opened the door. She was right, it was the handle of a dagger wielded by a thin man wearing a tall hat. Rafe had told her to expect him but she hadn't been prepared for the colorless eyes and hollow, sallow face. Behind him stood three other constables. She recognized the one with the bandaged arm from the alley. She averted her gaze and concentrated on hunching her back and squinting. Coupled with the darkening of her skin, it should be disguise enough. She hoped.

"I am Chief Constable Edmund Treece," the leader said. "I'm searching for two fugitives believed to be in this region. Did you see any strangers yesterday? One is a large man of around thirty years with black hair, the other a younger woman, much smaller with yellow hair."

Yellow! Her hair wasn't yellow.

"Very pretty she is," the injured man chimed in.

Treece hissed at him. Lizzy screwed up her face to deepen the appearance of wrinkles and distort her face shape. "I ain't been out for days," she said with a shaking, thin voice. With the wads of cloth in her cheeks, she even sounded like she had an accent. Upstairs, Rafe coughed a deep hacking cough. Then he spat. Treece and the others glanced at the ceiling. "Samuel's sick, see. That's me 'usband. Real sick. Got spots all over and can't keep nothing down."

The constables behind Treece recoiled and, as one, stepped back. Treece did not. He caught the good arm of the injured man, the one who could recognize Lizzy if he looked past the close cap covering her hair, the grossly padded clothing, and other elements of her disguise. There was no recognition in his eyes. So far. It would only take a small mistake on her part—a slip of the rolled-up shirt tucked under her bodice or the false moles falling off.

"We'll need to look through your house," Treece said.

He didn't believe her. *Oh God*.

"Not me!" one of the men said. "I'm not going in there." The others shook their heads too.

Treece gave them a look of disdain and pushed his way past Lizzy. He put the hand holding the dagger to his mouth and nose. "It stinks in here."

Lizzy said nothing. Let him think it was the scent of "Samuel's" illness and not the dead fish she'd found at the bottom of the yard and used to cover up the smell of charcoal and ash.

He went into the kitchen and came back a few minutes later. He paused at the stairs. Rafe coughed again, ending it with the very real sound of throwing up. Treece pulled a face. Clearly he didn't want to go up.

With a heaving sigh, Lizzy began the slow climb. "I gotta check he's not choking on his sick. You coming?"

She acted as if every step was an effort. In many ways they were. The closer she got to the landing, the closer Treece was to Rafe. It wasn't easy to disguise him with his size and distinctive looks, and Treece had such shrewd eyes, not like his constables, whose attentions were easily diverted by different clothes and a bit of face paint.

She stopped at the open door to the front bedchamber. Rafe lay on the pallet, his back to them. He seemed much larger thanks to the extra layers of clothing under the blankets. His body shook as if with an ague and he moaned.

"Turn him over so I can see his face," Treece said from the doorway.

"I can't move 'im. He's too big. Got so fat these last months, 'e did. Go in and take a look but don't get too close. I seen this sickness before. He's a dead man and most that get near will be too. I nursed a girl and boy once that had them spots on theirselves. Died, they did, but I lived, so I'll see this through too." She shuffled inside, her back stooped, and reached for Rafe's limp hand. She held it up for Treece to see the black fingernails and pustules on the skin.

He gagged and fled back down the stairs. "Come with me!" he shouted to her. "I'm not finished with you yet."

Rafe's fingers closed around hers. He didn't say anything, just held her tight. She winked at him and pried his fingers off. Slowly, she made her way down the stairs. Treece stood in the doorway again. His constables lingered out on the street, chatting to each other and already looking to the next house.

"Remove your hair covering," Treece ordered. "I want my man here to see you in your natural state." He beckoned the injured man to rejoin him.

"Me natural state, eh?" Lizzy chuckled. "Give me two shilling and I'll show you more than the 'air on me 'ead." Strange how she felt so unlike herself dressed as an old crone. The fear was still there, playing havoc with her nerves, but it was a different fear. It was fear for her life and not the fear of embarrassment. She could say the first thing that came into her head and not care about it being wrong or foolish.

The injured constable looked repulsed. "Believe me, it's not her, Treece. Let's go."

"In a moment," Treece snapped. "We must be thorough."

His companion rolled his eyes and sighed. "Better take it off or we'll be here all day," he grumbled.

Lizzy licked suddenly dry lips. She reached up and unpinned the cap. The thick braid of hair remained coiled upon her head. She'd wanted to cut it but Rafe refused and hid the sharp knives when she said she'd do it herself. The ash they rubbed through it would have to be enough.

"Told you. It's not her." The injured constable walked off to join his colleagues. Treece grunted and followed him. It seemed that was the only apology she'd get for having her morning disrupted.

She shut the door on them and sagged against it. She counted to ten then climbed the stairs. Rafe sat on the pallet and smiled through his pimply lips. He looked ill, which was precisely how he was supposed to look.

"*Give me two shilling and I'll show you more than the 'air on me 'ead,*" he mimicked. "The stage is missing its brightest star."

"Women aren't allowed to act."

"They're not supposed to be tiring house managers either, but you are."

"I'm not the manager, my father is. I'm his assistant."

He waved a hand and one of the pustules fell off. It was surprising it had lasted as long as it had, held on with a paste of flour and water. "You really were excellent," he said with a nod of approval. "I am in awe of your courage and ability. I couldn't have fooled them as well as you did."

"That's because you'd make a terrible crone."

He threw his head back and laughed, dislodging another pustule. She grinned. Perhaps she should stay in disguise. Samuel's wife was quite the feisty old crow. Lizzy liked her.

"I may be a poor crone, but I'm a great fishmonger's wife," he said.

"I've never seen a fishmonger's wife as big as you."

"You should go to the Low Countries. They breed them large there. The fish too."

She giggled, her anxiety eased by his ridiculous banter.

He stood and nodded at her hair, still uncovered. "You'd best keep it that way for today, to be safe. The rest of the costume too. I don't trust Treece."

"Nor I. Will you remain in your disguise?"

"No, I have a better one in mind for when I leave."

"Leave! You can't leave, they'll see you!"

"Hence the disguise. Don't fret, wife, I'll be quite safe."

"But why do you need to leave?"

"To find out what I can and get more supplies. Now, I'm starving." He shed a layer of his extra clothing. "Shall we see what delights the servants prepared for breakfast?"

She gave him a withering look but followed him down the stairs. Once in the kitchen, Lizzy removed the wads from the insides of her cheeks and the padding from beneath her clothes.

Rafe worked side by side with her to cook the bacon and warm the leftover pie. He chatted amiably and didn't mention her nightmare or their conversations about fear. Indeed, Lizzy didn't feel afraid of him at all as they ate together at the kitchen table. He was friendly, fun, and she was dressed as someone else, someone with a tongue in her head and the wits to use it.

Why couldn't she be like that all the time?

Seeing as she had a voice, she might as well say something. "How will we prove our innocence?"

He set down the piece of bread he was about to bite. "I'll take care of it, Lizzy, don't worry."

"Don't brush me aside, Rafe. I want to know what you think. And I want to know what you know."

His gaze met hers. "What makes you think I know anything?"

She hadn't but she did now. His lack of denial proved it. "I'm not a fool, Rafe. I might not talk much but I can think for myself."

"I know that."

"Then don't treat me like a child."

He pushed his empty trencher aside and leaned forward. "I'm sorry, Lizzy, I wasn't aware that I did."

She sighed. "You don't. Not usually. But over this matter...well, I know you're not telling me everything."

He sighed too and folded his arms over his chest. He no longer wore all the padding of his disguise and he'd removed the pustules so his face was once again handsome if somewhat troubled. "There is someone who wants me...punished. I think he's the one who claims to have witnessed us committing the murder."

"Who—"

"A former colleague."

"The madman you warned me about?"

He nodded.

"Why does he want you implicated?"

"A...business matter didn't work out in his favor."

"It seems an extreme measure of retaliation over a failed business agreement. Did he try to hire your services as a mercenary?"

"It's more complicated than that." He stood and picked up the trenchers and just like that she was dismissed. He'd told her nothing. Worse, he'd told her just enough to make her worry even more.

How far was the disgruntled man prepared to go for his revenge?

She snatched the trenchers off him and plunged them into the cauldron of water warming over the fire. "Is that where you're going? To confront this man?"

"I'm sorry, Lizzy, but it's for the best if I don't tell you. Trust me."

"Trust *you*? Ha!"

He sighed. "At least you're speaking freely to me now."

Yes, she was, she realized with a start. And it felt good too.

He came up behind her, very close. Every piece of her tensed deliciously, waiting for the warmth of his breath on her hair. None came. She glanced over her shoulder and caught him staring at the back of her bare neck, his fingers hovering as if he contemplated touching her there.

"I was just, er..." His face reddened and he strode out the back door.

She smiled and her irritation faded. *She'd* made *him* blush for once. It was quite a heady experience.

He came back in with an armful of wood. His face was no longer red, nor did he look at her directly. "Stay in your disguise for the rest of the day," he said.

"All day? Even if Treece doesn't return?"

"Aye. You talk to me easily dressed like that. I like it."

"Oh? You didn't seem to like it a moment ago."

He chuckled. "If we agreed on everything life would be dull. Now, about that fishwife disguise. Could you help me?"

She wiped her hands on her apron. "You'll need more than my help, you'll need a miracle." She grinned and he grinned back and the last of the tension vanished altogether.

Rafe stepped into the enormous skirt and Lizzy pinned it to size at the back. She helped him with the bodice and cloak and arranged a cap to cover all his hair then she stood back to survey her work.

"How do I look?" he asked.

"Like a man dressed as a woman."

"Not even an ugly woman?"

"Not yet. You need something down the front of your bodice." She went into the storeroom and considered all the items they possessed. The cheese and pigeon would be too smelly and lumpy but the grain would make a shapely chest. She tore off pieces from the sack and returned to the kitchen.

Rafe handed her the sewing kit and watched as she sewed the cloth into pouches.

"You're very good," he said. "Very fast."

"My sister, Alice, was better. Her stitching was the best in London and she had a flair for designing costumes and gowns."

"I remember Alice."

"Everyone remembers Alice," she said with a rueful smile. "Everyone noticed her. She used to think no one did but she was wrong. Being so tall and pretty and fair, how could she be missed?"

"Particularly by Lord Warhurst?" Mischief danced in his eyes. If *he'd* ever noticed Alice in that way, it certainly didn't matter to him now.

She smiled. "Especially him."

He fingered the first pouch while she sewed the second. "You're connected to nobility now. You could demand a better marriage for yourself."

"Better than James?"

He shrugged one shoulder without looking up. "If you wanted to. I'm sure Lord Warhurst could find you an eligible knight or baron in need of a pretty young wife."

She laughed. "They would be disappointed when all they got was a plain old seamstress."

"There is nothing plain or old about you. As to being a seamstress, Lord Warhurst wanted your sister enough to marry her and she was a tiring house assistant too."

"Alice is beautiful and fun and lovely."

He stared at her, his eyes very wide, not blinking. "And?"

She sighed. "I sound like I'm fishing for compliments and I'm not. Truly. But Alice *is* special. She worked hard to make herself a worthy companion for someone like Lord Warhurst. She practiced talking and walking like a gentlewoman every day from a young age. She learned to read and write much better than I, better than Mama and Papa. She's teaching our sister the art of being a lady up at Warhurst Hall. Jane will be the one to attract a noble husband with her high spirits and beauty. Everyone says so."

He spun the pouch on the end of his finger, round and round. He seemed entirely focused on it, concentrating to not let it fall. "You could too," he said quietly. "If you wanted to."

She shook her head. "I don't. Going up there and being so far away from home, in a world I don't really belong to...It isn't me. I'm happier here in London with Lord Hawkesbury's Players. Besides, I'm much too shy and awkward to turn into an accomplished lady. Jane is a far better choice."

"You're not shy and awkward now." The pouch flew off his finger and landed on the table. He left it there and regarded her through heavy lids.

"That's because I'm not being myself here." She waved a hand to encompass the house, her disguise, and his. "I'm dressed as an old crone, I'm being sought for murder, and I've spent the night alone with a...a man." A very handsome, virile man, she'd almost said. "Nothing about this situation is normal." She set down the finished second pouch. "You make it sound like you don't want me to wed your brother."

He snatched up the pouches and stalked off into the storeroom, lifting his skirts so as not to step on the hem. "Of course I want you two to wed," he tossed over his shoulder. "James needs you."

She sighed and instantly regretted it. It made it sound like she was having second thoughts about marrying him when she wasn't. She should be proud to be James's wife. She *was* proud. He was a good soul, kind and gentle.

Rafe emerged carrying the full pouches, one in each hand. He held them up. "Do you think they're big enough?"

Men! Always concerned with size. She took one from him, sewed up the opening, and swapped it for the other. She sewed that one closed too, then watched as he stuffed them down the front of his shirt. The bodice was tight enough to hold them in place.

He squeezed them and gave a nod of satisfaction. "Now do you think I'm ready?"

"Two more things. First you should wear the hat I found in the trunk. It has a veil attached to the back but it'll look just as good if you wear it back to front with the veil covering your face. That'll solve the problem of your very..." *handsome* "... masculine face and this morning's growth."

He rubbed his chin. "What's the second thing I need?"

"Me."

He stopped rubbing at the same moment his jaw dropped. "You are not coming with me, Lizzy."

"I am." She'd never felt so thrilled, so *alive*. It was like a pressure had built up inside her, so slowly she'd hardly noticed it, but now she was finally releasing it and she felt wonderful. Free. "I am in as much trouble as you and I want to do everything I can to clear our names. I think we should pay Sir Robert Blakewell a visit. He might know more about the situation."

"You know him?"

"We're distantly related and I trust him completely."

"No," he said emphatically. "It's too dangerous for you. I'll go alone."

"I'm in disguise, a better one than yours might I add." She brushed past him and fetched the hat from the dresser cupboard. "Don't worry, I won't hinder you and I promise I'll do what you say." She held the hat out to him.

He ignored it. "I'm not concerned about that. I am concerned about everything that could go wrong."

She waggled the hat and he took it. "Do you worry this much before every mission?"

He narrowed his eyes. "This is different."

"Just treat me like one of your colleagues."

"You are nothing like Orlando or Cole. They're not nearly as pretty."

She should have blushed but her face didn't heat. She curtsied instead. "That's because they haven't got the benefit of this disguise. Now, put the hat on and let's go."

He did and lowered the veil. It seemed she'd won that argument.

She put her own cap back on to cover her ash-gray hair and together they went out the back door into the yard.

CHAPTER 9

"**Y**ou are not to move from my side," Rafe said, hooking his arm through Lizzy's. She seemed even smaller and more fragile dressed as an old hag, but somehow less vulnerable. Perhaps because he knew the authorities weren't looking for a craggy-faced crone, but more likely because of the change in her manner. He'd often suspected there was a sharp tongue in her mouth, now he had the proof. She hadn't shrunk from him since donning the disguise, and she hadn't held back her opinions either. It had been a good thing, until she'd insisted on coming with him.

"Don't look around," he told her. "And don't forget to hunch your back and squint hard for those wrinkles."

"Anything else, master?" She closed both of her hands around his arm, clinging on. Part of her disguise or because she wanted to?

Why did he care?

"Or should that be mistress?" she went on. "Or Lady Beardly perhaps?"

He blew out a breath and the veil puffed up like a cloud. "I'll have you know I used to be a beauty in my youth. Skin like butter and hair of silk."

"On your head or chin?"

He laughed and squeezed her arm. How did James ever match wits with this woman? Or was she shy around him too? He hadn't seen them together long enough to know.

James. Rafe needed to see him. He'd planned on going to the Marshalsea today in his disguise but he couldn't with Lizzy in tow. He had to go soon, however, or his brother would starve or be beaten or both.

A dray pulled up in front of them and the driver offered the "poor old ladies" a ride into the city. Rafe helped Lizzy onto the back and they settled against the bales of straw. Behind them, caged hens protested the jerky start with a series of clucks.

"Any sign of Treece and his men?" Lizzy asked. She still held on to his arm. There was no reason to ask her to remove it.

Rafe scanned both sides of Borough High Street before he shook his head. "He'll be near, though. We haven't shaken him yet."

"I do not doubt it. A tenacious man, that one."

"Let's hope he's not too tenacious."

The dray rattled up to the bridge and they crossed the river into London proper. They'd agreed to keep away from their homes as it was likely Treece had a man watching them. Instead they would speak to Blake, a kinsman of her sister's husband. He would know for certain if Barker was the false witness, and if he didn't know, he could find out.

They hopped off the back at the corner of Thames Street and walked up to Dowgate, deliberately keeping their pace slow to avoid attention. So far they'd been left alone. No one seemed to notice two women, even though one of them was unnaturally tall and well built. It was a good disguise.

"You're swaggering again," Lizzy told him.

"I am not swaggering."

"You are. It's not feminine."

"No one could think me feminine, even when dressed like a woman."

"That's for certain," she muttered. "Just keep the veil low. One glimpse of that jaw and the illusion will be completely shattered."

"I have done this before," he ground out. "Successfully and without your help too."

Her step faltered. She looked up at him, squinting to screw up her face and add wrinkles to her otherwise perfect skin. "Why?"

"What?"

"Why have you needed to dress up?"

Bollocks. He'd said too much. "I can't tell you that."

"There is an awful amount of your past which you refuse to talk about."

"For your own benefit."

"Why not let me judge that?"

"No."

"No?"

"Lizzy, do you think you could *pretend* to be demure and fearful again? Life was so much easier before you became this character."

She stiffened and let go of him. "I...I'm sorry, I..."

He stopped and she stopped too. He touched her chin to force her to look up at him but even though her head lifted, her eyes didn't meet his. "It was a jest. Do not stop being who you really are. Understand?"

She nodded, but he could see she wasn't convinced. For one thing, she said nothing. For another, she walked off. No more linked arms. He cursed himself. One day he would be able to say what he liked to her and she wouldn't be afraid of him.

They made it to Blakewell House but the steward told them to use the back entrance and speak to the cook. The cook let them wait in the kitchen while she sent a maid to fetch the master. Moments later Sir Robert Blakewell entered with a little girl attached to his leg.

Lizzy beamed at the child. The girl clung tighter to her father and turned her head away.

"Annie, it's me! Aunt Lizzy."

Blake stepped closer, eyes narrowed. "Good lord, so it is!" Apparently the child was satisfied too because she stretched her small arms out and Lizzy took her. The girl wrapped her entire body around Lizzy and hugged so tightly Rafe thought he might need to separate them.

"Lizzy, thank God," Blake said on a breath. "Are you all right?"

"Perfectly well, thank you. Do you know James's brother, Rafe Fletcher?"

Blake nodded a greeting. Rafe nodded back then realized his veil was still lowered, so he lifted it. Blake smothered a laugh. "You are an ugly woman."

Rafe batted his eyelashes. "You should have seen me in my youth."

Blake cracked a smile. "I'm sure men were throwing themselves at your feet."

"Why wouldn't they?" Rafe said, playing along. "A big, strong wench like me would be a godsend to any shopkeeper. How many women do they know who could lift a barrel with one arm and a basket of fish in the other?"

Blake laughed. "I'm glad Lizzy is with you. It eases my mind somewhat."

Lizzy glanced back and forth between them, frowning. Rafe wondered if he was the only one who noticed the uncertainty in her eyes.

"Is Min home?" Lizzy asked, jiggling the child on her hip. "Or the boys?"

Blake shook his head. "The boys are out riding with their instructor and Min's meeting Style about her next play."

Lizzy's face lit up at the mention of Style. "How are the players faring? I miss them so."

"They miss you too. They're very worried. The authorities have been crawling all over the Rose, asking questions, going through your things looking for clues to your whereabouts." He tilted his chin at Rafe. "They've been to your place too, looking for James to ask him questions about you."

"He's away," Rafe said quickly. "He charged me with taking care of Lizzy in his absence."

"He's conducting business for his master," Lizzy added. She handed little Annie back to her father and promptly sat on the bench seat alongside the table.

"Lizzy?" Rafe asked. "Are you tired?"

"Cook, bring Lizzy something strong to drink," Blake said. The cook scuttled out of the kitchen, wringing her hands in her apron.

"I'm well enough," Lizzy said, rubbing her forehead. "Just worried." She looked up at Blake. "My parents...?"

Blake sat beside her, straddling the seat to face her. "Don't fret." He clasped her hand in his own and gave her a reassuring smile. "Min and I are taking good care of them. They're worried, of course, but you need not fear for their comfort in your absence."

She gave him a watery smile in return. "Thank you, Blake, you and Min are so good to me."

"We're family."

"Not quite," she said but kept smiling.

"We are. The children call you Aunt Lizzy, that makes you family. Now, you just let Rafe protect you. If I'm not mistaken, he's the sort of man who'd be good to have on your side in a situation like this."

Again she frowned and glanced quickly between Rafe and Blake.

The cook returned with a tankard and handed it to Lizzy. "Drink up now," she urged with a flap of her apron. "You'll feel better with some of this in your belly."

Rafe shrank back and watched the scene like he was in the audience of a theatre and they were actors. They played their parts perfectly. The motherly servant, the sweet little girl, and a man and woman who clearly cared for one another.

A dull ache pressed down on him and he sagged against the wall under its weight. It wasn't that Lizzy and Blake looked at each other adoringly. There were no simpering, longing gazes. It was the trust in her eyes, and the faith. As if she knew without a doubt that Blake would take care of things if she let him, and that he would never let her down.

She should be looking at Rafe like that.

They were in this together after all. He was the one who always took care of things. He'd taken care of his brother and mother up until he'd left, then he'd taken care of whatever task he was paid to do. He was bloody good at it too. Efficient and fast, leaving behind no mess and no mistakes.

Not until Barker.

He closed his eyes. Breathed deeply, emptying his mind of all except what was important—protecting Lizzy and stopping Barker. He opened his eyes again and the strange aching sensation was gone so that he could watch them objectively. Blake was talking to her, reassuring her again about her parents. She listened, thanked him over and over, and asked questions. She leaned forward and kissed him on the cheek.

Just like that, the ache returned heavier than before. Rafe couldn't breathe from its oppressiveness. "Tell us what you know about the witness, Blakewell." It came out rougher than he meant it and both Blake and Lizzy glanced at him with uncertainty. "Have you heard anything?"

Blake stood. "As soon as I heard what had happened, I went to the sheriff's office. The sheriff is a good, honest man, and a friend." He shook his head. "But he couldn't tell me who claims to have seen the murder. The name has been kept even from him. For the witness's own protection, apparently."

"His own protection?" Lizzy frowned. "But who would... Oh." Her gaze lowered to her lap but not before she glanced at Rafe beneath her lashes. Her fingers twined together, the knuckles white. She thought he would hurt the witness to get him to retract his statement. Perhaps even kill him.

She was right. He would. Did that make him a monster?

It seemed it did, in her eyes.

Blake cleared his throat. "I'll keep asking. Someone might know something."

"Thank you," Rafe said. Blake appeared to be a good man, capable, someone you wanted on your side. Rafe would have to trust him.

"I did learn one or two things that may help." Blake glanced at his daughter, playing with a wooden spoon and pot the cook had given her, and beckoned Rafe out of ear-shot. "There was no weapon found in Gripp's office, but he was killed cleanly with a blade to the throat."

Clean meant the murderer knew what he was doing. "Anything else?"

"I asked some of the people who worked for him if they saw anything. It seems many of them saw you and Lizzy with Gripp that morning but no others either arriving or leaving after you. Not much help, I'm afraid."

"Actually that's very helpful."

Blake raised an eyebrow in question but Rafe told him nothing. No one in London knew about his job as an assassin working for Hughe. And no one must find out, not even James. If they thought he was little better than a thug when he was a mercenary, what would they think knowing he'd been an assassin? James would be ashamed of him, Lord Liddicoat would end his employment before it began, the Privy Council would want to either recruit him or behead him, and Lizzy... Lizzy would be even more afraid of him. No one must know. Besides, Hughe's, Orlando's, and Cole's safety depended on their anonymity.

He had to stop Barker.

"Lizzy," Rafe said, "we must go."

She nodded sadly.

"Wait here," Blake said and left the kitchen.

Lizzy rose. "I need to speak with Blake," she said and followed him out.

"She'd make a good mother, that one," the cook said, picking up the little girl.

"Uh, yes. A very good one." Rafe coughed and crossed his arms but that made one of his grain-breasts shift to the left. He dug a hand down his bodice and rearranged it.

The cook erupted into a fit of snorting giggles.

~ ~ ~

"Blake," Lizzy said upon entering his study. "A word, if you please."

"Of course," he said, unlocking a casket on the desk. When she didn't respond, he glanced up. "What is it, Lizzy?"

"You don't seem too concerned that Rafe and I are forced to spend time alone with each other."

"Are you worried he'll betray his brother's trust and…" He cleared his throat and the skin above his ruff reddened.

"No! Not that. But…do you know the story behind his departure from London years ago? You can't possibly or you wouldn't be so relieved that he is with me now."

Blake replaced the casket lid and came around the desk to hold both her hands. "I know what happened. As much as anyone does, that is."

"And you're not afraid?"

He smiled. "I'm not afraid. You were a child then and probably weren't made aware of all the facts. Perhaps if you were, you'd feel safer around him."

"The fact is, he almost killed his own stepfather."

"True, but he never hurt anyone else, including James or any of the witnesses to his crime."

"What about the fights he was rumored to have started at the alehouses before that day?"

"I thought we were dealing with facts, not rumor. Listen, Lizzy, Rafe Fletcher is a capable man and that's what you need now—someone who can take care of you. Besides, if James didn't trust him, he would hardly have asked Rafe to take care of you in his absence."

It was a point that had bothered her for some time, and still didn't quite make sense. Of all people, James knew what his brother had done, knew about his tendency to violence. Being capable had nothing to do with the equation. Rafe was capable of a lot of things, killing being one of them.

Blake returned to the desk and filled up a pouch with coins from the casket, then walked with Lizzy back to the kitchen. She was still deep in thought when they rejoined Rafe and the cook. He smiled at her. She didn't smile back.

"Your left breast is higher than your right," Blake said to Rafe. He held out the pouch. "For supplies or bribes. Cook, make up a parcel." The cook, still chuckling into her chins, disappeared into the adjoining storeroom. Blake jiggled the pouch again.

Rafe shook his head. "I can provide—"

"Thank you," Lizzy said, taking the pouch. She arched a defiant eyebrow at Rafe. "We'll pay you back when this is over." She bobbed down and kissed Annie on the top of her head. "Say hello to your mama for me, little one."

Blake clasped Lizzy's shoulders and kissed her cheek. His lips came away smudged with the black charcoal she'd used to define the creases around her mouth.

"G'bye, Uncle." Annie reached up with both arms, her pale little face watching Rafe intently. "I'm not your uncle," he said, squatting in front of her.

Her big blue eyes swept across to Lizzy then back to Rafe. Did she think them married? "G'bye, Aunt?"

Blake and the cook erupted into laughter. Lizzy grinned behind her hand.

"I told you it was a good disguise," Rafe said, taking the parcel of supplies from the cook.

They said their good-byes and left through the servants' door. Rafe checked the street for signs of anyone watching then hooked his arm through Lizzy's and walked her back the way they'd come.

"He's a good man," she said wistfully.

"Yes," Rafe said.

"Rafe."

"Yes?"

"Can you not squeeze my arm so hard? I can't feel my fingers."

He let go. "Apologies."

They walked until they reached the river, the silence long but not uncomfortable. It was easy and uncomplicated and made the stroll pleasant. They could have been promenading around manicured gardens instead of down hilly Dowgate Street to the grimy warehouses and shipyards along the Thames.

"What shall we do now?" Lizzy asked him when they reached the junction with Thames Street.

"Now we get supplies on the other side of the river. This parcel won't be enough."

"We're not going to investigate further?"

"No. There's nothing further to learn. Blake told me everything I need to know."

"It's him, isn't it? The man who wants his revenge on you. You're sure now."

He nodded. "I'm sure."

"Then you can go to the authorities! Tell Treece. Tell Blake to speak to his friends in the sheriff's office and give them the man's name."

He caught her cheeks and caressed his thumbs along her mouth to calm her. Her eyes remained wild inside her disguise, but with urgency and frustration, not fear. "Not here." He took her hand and they walked through a muddy alley that stunk of dead fish until they reached the water's edge.

A waterman spotted them and rowed his wherry to the nearby waterstairs. "Eastward ho! Westward ho!" he shouted.

Rafe held up his hand for him to wait. "I can't tell them anything," he said to Lizzy.

"Why not?"

"Because I need to take care of this on my own. Quietly."

She snatched her hand out of his. "And how do you propose to do that? Or are you a witch beneath that disguise too?"

He deserved that barb. He deserved all the anger she could muster toward him. She was afraid for herself and her parents and perhaps feeling helpless, all thanks to Rafe. If only he'd done his duty properly in Cambridge, none of this would have happened and Barker would be dead.

"It's something I must do alone. For now, we buy supplies then return to the house."

They caught the wherry across to the other side and alighted at the bankside waterstairs near the theatres and bear-baiting pits. Rafe paid the waterman with Blake's money then helped Lizzy out of the boat. When he let her go, she stumbled on a slippery stone and he reached out to catch her. She pushed his hand away, steadied herself, then walked off.

He deserved that too.

He glanced around to see if anyone had noticed the unnaturally nimble elderly woman. Most people appeared to be heading toward the Rose or the inns, but lingering in the yard of a nearby church he saw a man on his own. He was short and thickset with a fat, crooked nose. He lounged against a tree trunk, picking his teeth with his thumbnail. An idle man waiting for a friend. Then Rafe saw his eyes. They were fixed firmly on Lizzy.

Rafe gave him a wide berth and directed her toward Borough High Street. It was market day and apart from the usual shops and industry, there were carts and temporary structures set up to sell everything a busy Londoner might need. They purchased bread, pies and tarts, sliced pork and beef, fish because it was a fish-eating day, eggs, spices, and fresh vegetables. Lizzy stopped at a lopsided cart filled with rags and old clothing, gloves, hats, and shoes.

"Good for disguises," she said. She paid the saleswoman who looked more aged than Lizzy pretended to be, and set off alongside Rafe.

"We should buy some ale," he said when he spotted a tavern.

"Wait until we're closer to the house. Bottles will weigh you down and you're already as laden as a packhorse."

She was right. They weren't out of danger yet and he needed to be swift if necessary. The fat-nosed constable wasn't in sight but that didn't mean he wasn't near. The theatres were still very close, which meant Lizzy's friends were too. If Treece had any sense—and Rafe suspected he was not a stupid man—he would be watching Lord Hawkesbury's Players and the Rose day and night. Lizzy and Rafe were probably safest staying on the busiest stretch of road.

"Shall we ask one of these carters for a ride up to the house?" Lizzy asked. "You cannot carry everything on your own the whole way." The carters were mostly farmers leaving the market and heading south to their farms, their goods sold and their carts empty.

He hefted the two sacks, one filled with food, the other with clothes. "You doubt my strength?"

"I doubt your reasons for purchasing so much. We'll never eat all that food before it turns rancid."

He didn't plan on only the two of them eating it, but he couldn't tell her that. "I'm hungry."

They set off down Borough High Street but he paused outside the gate to St. Thomas's Hospital and looked back to check if they were being followed.

"What is it?" she asked.

At first he didn't see anyone suspicious but then he spotted Fat Nose inspecting the wares at the rag and clothing cart. He was speaking to the old woman and she shot them a curious glance, a sure sign that Fat Nose was asking her questions about them. Rafe had underestimated him. He must have seen Lizzy stumble at the waterstairs after all, then pick herself up the way a young woman would.

"Rafe," Lizzy whispered. She'd spotted him too. "Rafe, what shall we do?"

"Be calm. If we quicken our pace then we look guilty and ruin our disguises completely. There's still a chance he thinks we're simply a pair of aged women. Walk like your back aches then turn into the first lane we come to."

"Shouldn't we stay on the high street?"

"Not now that he's seen us. If he raises a hue and cry out here we won't be able to get away. Our disguises won't matter."

"Through here then," she said, nudging him toward the stone arch of the hospital gate. "It opens onto a courtyard, but there's another gate on the other side that leads to a lane. I've been there before."

Rafe glanced around once more before following her through the arch. He counted another four men watching them from across the road. One was the tall, lanky frame of Treece himself.

Bloody hell.

He followed Lizzy through the gate, then urged her to hurry. God knows how women ran with so many layers of underskirts, but he managed it with only a few curses and Lizzy did so with none. They bypassed the hospital buildings and headed to the far wall and the second gate. Once through to the alley, Rafe felt happier. Shadowy, narrow spaces suited him better than open ones with witnesses.

But the alley was a dead end in one direction. The other led back to the high street. It was the only exit.

Footsteps thundered across the hospital cobblestones. It sounded like an army. Rafe and Lizzy could risk running to the high street but Treece would probably have set someone there to stop them. Perhaps Rafe could use his favorite trick of catching the beam of the overhanging story and lift Lizzy up. No, there was no time and he'd have to drop their supplies, leaving a clue as to where they'd gone.

They were trapped. He would have to fight his way out of this one with only the dagger strapped to his forearm and his fists. Why the hell didn't women carry swords?

The footsteps became louder, dangerously close.

"Back against the wall," he growled to Lizzy. "And whatever you do, stay there." When she didn't answer, he glanced over his shoulder.

She was gone.

CHAPTER 10

"In here." Lizzy pulled Rafe through the door, closed it, and slid the bolt across. She listened. For several moments all she could hear was the pounding of the blood between her ears and her own breathing. Rafe didn't seem to be breathing at all. Then came the sound of running footsteps on the other side of the door.

"Which way?" someone shouted.

"Where did they go?" asked another.

The door handle twisted, rattled. The *thump thump* of a fist on wood made her jump. How long would the bolt hold?

She signaled to Rafe. They left the small room, which appeared to be used as a closet for storing coats and boots, and made their way into the adjoining kitchen. It was empty and the ashes in the fireplace were an old, cool gray.

"Whose house is this?" Rafe asked from behind her.

"Shhh." She led him past the winter parlor and through to the main parlor at the front of the house. It was also empty but the embers in the fireplace glowed orange. "Lo!" she called out softly. "Anyone home?"

"Away from the windows," Rafe said and steered her toward the stairs.

"Is someone here?" came a woman's voice from the top of the staircase.

Lizzy looked up at the pretty girl with milk-white skin and a thick rope of wheat-colored hair drooping over her shoulder. "Kate? I don't know if you remember me but my name is Lizzy Croft. I'm a friend of Will Shakespeare's from the theatre. I came here once to deliver a message to him."

"I'm terrible with faces," Kate said. "Will!" she called out. "Will, someone here to see you."

"He's here?" Lizzy couldn't believe her luck. Will would help. The playwright had an ingenious mind; he'd think of something to say to Treece to get rid of him.

A fist pounded on the back door through which they'd just entered. "Open up!" someone shouted.

"Who the bloody hell is that?" Kate asked, coming down the stairs. She wore a housecoat over a shift. Both were open at the top, revealing a lot of creamy flesh. Behind her Will Shakespeare appeared in nothing but a shirt reaching to his knees. His feet were bare.

"What's going on?" He rubbed his eyes and squinted down at Lizzy.

"Will," she said. "It's me, Lizzy Croft, and this is my friend—"

"Lizzy!" Will gasped. "What in God's name are you doing here? They're looking for you everywhere!"

A fist pounded on the door again. "Open up! Now!"

"Keep your hose on!" Kate shouted back as she passed Lizzy on the bottom stair.

More pounding, this time on the front door. "Go delay them," Will told Kate.

Kate *humphed* and turned her glare onto Rafe as he and Lizzy ran past her up the stairs.

"Our apologies for the intrusion," Rafe said with a nod of greeting.

Kate's jaw dropped and her eyes nearly popped out of her head. "You're a..."

"An ugly woman. Thank you, so I've already been told."

"I...I..."

At the top of the stairs, Lizzy clasped Will's hand. "We need your help," she said, but Will was already pulling her across the landing.

They entered a bedchamber and he pressed a panel of the wainscoting. Nothing happened. He clicked his tongue. "It's here somewhere," he muttered and pressed another panel.

Down below, footsteps drummed across the floor. Treece shouted at his men to search then he shouted at Kate. "Has anyone come in here? Two women, one big, one small?"

Kate's answer was muffled.

Please don't betray us. Lizzy had met Will's mistress only once and very briefly. She owed Lizzy no allegiance. Whether she owed Will enough to harbor fugitives in her house was another matter.

"They're not down here," a man called out.

"Upstairs then," Treece answered him.

Lizzy's blood went cold. She willed Will to hurry, to *do* something, to use his creative mind to save them. Rafe lowered the sacks. Readying to drop them and fight?

"Ah." Will's murmur was punctuated by the soft click of the panel opening.

There was no time to think as he gripped her arm and threw her through the small door. She had to duck and Rafe had to bend almost double, but once inside they could stand albeit not move. Will closed the panel and darkness embraced them. She couldn't even see a crack of light shining around the door.

For a moment the only sound was her own breathing. Rafe was silent but his arm touched her. He must have put the sacks down, because his hand found hers. She held on tight, giddy with gratitude that he was with her.

Giddy with fear.

The silence was shattered by Treece's voice ordering his men to search the bedchambers. Footsteps muffled by the floor rushes *thumped* past their secret door. Lizzy held her breath, closed her eyes, and prayed.

A moment passed. Two. Three.

Rafe's hand squeezed hers. She leaned into him, soaking in his confidence and the comfort he exuded just by being there. He pulled her into his chest, lumpy from the grain-filled sacks, and massaged the back of her neck.

Without thinking, she wrapped both her arms around him and clung on, desperate to hold on to the one sure thing in a life that had quickly gone from normal to insane. It felt so right and so good that surely there was nothing wrong with taking comfort from someone who shared the same dangers.

The footsteps left. Treece's men informed their leader that they'd checked everywhere and found no sign of "the murderers."

"Murderers!" Kate's exclamation was quickly followed by Will saying, "Bloody hell! You won't find any murderers in here. We're good English subjects. We don't harbor that kind."

More silence. What was happening? What was Treece doing?

Rafe stopped massaging and a small whimper escaped her. Tears welled. *Don't stop. Please hold me.* As if he could read her thoughts, his big warm hands caught her cheeks and drew her face up.

Then he kissed her.

Shallow, teasing kisses so tentative it was hard to imagine they came from the big, brusque man. But they did and they were oh, so good. But not enough. Not nearly enough.

More...

She wanted to taste him, feel his lips everywhere. Heat spiked through her and she tingled all over. It was like she'd been rolling around in the snow then plunged into delicious warm water.

Her heart pounded in her chest and he pressed her against him. His hands seemed to be everywhere—on her face, back, shoulders, digging through her hair, cupping her behind.

It was madness and she didn't care.

The door jerked open and they sprang apart, or as far apart as the space would allow. Rafe snarled and grabbed the shirt of the man standing there but when he saw it was Will he let go.

Lizzy pressed herself back against the wall for balance. The world had tilted and she needed to hang on or she'd slide off.

"Well," said Will, glancing from one to the other. "Interesting what fear and confined spaces can do." He broke into a grin. "You can come out now, if you want to. They're gone."

Rafe snatched up the sacks and pushed past Will. Lizzy followed and watched him stride to the door, checking his surroundings. His face was pale and drawn. He looked ill, but his eyes were darker and fiercer than ever.

Kate passed him coming in. "Is he in disguise or does he always dress like that?" she asked Lizzy, a wry smile on her lips.

Lizzy tried to think of something witty to say but her mind failed her and her voice probably would too. So she lifted one shoulder and shook her head.

Kate looked to the large bed with its rumpled covers. "Where *were* you two hiding?"

"Not under there." Will sighed. "I suppose I'll have to show you now."

"Show me what? What have you been keeping from me, William Shakespeare?" Even with hands on hips and an expression that could wither a tree, Kate managed to look beautiful. "Well?"

"Don't frown so, my sweet shrew. If the wind changes, your pretty face will stay like that forever."

"There is no wind in here. And you are not so high and mighty that you can speak to me like I'm no better than a speck of dirt on your hose. I can find myself another man who won't treat me with such, such...rudeness! One who won't write trite plays about me either."

"Trite? Ha! You loved it and loved your part in it even more."

"Only up until the heroine capitulated. I would never do that."

"I know," he muttered.

Lizzy dared a glance at Rafe to see what he thought of the lovers' spat, but he was too busy looking out the high window and didn't seem to have heard any of it.

Will blew Kate a kiss. "Calm yourself and look at this." He opened the secret door again and Kate gasped.

"All the years I've lived here and I never knew it was there!" She poked her head inside. "How did you come to know of its existence?"

"The landlord showed me when I first rented the house for you. This humble little abode was built by Catholics who found themselves in need of hiding a priest on occasion. Good, isn't it?" He looked very pleased as he shut the door again. It was so well concealed it was impossible to know there was an opening hidden among the wainscoting panels at all. "The trickery and ingenuity that spring from desperation and fear never fail to intrigue me. Take a look at these two." He indicated first Lizzy then Rafe. "Your disguises are extremely good. Your skill is to be applauded, dear girl."

"I'm afraid they're useless now," Lizzy said. "Treece and his men have seen us."

"Ah!" Will held up a finger and raced out the door.

Lizzy looked to Kate but the other woman merely shrugged.

"Did you really kill someone?" Kate asked. She was looking at Rafe but he either didn't hear or was ignoring her.

Lizzy answered for him. "There's been a terrible misunderstanding, which we are trying to fix before..." Before it was too late and they were arrested, tried, and hanged.

Will returned with his arms full of hats, wigs, and a beard. "You can borrow something of Kate's," he said to Lizzy, "but I'm afraid your friend's size is a difficulty. I keep a set of clothes here for myself, of course, but none will fit him. Nor will Kate's and not even your skillful fingers will be able to alter them to suit."

"I bought some on our way here," Lizzy said, relieving him of the wigs and beard. "One of the sacks contains all I'll need for him, but these are perfect! I'm amazed you keep such things here."

Kate licked her top lip. "He likes me to alter my appearance for—"

"I'm looking after them for our tiring house manager," Will cut in with a sharp glare at Kate. "As you know, we are in a somewhat heated discussion with the Theatre's landlord over our lease." He shook his head. "The less property we keep there, the better."

The Theatre had been the first dedicated playhouse but the land's owner was not keen to renew the agreement that saw Lord Chamberlain's Men performing there. Without access to their theatre, the troupe was experiencing some financial difficulty, so Lizzy had heard. It was even more amazing then that Will, a sharer in the company, could afford to keep his mistress in a house, albeit a modest Southwark one.

"Let us see what you have in that sack of yours," Will said, picking them up. "You'll have to stay awhile anyway, so you might as well dine with us. What say you, sir?"

Rafe turned away from the window and gave a nod. "I say you are a good man to help us. We're grateful to you and your friend for harboring us. If you don't mind our company until nightfall then we'll be indebted to you. The danger isn't over yet."

"That is quite an elegant speech," Will said. "And nicely spoken too. If ever you need a new profession, you should consider a career onstage. What is it you do now? Aside from running from the authorities, that is."

Rafe gave him a darkly humorous laugh. "I fix things for people."

"Ah. Like a stagehand."

Rafe extended his arm. "Rafe Fletcher."

"Will Shakespeare, player and playwright." Will nodded a greeting and introduced his mistress, Kate Manderring. Before he'd finished, Kate hooked her arm through Lizzy's and led her out to the landing.

"Come help me in the kitchen," she said.

"Yes, please," Will pleaded from behind them. "Show her what to do with the pots and pans, Lizzy."

Lizzy smiled, her fears fading quickly. "Ha!" said Kate. "I'll learn what to do with them when you make me your wife, William Shakespeare."

"I already have a wife," he said without a hint of apology.

"So he says," Kate muttered. "But has anyone ever seen the wench?"

"She doesn't live in London."

"And yet you do. What a convenient marriage."

"The best kind."

In the kitchen Lizzy found herself working alongside Rafe after Kate declared she couldn't cook an egg let alone an entire meal. It seemed she usually bought cooked pies or roasted meats from one of the local cookshops. It was just like being at Hughe's house with Lizzy and Rafe quietly preparing the food without getting in each other's way. The only difference was that behind them, seated at the table, Kate and Will went through the sacks and discussed how to make good disguises out of the old clothes and rags. Occasionally their chatter stopped. Lizzy only made the mistake of turning around once and wished she hadn't. Seeing the amorous couple kissing only reminded her of the one she'd shared with Rafe.

She could not think of that. Not now. Not later. Not ever. She didn't even like him much, and she certainly didn't trust him. Besides, he was James's *brother*. No wonder Rafe hadn't said a word to her since emerging from the priest's hole. He must feel as despicable as she did. At least they both regretted it. That was a good thing. It meant there was no chance they would kiss again.

They dined on fish together at the kitchen table and afterward they all helped Lizzy create some new clothes for Rafe. By late afternoon, they'd finished. Somehow Lizzy managed to measure Rafe yet not touch him with any intimacy. It also helped that she didn't look him in the eyes.

"That's him done," Kate said, folding up the new woman's skirt and bodice they'd made for him. "Now for you, Lizzy. I have just the thing in a trunk upstairs."

The two of them got as far as the bottom step when a knock sounded on the front door.

Lizzy's heart slammed into her ribs. The women looked at each other. Rafe came out from the kitchen, Will at his heels.

"Upstairs," he hissed. *"Now!"* He grabbed Lizzy's arm and together they raced up. He found the secret door and she stepped inside. He followed and pulled it shut.

Lizzy strained to hear sounds of footsteps or talking beyond the wall but there was nothing. Only their ragged breathing filled the silence. She itched to reach out for Rafe's hand, to get some comfort from him, but she dared not. Disaster in the form of their kiss had followed the last time she did that.

Without warning, the door suddenly opened. A scream caught in her throat and she shrank back.

Will's face beamed at her. "Be calm," he said. "Look who's here!"

"Lizzy, thank God you're all right!" The refined, delicate features of Antony appeared around Will.

"Antony," she whimpered. "It's you." She clutched at the hand he extended and gratefully received his hug. She might have even cried. Just a little. But it was Antony after all, so it didn't matter, and it felt *so* wonderful to see him. She hadn't realized how much she'd missed her friend.

"You trust him?" It was Rafe, standing close behind her. Or rather, looming over her.

"Yes," she said, wiping her cheeks. "Absolutely."

Antony glanced over her head at Rafe. He cleared his throat and set her aside. "Have you been taking good care of her? Because if you haven't..." His threat ended on a swallow and no one expected him to continue. Because what would a man who liked to dress as a woman say to a mercenary like Rafe? *I'll claw your face with my fingernails?* The fact that Rafe was actually the one dressed in skirts and a bodice was an irony not lost on Lizzy. She giggled, a reaction in part to the absurdity of it, but mostly due to relief. Antony had arrived and Treece had not.

"Something funny?" Rafe asked.

She bit the inside of her cheek to control the smile and shook her head.

"So be it." He lifted his skirts and strode to the door. "We *men* will be downstairs while you ladies find a new dress."

Antony raised both eyebrows and appeared to be holding back a grin. Will paused at the door and said, "He's including you when he says men, Antony."

"Barely," Kate muttered, lifting the lid on a trunk.

Antony made a rude gesture at her back. "Including you in the ladies part was more than a gross exaggeration, it was an insult to all true ladies."

Kate flicked a hand, dismissing him, and he left with a wink at Lizzy. Kate beckoned her over to the trunk and pulled out a black skirt and a black, burgundy, and cream bodice with a swirling pattern through it. A simple outfit for a simple woman. Perfect.

"Thank you," Lizzy said, holding it up. "We are of a size so it should fit."

Kate eyed Lizzy's chest. "Hmm. We shall see. Try it on. Here." She fished out a shift and hose from a different trunk.

"Are you sure?"

"Quite sure. Besides, I shall have your clothes in exchange until you can return these."

Lizzy's gown and bodice weren't particularly fine but they were as good as the ones she was borrowing and Kate could pin them to fit.

"Let me help you." Kate laid out her clothes on the bed while Lizzy removed her old crone's disguise. It was a relief to shed the extra padding. Once she was dressed in the clean hose and shift, Kate stopped her from donning the rest. "Let me fetch water and we'll wash the ash out of your hair first." A few moments later, she returned carrying a basin of water and a cloth. She carefully removed the charcoaled lines from Lizzy's face then helped rinse her hair. After Lizzy dressed, Kate gave her a thorough inspection which began and ended at her breasts. "Well. Perhaps we're not of a size after all."

Lizzy looked down at her chest. The shift sat low, barely covering her breasts, and the tight bodice pushed them up. "I think I should put my old clothes back on."

"Absolutely not!" Kate caught her hand and dragged her to the door. "It's a wonderful disguise."

"But I will attract too much attention dressed like this."

"Your titties will, not your face. The constables won't look above your neck. What better disguise is there?"

Lizzy reluctantly followed her down the stairs and entered the kitchen, interrupting the card game between the three men. Will, the first to look up, made a strangled sound in the back of his throat. His eyes widened and a bead of sweat popped out on his high forehead.

"Um..." he said.

"Well," said Antony. "All this time and I never knew you had *those*."

"Ha, ha," Lizzy said, one hand on her hip. She glanced at Rafe. He simply stared back, first at her chest, then at her face, then at her chest again. His Adam's apple bobbed furiously until he looked down at his cards. He threw one on the table.

Antony gave a triumphant snort. "That's all you've got? Come on, Shake, your turn."

Will threw all his cards on the table. "I'm out."

Antony whooped with delight and put down a card. "You both owe me five thousand pounds."

Will's head whipped around. "What?"

"Ah, so you *are* listening." Antony gathered up the cards. "Which is more than I can say for him." He nodded at Rafe.

Rafe passed a hand over his eyes. "My apologies." He stood. "I'm hungry."

"There's a lot of food in the sack," Lizzy said.

Rafe nodded without looking at her.

"Or there's some bacon left over from breakfast," Will said. "I think we have cheese and bread too. Kate?"

"Aye," she said and disappeared into the storeroom.

Lizzy sat on a stool near the fire and dried her hair, running her fingers through the long strands. She glanced at Rafe beneath her lowered lashes but he was once more sitting at the table, angled so his back was to her. Antony was trying to interest him in another game of Primero, but Rafe shook his head.

"You have lovely hair," Will said, watching her.

"Thank you, that is very sweet of you to say so."

"You make it sound like I don't mean it."

She shrugged. "You've seen my sister's hair. Mine is like dirty snow next to hers."

"Alice's?" Will almost shrugged, almost nodded, but didn't really do either. "It's different from hers, neither better nor worse."

She smiled. "You're very diplomatic."

"Not at all!" The playwright looked offended. "I believe it wholeheartedly."

"I never met your sister," Antony said, shuffling the cards. "Either of them. Are they truly both beautiful?"

"Yes," Lizzy said.

"Not in the classic sense of beauty," Will said with a glance toward the storeroom door and Kate. "But their faces were ones you could look at all day long and not tire of the sight. There was always something different about them, something unique and intriguing. And their eyes! Captured your imagination, those eyes did." His own eyes had a faraway look in them.

"Well," Antony said. "That is quite a compliment coming from you. I wish I could meet these intriguing sisters of yours, Lizzy. What say you, Rafe? Is that how you remember them?"

"I hardly recall," he growled. "They were just girls when I last saw them."

"Not Alice," Will said. "She would be about the same age as you?"

"She was already a grown woman when Rafe left London," Lizzy said. "I'm sure he must have noticed her." She tried to put a laugh into her tone but her words still sounded forced.

Rafe half-turned. His profile was dark and his jaw set like stone. "I didn't notice her. I was too busy."

"Too busy to notice a beautiful woman?" Will laughed and caught Kate around the waist as she walked past him carrying a trencher laden with bread and cheese. She giggled and kissed the top of his balding head. "Then you are a man made of strong stuff."

"Or soft," Antony said with a sly grin.

Rafe said nothing and the silence quickly frayed. Will and Kate separated and Antony concentrated on fanning the cards out and closing them again. It took all his attention. Lizzy stared into the fire.

"You shouldn't think yourself less than your sisters." Rafe's voice was quiet but drew everyone's attention with its golden tones. "You're not, neither in appearance nor in any other way." And with that, he helped himself to a piece of bread from the trencher.

His words raised Lizzy's spirits. At first. Then they came crashing down again. On his own admission, he hardly remembered her sisters, so his favorable comparison was simply a kindness. "Thank you," she said all the same.

It felt like a light had gone out within her.

They ate supper and Lizzy asked Antony about the company. She missed them so and he told her they missed her equally as much. They were all very concerned. "Even Style," he said. "I think he feels responsible."

"He should," Will said, tearing apart a piece of bread. "None of this would have happened if it wasn't for his petty feud with Gripp."

"What's done is done." Lizzy sat at the table with them, her dry hair falling down her back. "Rafe and I must find a way out now."

Will shook his head. "It's hopeless. You should catch a ship to France or the Low Countries."

"No." Rafe spoke with such finality that no one contradicted him. "Lizzy belongs here in London. I will set things right for her."

That brought more silence down on them until Antony said, "Style is offering a reward to anyone who can name the true killer."

"Really?" Lizzy stared at him. "*Roger* Style?"

Antony nodded.

"And he's offering real money?"

"Three pounds."

Will paused with a slice of cheese halfway to his mouth. "Perhaps I should start an investigation of my own. Keeping a mistress costs a fortune."

"You get more than your money's worth," Kate said, hands on hips.

They finished their supper and Rafe declared it was dark enough for them to leave. "It'll be safe now." He gathered up their sacks and thanked their hosts.

Lizzy kissed Kate and Will on their cheeks and hugged Antony tight.

"Take care," he said, hugging her a second time. When he drew back there were tears in his eyes.

"I will."

"I'll call on your parents every day. Do not worry about them, just worry about keeping away from constables."

She nodded. He was so good to her. She hugged him again. When she finally pulled away she caught Rafe watching her. He had that odd expression on his face again, dark and cold like a looming winter storm.

"Let's go," he snapped.

She followed him out the front door, Kate's cloak clasped over her breasts, and wondered how she would fare spending another night in the presence of Rafe Fletcher.

CHAPTER 11

Lizzy fell asleep almost as soon as she tumbled into bed. She awoke some time later in a tangle of blankets, shaking with cold and fear. She'd dreamed about Rafe again and the day he'd left London seven years ago. The cold, dark look in his eyes haunted her even now that she was awake. She told herself he wasn't always like that. He'd shown kindness to her since his return.

Yet...

What would happen if she did something he didn't like? How far would he go? How bad would she need to err before he turned violent?

"Lizzy? Is everything all right?" He stood in the doorway dressed in his new clothes. Unlike the night before, he did not have a blade in his hand and he did not rush in thinking she was in danger. He merely hovered at the edge of her bedchamber, a powerful presence in the darkness. Surprisingly, it brought her comfort.

Would she be forever undecided between her fear of him and her trust in his ability to protect her?

"Yes," she said. "It was just another dream."

He stepped closer but kept back a little from the bed. "It might help to talk about it."

"I don't think so."

He was silent a moment then, "Did you have these nightmares at home?"

"No." She got out of bed and untangled the blankets. By the light of the moon she could see his face was turned to her, watching. His eyes may have been shrouded in shadows but she didn't need to see them to know desire dwelled in their depths. She could *feel* it vibrating off him.

Too late she remembered the new shift didn't modestly cover her breasts. Did his vast catalog of skills stretch to seeing in the dark? There had been no doubt at Kate's house that he'd noticed her cleavage. Everyone had.

"I'm sure it's because of the danger we're now facing, and the uncertainty," she said.

"Hmm? What's that?"

"My bad dreams are caused by our current danger."

He cleared his throat. "You're right. It's nothing to do with—" He sucked in a breath. "With anything else."

Neither of them spoke or moved. Perhaps he would come back to her, comfort her, assure her all would be well again. Kiss her.

Heat spread from her breasts to the tips of her ears and down to her toes. Her nipples tightened, tingled, strained against the shift. Thank goodness for the darkness.

Rafe reached up to the door frame as if he needed it for balance. "Lizzy..."

Now. Come to me. Here. "Yes?" she asked, breathy.

"Lizzy...I'm sorry for what happened at Shakespeare's house. I should not have..."

He was sorry for the kiss? "Oh. Yes, of course. I'm sorry too." Sorry she had enjoyed it so much and hadn't wanted it to end. Sorry she could not get it out of her head, despite her nightmare, despite being afraid of this man.

"James would kill me if he knew I'd forced myself on you."

Oh lord, poor dear James. Guilt stabbed her squarely in the chest. "Kill you," she said dully. "Yes. I mean, no. James wouldn't do that. He's not violent at all." She rubbed her forehead. What had come over her? Kissing Rafe, forgetting about James...what sort of woman was this escapade turning her into?

He turned away and rubbed a hand through his hair. "No, he's not. He's a good man, a good brother. The best."

He stalked off before she could say good night.

~ ~ ~

It hadn't been easy to leave the house without Lizzy. Rafe had to convince her he was simply doing a check of the vicinity to see if Treece and his men were still in the area. She'd thought it best if he dressed as a woman again, and although he protested, he knew she was right. He used the new gown she'd stitched for him and a long, dark wig borrowed from Shakespeare. From the expression on her face when he asked her how he looked, he guessed the disguise hadn't improved his appearance. At least he looked different enough from the day before that Treece wouldn't immediately recognize him.

He walked with a basket over his arm down Borough High Street toward the Marshalsea prison. Lizzy had thought the basket empty under the cloth covering, but he'd laden it with food for James and the other prisoners. He hoped it was enough.

He also hoped his brother was still alive.

There was no sign of Treece or his men on the way to the Marshalsea but he doubted they'd given up, not after getting so close the night before.

A bored guard let him into James's cell after he told him he was James's mother. Either he didn't look too closely at the face beneath the wig or he simply accepted that James came from ugly stock.

The same four prisoners were in the cell. The ogre and the other two looked up from where they sat or lay on pallets and quickly dismissed him as someone they didn't know. Good. It meant the disguise was effective.

James did not look up. He lay on his pallet, his back to the entrance, his legs curled up in front of him. Rafe's first instinct was to tell him to roll over and never leave his back exposed like that to the other prisoners, but the advice died on his lips.

An ice-cold lump formed in his gut. James wasn't moving.

Rafe approached him carefully, keeping one eye on the ogre, who appeared to go back to sleep. The other two men played cards in the corner, their faces hollow amid the griminess, their eyes sunken but watchful.

Rafe knelt down and peered at James. A dark bruise spread across his jaw and his lip was cut. *Fuck. Fuck, fuck, fuck.* He set down the basket but instead of reaching for James, he strode over to the big prisoner and picked him up by the front of his jerkin. The man's eyes sprang open just in time to see Rafe's fist smashing into his nose. He roared in pain and clutched his face. Blood oozed between his fingers.

God, that felt good.

"Bitch!" the giant protested, rubbing his face. He got to his feet, flexed his shoulders, and stretched his neck. Rafe glanced at James.

His brother sat up and tucked his feet in. His gaze swept over Rafe to the oaf and then to the others. He said nothing, only hugged his knees to his chest. He didn't give Rafe a second look.

"James," Rafe said. "It's me."

James squinted at him. The big prisoner looked hard at Rafe and burst out laughing.

"God's wounds, it's your brother," he said to James. "About time you came again. Thought you'd forgotten about us, hadn't we, boy?" He tore the cloth off the basket and bent to look inside. "Got any apples for me today, big brother?"

Rafe kicked him in the gut and the oversized body smashed into the wall with a satisfying *thud* near the card players. They scrambled out of the way like rats set upon by a cat.

The ogre groaned and coughed. Finally he rolled over and sat up. "You're one ugly wench, you know that?"

Rafe joined his brother, keeping an eye on the big prisoner who remained sitting on the packed-earth floor.

"Are you well?" Rafe asked.

James stared at him. Then he started laughing. "He's right, you are ugly," he said. "Nice hair, though."

"Thanks. I spent all morning brushing it."

James grinned and Rafe grinned back. The other man gave a grudging laugh but didn't rise.

"Answer my question," Rafe said, "or I'll be forced to beat someone up again."

James rubbed his jaw. "Do I have a bruise?"

"Just a little one." It wasn't little, it was large and purple. Rafe shot a glance at the big prisoner who cast a grimace back.

"I'm all right," James said on a sigh. "Starving, though." He checked the basket and groaned the way a man does when he sees his lover naked for the first time. "I love you, brother." He pulled out a pie and bit into it. His eyes fluttered closed in ecstasy as crumbs dropped onto his lap.

The other three prisoners descended on the basket like bees to the first spring blossoms. Rafe pulled it away from them.

"I want a promise that you will leave my brother alone." He spoke to them all but he looked straight at the giant.

The man nodded quickly. Rafe pushed the basket toward him and he dove in with both hands and pulled out the other pie. The two quiet, hollowed-out prisoners had their turn next. Rafe let them all take their pick but he made sure James received the most.

The food would only be enough to last them the day, he realized. They were all starving, which meant Rafe was probably the only one bringing in food for all four. They'd be dead if it wasn't for Rafe. At least James didn't look to be the worst off, despite his bruise. His eyes weren't as sunken as the two smaller prisoners, nor did he look as tired or his bones as sharp. Those two ate the food so quickly they couldn't have chewed properly let alone tasted it.

Rafe waited until the basket was empty before shooing them all away. "I want to speak to my brother in privacy."

They moved to the far side of the cell, no questions asked, even the ogre.

"What happened?" Rafe asked James. "He hit you?"

James licked his finger and touched it to the crumbs clinging to his jerkin. "Aye." He sucked the crumbs off his fingertip. "After you left that day. He wanted the last apple. So did I. He hit me, I gave it up." He shrugged.

"A wise decision." But it galled Rafe to say it.

"Rafe?"

"Hmm?"

"I know we've grown apart these last few years, and that we hardly know each other anymore. But tell me...have you changed so much that you now like wearing women's clothes?"

Rafe chuckled. "It's a disguise."

"A good one. I didn't recognize you. But why do you need a disguise? Does this have anything to do with your new employment with Lord Liddicoat?"

What exactly did he think Rafe's new job entailed? "No. I don't start there for a few more days."

"Oh." James tapped his fingers on his knee. "So he wouldn't let you begin earlier?"

"No."

"Then how did you buy all this food?" James looked Rafe up and down then screwed up his nose. "Good lord! You didn't..." He fingered Rafe's skirt. "...you know."

Rafe chuckled. "Would you pay to be with a woman who looked like me?"

"Not even if I was desperate." He nodded at Rafe's wig, an impish smirk lighting up his face. "Perhaps if you were fair like Lizzy."

Like Lizzy, with her beautiful "dirty snow" hair as she'd called it, falling down her back, over her shoulders, brushing her nipples. *Christ.*

He shoved the image out of his mind. It was beyond wrong to picture his brother's intended naked and writhing and...

Bloody hell.

"Are you going to tell me how you got the money?" James asked. "Did you ask the Crofts after all?"

"No."

James's gaze slid to the other prisoners. He sighed. "Can you come back every day from now on? Or every second day, instead of forgetting about me then turning up dressed like the offspring of a she-monster and Briggs there." He jerked his head at the ogre, who cracked open an eye at the mention of his name. His nose had stopped bleeding but his face and clothes were covered in his blood. He wasn't a pretty sight. "So why didn't you come yesterday?" James asked, his voice cracking with indignation. "Or the day before? I could have been eaten alive."

"The wardens won't let them eat you," Rafe said. Not in a civilized city like London, but some of the prisons he'd seen in Moscow would be a different story.

Rafe stretched out his legs and crossed them at the ankles. He wanted to tell James to mind his own business or that he'd been too busy. Those were the responses he would have given to anyone else who'd asked him what his movements were. But that was in the past, and James was his brother.

If Rafe was going to start afresh in London, he needed to be honest. Well, a little bit honest. James wasn't ready to hear the whole truth of his past. Nor was Lizzy for that matter, or her parents, or anyone. And Rafe was positive he wasn't ready to tell them.

"I'm sorry," he said. "I intended to come in every day, but... something happened." He glanced at the ogre, who appeared to be sleeping again but Rafe suspected he was trying to listen.

"Something happened!" James echoed. "Something *happened*? I know what I'm about to say may sound selfish, but... what could possibly be more important than keeping me alive? Finding the right gown to match your eyes?"

James may have been Rafe's brother but he could have benefited from a thumping to shut up that smart mouth of his. Rafe crooked his finger to get him to lean in close. With total trust, James did as he was told.

"I'm avoiding the authorities," Rafe said.

"That explains the disguise. So what did you do?" He nodded at the empty basket. "Steal that food?"

"I know how to take food without getting caught. I also know how to kill someone without getting caught. The witness is lying."

Rafe could see the moment his words sank in. His brother's jaw went slack and his mouth swung open. "But...you mean...you're wanted for murder?" He whispered the word, thank God. No reason to let the others know.

Rafe nodded. "I didn't do it, but someone says I did. I have a suspicion who. When I find him this will all be cleared up."

James looked at him for a long time. Just looked. Rafe knew what he was thinking—that he really would need to murder someone to clear his name, that someone being Barker.

It did seem like the best way. Perhaps the only way.

"Bloody hell." James rubbed his stomach and closed his eyes.

"Do you feel sick? You shouldn't have eaten so fast."

"No, fool!" James's eyes snapped open. "I'm worried about you. You can't come back here, it's too dangerous."

Rafe twirled a strand of his dark wig. "Not if I wear this."

"Then you're an even bigger fool than I thought." He nodded at the other prisoners. "They know who you really are and others might too. How long will it take the authorities to realize I'm in here? They only need to make a few inquiries and they'll find out. And then how long will it take them to ask my friends over there some questions?"

Rafe had to hand it to him, James was thinking clearly at least. "Don't worry about me. I'll take care of myself."

James clicked his tongue and sighed. He leaned his head back against the wall and Rafe thought the conversation at an end. He was wrong.

"Are you able to get word to Lizzy?" James asked.

"Ye-es," Rafe hedged. "Why?"

"To tell her I'm in here. She can bring me supplies instead of you."

"I thought you didn't want her to know you were here. Your stubborn pride was stopping you, I believe."

He sighed again. "I give you my permission to tell Lizzy now. There's no one else."

How could Rafe put this in a way that his brother would understand? "No."

"No?" James shrugged, shook his head. "Why not?"

"Because I don't think we should bother her."

James's eyes bulged. "You don't think we should *bother* her? Rafe, this isn't a trivial matter. I need to eat, but you can't bring me food anymore."

"I can."

"And you think I'm the stubborn one." James blew out a breath. "Rafe, I know I didn't want her to know about me being in here. I was embarrassed, I admit it. I adore Lizzy. She's so good, so perfect in every way that I was afraid..." Another sigh. "I was afraid she'd think me worthless, so much so that she'd not want to marry me."

"You haven't proposed yet."

"No-o, but there's an understanding between us."

Not the same thing. Not nearly the same. But Rafe held his tongue. Indeed, his tongue suddenly felt thick in his dry mouth. He swallowed twice before he could go on. "If she loves you," he said, staring down at his hands in his lap, "she wouldn't care that you made some mistakes and ended up in here."

"It's not about love, it's about respect."

Rafe blinked at James. "What?"

"I want her to respect me. As well as love me, of course."

"Of course," Rafe repeated quietly. "Of course. And she does love you. I'm sure of it."

He pursed his lips. He must never tell James about the kiss he'd shared with Lizzy. It had been so very, very wrong. The fact that it had felt right made it even worse. "But I'm still not going to tell her."

James threw up his hands. "Why not? I know I said not to at first, but the situation has changed. You can't risk your life coming here anymore. And I need to eat."

"I'll take care of you. Lizzy doesn't need the extra worry."

"Why, what has she got to worry about? She has a nice life working at the tiring house and taking care of her parents in the evening. They're not demanding people, the Crofts, they're good folk and don't put any pressure on her whatso-ever."

Rafe said nothing. The authorities would soon discover he was in the Marshalsea and they would use that knowledge to flush Rafe out. He couldn't risk Lizzy coming and the only sure way to do that was to not tell her.

"Rafe, listen to me." James was up on his knees, pleading. "It's too dangerous for you to come here anymore. Lizzy is the only one." He blinked rapidly. "I have many acquaintances, but no other true friends. Not ones I can trust."

Rafe put a hand on his arm. "Don't fret." There was nothing else to say. They were going around in circles and it was time for him to leave.

But James wouldn't stop. "You always take care of me, Rafe. Let me worry about you for once. I want to stop being an extra burden to *you*."

Rafe's heart swelled. He squeezed James's arm. "You're not a burden, little brother. Not in the least."

"Look," James said with gritted teeth. "I *need* Lizzy. She makes me feel better about myself." His voice turned soft. "She's the best thing in my life. Actually, she's the only good thing in my life at the moment. I *want* to see her." His eyes filled with tears. "I need her, Rafe. I need to speak to her, hear her voice."

And kiss her again, and hold her until she falls asleep in my arms. But James didn't say it and the words echoed in Rafe's suddenly empty head.

"So really, you'll be doing me a favor by telling her I'm here. She'll be such a great help. She always gives sage advice. I love her for it."

"Love." Rafe's gut twisted. He blinked, tried to grasp at a thought fleeting through his mind but couldn't. Thinking had suddenly become like wading through a swamp.

"Watch out!" That was James.

The fist that smacked Rafe in the cheek belonged to the ogre. He hadn't seen it coming. His head hit the wall behind him and everything went black. If the other man, Briggs, hit him again, Rafe wouldn't be prepared.

But he didn't and Rafe's sight cleared. Briggs extended his hand to help Rafe stand. Rafe took it.

"What did you do that for?" James asked, also standing. "He brought us all food. You should thank him, not hit him."

"My nose hurts like the devil," Briggs said with a shrug. He gave Rafe a nod. "We even?"

Rafe nodded back. "Thank you," he said.

Briggs screwed up his face. "Why?"

For knocking sense back into me. "Never mind. James, I have to go. Take care of yourself." He gave Briggs a glare. "Any more bruises or cuts on my brother and I'll kill you next time. Understand?"

The prisoner grunted. "Come back sooner and I won't feel like hitting someone."

It was the closest to a promise Rafe was likely to get. He fared James well and left the cell. A few minutes later he was outside the Marshalsea and heading back up Borough High Street to home.

Every part of him alert, he scanned the road, doorways, and windows of shops and houses for Treece or his constables. And then he saw someone—a hooded and cloaked figure watching him from the other side of the road.

The figure had the same build as Barker, and he'd just seen Rafe leave the Marshalsea.

CHAPTER 12

Lizzy wrapped the beef up in a cloth and returned it to the storeroom with the bread and jug of ale she'd set out for Rafe's dinner. She didn't want to waste it. There was little else to do after that so she set about scrubbing the storeroom. Years of dirt had settled into the grooves of the wooden dresser and a patch of mold had taken over the far corner. The work was hard and her back ached by the time she'd finished, yet it didn't stop her from thinking about Rafe.

Where was he? Why hadn't he returned? And why did he need to take some of their food with him?

Why had he kept his mission a secret from her?

The niggling thought that he had left her grew into a gnawing fear by the time daylight slipped away. It fought for supremacy with her other fear—that he was hurt and unable to get home. She wasn't sure which scenario she preferred. She didn't even know where to start looking for him.

But she could still look. It was better than cleaning.

~ ~ ~

Rafe was tired of walking and not getting anywhere. He'd crossed the city twice with bloody Barker dogging his every step. The bastard didn't show his face but Rafe caught glimpses of the hooded figure and he had the same height and build as Barker. Besides, if it had been Treece, a hue and cry would have been raised immediately.

On Thames Street, Rafe decided to end it. He was tired and he wanted to go home. Lizzy would be worried. Hopefully. Was it wrong of him to want her to be concerned?

Probably. All the thoughts he had regarding Lizzy were wrong.

Finally, in an alley behind the Men at Arms Inn, he found the perfect place to flush Barker out. Squeezed between two wide, squat houses was a tall tenement that was narrower at its base than its top so that it looked like a tankard of ale with froth swelling over the rim. Boards covered the ground-level windows, and holes pockmarked the daub plaster. The door unlocked easily. Opposite the house on the other side of the alley stood three barrels, most likely belonging to the Men at Arms. There was nothing else nearby that could be used as a hiding place.

He went inside.

The abandoned building was in worse condition than it appeared from the outside. Half of the ceiling separating the ground and first floors was missing and the jagged broken ends of the other half looked unstable. Rafe climbed the stairs and tested his weight on them. They creaked and made snapping sounds but held.

He glanced down at the door. His pursuer did not enter. Good. Barker was behaving exactly as Rafe expected him to. He climbed back down, sat on the floor, and waited.

When nightfall came, he peered out one of the second-story windows. The street below was dark but he could see the barrels clearly enough, and the space behind. Empty. Whether someone had hidden there during daylight and watched the front door, he could only assume, but there was no other vantage point from which to spy on the house and Barker needed to spy on it. He must have left to alert Treece, in which case it was time for Rafe to go.

Rafe twisted and looked up. The overhanging roof was just close enough for him to catch hold of the edge. Two tiles came away in his hand before he found a good grip. Using the windowsill as leverage, he swung up onto the roof then slid down the steep pitch to the neighboring roof a level below. He landed softly in a tangle of skirts.

Picking them up in one hand, he scrambled to the roof's apex and slid down the other side. He did the same on top of the next house and the next, silently thanking London's carpenters for building houses so close together.

By the time he got to the last house, he was sick of clambering about in women's clothing and decided he'd gone far enough from the abandoned building. He lay flat on his stomach, put one hand to his wig to hold it in place, and leaned over the roof's edge. One of the shutters on the nearest window was open and, still hanging upside down, he peered inside.

The room was a bedchamber and inside stood a man wearing a shirt and nothing else. He bent over to put a log on the fire and the sight made Rafe wish he'd chosen a different window.

But there was nowhere else to go. He could only return the way he'd come, across the roofs, or jump from a height of three floors to get to the street. Not impossible but broken bones were likely.

In the distance, he could just make out the excited voices of men with the scent of a hunt in their nostrils. Treece's constables, and hopefully Barker too. The banging of their clubs on posts or walls echoed through the crisp evening air. They were close.

He had to go in.

"Lo," he called through the open half of the window.

The man farted as he straightened. "Who's there?" He looked around, squinted, and picked up the candelabra.

"Over at the window," Rafe said. "I mean you no harm but I need to come inside and go out through the front door."

The man held the candelabra up to the window. It swayed and so did he. He was drunk. "Good lord! You're a...a..."

"An ugly wench. I know." Rafe opened the other shutter and flipped through the window, sliding at the last to get all of his body in. He landed on the rushes, his skirts halfway up his thighs but his wig miraculously still in place.

A pair of knobby knees and hairy legs stood beside him. "You hurt?" the man asked. He offered his hand and Rafe took it to get to his feet.

"No."

"Huh." The man belched and wiped his mouth with the back of his sleeve. His breath reeked. Definitely drunk.

"Thanks for letting me in." Rafe gave him a nod and made for the door.

"Wait!"

Rafe waited. Listened. The pursuers' voices were in the street, laughing and talking over the top of one another. The thrill of the hunt was in them. It could make men wild. He returned to the window and closed the shutters to muffle their sounds. "I must go," he said.

The man blocked the doorway. He was of middling height and age with a barrel-sized stomach and bulging neck. How those thin legs held him up was a mystery. "Not yet," he said.

Rafe didn't want to forcibly move him aside after the man had allowed Rafe to enter his home. "I'm in a hurry."

The man's eyebrows rose up then drew together. He squinted. "You have a low voice. And you're tall. I've never seen a woman as tall as you."

"Nor are you likely to. I'm an oddity."

The man sighed heavily. "So am I. I have a strange growth."

"Pardon?"

The man poked the middle of his chest. It wobbled beneath his shirt. "Right here. My wife, God rest her bitter, wretched soul, used to laugh at it." He shrugged. "So there you have it. What say you?"

"About what?" Rafe cocked his head to the side. It was impossible to determine what was happening in the street but he couldn't stay any longer. If Treece and his men weren't in the abandoned house they would be soon and then it would be too late. "Never mind, I must go." When the man didn't move, he shoved him gently to the side. The drunk swayed and took a step away from the door.

"Don't go, gentle lady!" he called after Rafe. "I don't mind how ugly you are! Truly I don't. I'll blow out the candles so we don't need to look at each other."

"That's very kind of you," Rafe said as he ran down the stairs.

"I'll pay you!"

"Not enough, I'm afraid."

"Oh."

The heavy sigh followed Rafe through the house to the front door. He listened then opened it and ran down the street. He just managed to sink behind the barrels opposite the abandoned house before Treece's men entered the alley. He watched as they filtered into the house, clubs in hand. One stayed behind, silhouetted by the moonlight. Rafe knew that tall, solid frame, the longish hair, the cocky stance.

Barker.

Rafe crept out of his hiding place and went silently up behind him.

Not silently enough.

Without warning, Barker spun around and struck out. Rafe ducked and kicked, knocking Barker down. Before he had a chance to recover and call for help, Rafe punched him in the jaw. Barker's head smacked back against the ground and his eyes fluttered closed. He was out.

Rafe couldn't kill him or confront him there in the street. He needed to take him somewhere he wouldn't be seen. If Barker turned up dead, suspicion would immediately fall on Rafe.

Rafe picked him up and hoisted him over his shoulder. There wasn't much time. The men were already shouting back reports to each other that no one was inside. Rafe ran up the street, down another, up one more until he found one that led to a set of waterstairs near the construction of a new brick warehouse. Barker was heavy but he'd carried heavier loads. Rafe threw him into one of the wherries tied to the jetty then gathered up some bricks and sacking. He climbed into the boat. There were no oars, the watermen having removed them for safekeeping overnight, so he simply untied the vessel and let the current take them.

When they were safely away from the waterstairs, protected by darkness, he looked down at his companion. He was quite sure Barker had woken up. "Catch you unawares, did I?"

Barker opened his eyes and rubbed the back of his head.

"I expected more of a fight from you," Rafe said.

Lightning quick, Barker reached inside his boot. He found nothing.

Rafe held up a long dagger. "Looking for this? I also removed your sword and the blade strapped to your forearm."

"Fuck you." Barker spat. He tried to sit up but Rafe pinned him to the damp bottom of the boat with his foot. He pressed the blade to Barker's inner thigh. If his quarry moved an inch either way, Rafe would castrate him.

"I'll kill you," Barker snapped.

"Not if I kill you first."

"Is that what those bricks are for? To weigh down my body after you stab me?" It was too dark to see the detail of Barker's expression but Rafe could hear the bitter sneer in his voice.

"It seems fitting to drown you a second time." Rafe kept his voice light, but all he felt was heaviness. While Barker hadn't been a friend like Cole, Orlando, or Hughe, they'd been on missions together. They'd fought alongside each other. They'd killed together. Nothing forges a link between men like living through danger and depending on each other to come out the other side with all limbs and lives intact. Nothing.

Barker had broken that link by threatening to sell the names of Hughe's guild of assassins to their enemies. Hughe was understandably angry and wanted him stopped in the most permanent way possible. Still, Rafe wished Hughe hadn't chosen him for the task. He respected Barker. At least, he had. Not anymore.

"I was relieved to learn you hadn't drowned in Cambridge," he said.

Barker said nothing and it was too dark to tell what he was thinking. Most likely his face would give nothing away. Barker was like that. Whereas the others in the guild could shut down their emotions when necessary, Barker was winter-cold all of the time. He never joked, never mocked the others about a woman, rarely shared anything about his life outside of the band. He'd mentioned a sister once, and it was to this sister that Rafe had given all his savings upon Barker's death. Or what should have been Barker's death.

"I'm sure you were," Barker said. "As relieved as I am to have you thrusting a blade between my legs."

"I never wanted you dead."

"Then why try to kill me in Cambridge?"

"Orders."

"And you always follow orders," Barker said. "Hughe has you twisted around his little finger. If he asked you to turn those blades on yourself, you'd do it and not ask why."

"You're a fool, Barker. Hughe saved you. He saved all of us. If it wasn't for him, I'd have gone out of my mind by now or I'd be dead."

"Saved you? Ha! I didn't think you such a fool, Fletcher."

"Whether you like to believe it or not, he saved you too. He saw something redeemable in you when he took you in. And you betrayed him. He has a right to want your head on a pike."

"A right?" Barker scoffed. "By whose authority? He's an outlaw, Fletcher. We all are. The law would string us up by our necks in no time if they knew what we've done."

He was right, of course. The authorities wanted to catch them. Some of Rafe's missions had ended the lives of those very authorities who'd literally gotten away with murder, or worse, because of their powerful positions.

"Go on then," Barker said. "Kill me here, now. I know you want to."

Yes, Rafe wanted to. It was the only way out of the mess Barker had created. But no matter how fast Rafe was, Barker was equally fast. Rafe could not kill him without first distracting him.

"You know I'll go after your sister when I'm done with you," Rafe said. "An eye for an eye. You hurt the people I care about and I'll hurt the one person you care for." The night closed in, smothering the splash of fish and chirps of insects so that the wherry was surrounded by a disorienting silence. Rafe held his breath. He'd gone too far. Not even he would believe such a threat; Barker surely wouldn't.

"She was a nice girl," he said casually before Barker could doubt. "What was her name again? Meg? Mary?"

"You're mistaken," Barker said in a voice as thick as the windless air. "I care for no one. I also know you gave my sister money, and I can't see the man who did that going after her for revenge. That's the problem with you, Fletcher. The problem with all of you—too much conscience. It makes you weak."

So much for using her as a distraction. Rafe had to keep him talking, had to wait until he let his guard down. "Why are you doing this, Barker? I don't believe it's for money. Hughe paid us well."

"You're right, it's not for money. It's for revenge. As soon as my identity was compromised, Hughe wanted to cut me loose. He wanted to forget about me. So much for the savior you paint him as," he spat. "He's not interested in saving anyone except himself. Why do you think he never undertakes any of the missions personally?"

"He can't. He's too recognizable. Everyone in England knows Lord Oxley."

"You're his tool, Fletcher, nothing more. You do the work Hughe won't because his head's stuck too far up his own arse."

Rafe would have laughed except it was no joking matter. "He had to cut you loose from the guild. With your identity compromised, our enemies would come after you. They find you, they find all of us."

Barker gave a humorless chuckle. "The amusing thing is, it seems my identity wasn't compromised after all. No one has tried to arrest *me*."

"Not yet, but when the kinsman of your last target saw you, you opened yourself up to the possibility. It's only a matter of time before he discovers your identity. You need to lay low, Barker, and we had to distance ourselves from you."

"Bah! He saw my face only. He'll never link what he saw to my name."

"Perhaps. So why haven't you followed through on your threat and sold our names? As far as I know, I'm being pursued for the murder of Walter Gripp only."

"Because it occurred to me there would be questions about how I came to know of Hughe's guild of assassins. I would throw suspicion on myself. This way, I am an innocent bystander who happened to be in the wrong place at the wrong time and I get the satisfaction of seeing you truly suffer."

Rafe wanted to wipe that smugness out of his voice with his fist. "You did do it, didn't you? You killed Gripp? That's low, Barker, even for you."

"He had no wife, no children, no siblings, or parents living. He was a petty-minded man, and not well liked."

"You think that justifies it? We had more reason than that for every life we took. Much more." When Barker didn't respond, Rafe said, "So that is all the reason you'll give? You have nothing more to add?"

"I do, actually. I want you to know that I'm going to ruin you. All of you. One by one, starting with you of course, since you tried to kill me. I think I'll end with Hughe. Let him watch his beloved friends fall first."

A flash of red flared before Rafe's eyes, not blinding but blanking out a part of him so that all he could think of was silencing Barker's sneering mouth. Hurting him. His fingers twisted on the knife handle. He could feel his own fingernails digging into his palms but he couldn't help it, couldn't control the fierce anger raging inside like a monster. Didn't want to.

"You do realize killing me won't set you free," Barker said. "My witness account has been written down. In the event of my death, it stands." His teeth flashed white in the darkness. "What a dilemma facing you. What will you do?"

Kill you anyway and worry about the written account later.

"There!" came a shout from the waterstairs on the northern bank. "Treece, they're on the river!"

Rafe glanced at the men silhouetted on the bank. A foolish mistake.

Barker caught Rafe's hand and snapped it back. Pain shot through Rafe's wrist, up his arm, but he held onto the knife.

Then more pain, white hot, ripped through his side. Burning, burrowing deeper. He touched his waist and his hand came away sticky. He registered the twisted smile of satisfaction on Barker's face, the knife in his hand, and wondered where it had been hidden.

He fought the pain, tried to stay in control, but his side felt like it was on fire and his mind drifted.

Focus.

Lizzy.

He set his feet apart to steady himself in the rocking wherry but then Barker shoved him and Rafe fell into the ink-black water.

CHAPTER 13

It was cold. So bloody cold and wet, like he was falling through crushed ice. It seeped into Rafe's bones, wrapped itself around his body, filled him up.

But it was the cold that saved him. It woke him with a jolt. He kicked out, instincts pulling him to the surface. He fought the instincts like he'd fought to survive and swam straight ahead, not down or up, just kept going forward in the freezing blackness. His chest burned. The desire to take a breath was the most painful thing he'd ever experienced. Worse than the pain of his side, which had gone numb.

With his body screaming for air, he finally surfaced. Slowly, carefully, just his nose, mouth, and eyes poking above the water. He sucked in wonderful, delicious air and got his bearings. The reedy bank was surprisingly near and Barker's wherry far away, farther than he'd hoped. Barker was standing and seemed to be peering into the water. In the distance, someone shouted but it was too far for Rafe to hear the words.

Barker shouted back, "No!" in answer. That meant Rafe was on the opposite bank to Treece and his men. Another blessing. He was out of immediate danger and closer to home. Closer to Lizzy.

He wanted to see her so much, *needed* to see her. The need overrode everything else, even the ice in his veins. He had to get back to the house.

~ ~ ~

Lizzy had never felt so powerless. She hated it. It was dark and Rafe still hadn't returned, but worse than that, she didn't know where to begin looking for him. He'd not given her any clue as to his route. That didn't stop her from trying. She wandered around the streets in her disguise, but there was no sign of him, so she returned to the house and waited. Waited and hoped and worried.

What if he did not return?

The thought nibbled at her but she did her best to ignore it. No easy task when there was nothing to do. She'd already cleaned the house from top to bottom. She was contemplating scrubbing the floor again when Rafe stumbled through the back door.

"Rafe!" She caught him but his weight was too much for her and they both landed inelegantly on the kitchen floor, his head in her lap. "You're wet." And exhausted and—covered with blood! "Dear lord, you're hurt! What happened? Where is the wound?"

He answered with a grunt and opened his palm to reveal a small earthen jar and a rolled-up cloth.

She took them. "What are these for?"

He pulled away the tatters of his disguise, red from his blood, to reveal a gash in his side.

Lizzy swallowed her gasp. The wound was puckered but had been washed clean and the bleeding seemed to have stopped, a small mercy.

She touched the skin near the wound and he sucked in air between his teeth. He felt as cold as a lump of ice. "Did Treece do this?" Her voice shook.

"No."

She didn't press him for details. That could wait until later. She opened the jar and sniffed the paste. It contained marigold and rosemary and other herbs she couldn't identify. "Where did you get it?"

Keep him talking, don't let him fall asleep, or she might not be able to wake him. Talking also kept her mind off the horror and fear creeping insidiously through her, threatening to turn her into a blathering mess. She had to be strong for him, had to take care of him.

"An apothecary…on High Street." Another shiver racked him—she could feel it through her own body.

"Well he could have helped you warm up before sending you on your way."

"He…wasn't there."

So he'd stolen it. Goodness knows how he'd managed that without making a sound in the condition he was in. She gently applied the paste to the wound. He winced and shivered again but made no sound as she wrapped the bandage around his middle.

Now came the difficult part. "We have to warm you up."

She added more logs to the fire then fetched the blankets from the bedchambers. The kitchen was already warmer when she returned but Rafe was still pale, still shivering. He lay on the floor, his eyes closed, his arms folded around himself. She helped him to sit, propped him against the wall, and tore the remnants of the wet bodice and shift off and threw them away. They landed with a *splat* but she had no idea where. She was much too distracted by the sight of Rafe's bare chest and shoulders to notice or care.

Magnificent.

All those muscles gently undulating across his shoulders and down his arms. Thick and powerful. Smooth, except for the occasional scar. She had a strong urge to trace them with her fingertip, especially the one that disappeared beneath the waistband of the skirt he wore.

Her mouth dried. She licked parched lips.

Rafe's mouth quirked up on one side. His eyes fluttered closed and his breathing became heavy but regular. "Now for the skirts," he mumbled.

"Um…" She sounded like a half-wit.

He shivered again and his lips were a dangerous shade of blue. She wrapped one of the blankets around his shoulders, covering up all that lovely skin and much of his lower body. For a moment she just held the blanket there, held him against her, comforting him as he had comforted her many times. It felt so good to be close to him, to feel his life force, to know he was safe, and it took all her strength of will not to kiss him with the sheer, heady rush of relief.

She tore herself away and together they managed to get his skirts off without her seeing more than his muscular calves.

He shuddered again and she forced herself to think of his well-being and not about the way he looked. He lay down and she tucked another blanket around him. "Better?"

"No," he mumbled, sleepily. "Cold."

She placed another blanket over him, the last, and went upstairs to fetch the pallet from his bedchamber. She laid it on the floor in the kitchen and helped him onto it. At least the straw would offer some protection from the cool flagstones. But it didn't seem to be enough. He was still cold to the touch and his body shook uncontrollably.

"We need to get you warm," she said.

His eyes were closed and he didn't respond. He was unconscious. It took her all of a moment to decide to remove her clothes, except for her shift, and slip under the blankets alongside him. He was asleep and would likely remain that way well into the morning, giving her enough time to dress before he awoke.

She lay carefully down behind him. His buttocks nestled against her thighs, silky smooth yet firm. Her breasts pressed against his shoulder blades and she circled her arms around him, just above the bandaged wound. A tremor coursed through him and she tightened her hold, soaking up the chill and drawing it into her own body. She was warm enough for both of them. Indeed, heat rolled through her, pooling between her thighs. She pressed her lips to his shoulder and managed to refrain from sinking her teeth into him like she wanted to. He sighed a deep, satisfying sigh, and his muscles unclenched as he relaxed.

Lizzy sleepily nuzzled the back of his damp head and closed her eyes. Her fingers crept down. Just an inch or two past the bandage, locating that scar. The smooth line traversed taut muscle and sinew and disappeared into a thatch of hair where it seemed to stop. What lay below was not affected.

What lay below...

Her fingers reached lower. Lower. And then she felt it. The thick root of his appendage, buried in the wiry hair. She felt along it, marveled at the smoothness, the ridges, and the size. It was bigger than she expected. And getting bigger.

Oh my!

She withdrew her hand to his waist and held her breath. He was still breathing evenly, still unconscious. She buried her face in his neck again and thanked heaven he hadn't woken, that he didn't know how much she wanted to touch him down there again. It would be utterly humiliating. Yet she could endure any kind of humiliation now that she had him back, safe and alive. She'd been sick with worry, but he'd come home and all was well again.

Home.

It was not home. The house was a temporary haven from their pursuers, nothing more. But it *felt* like a home because Rafe had returned. She was going to take care of him until he was well again.

~ ~ ~

Rafe awoke as dawn cast a golden glow through the kitchen. It took a moment before he registered that he was lying on a pallet on the floor, wrapped up in blankets and...Lizzy.

They faced each other, her head cushioned on his upper arm, her eyes closed in deep sleep. She wore only her shift, bunched up to her thighs. Her breasts were squashed into his chest and he silently groaned with the agony of not looking down.

Bloody hell, how was he expected to control himself with her lying almost naked beside him? He was no saint.

He closed his eyes and pretended to be asleep to avoid any awkwardness when she awoke. But she didn't wake.

He tried thinking about his injury. It still ached but no longer throbbed. The paste in the jar labeled WOUND HEAL had worked better than he expected. As long as it didn't become infected, he wouldn't be hindered in any way. Lizzy had done a good job of bandaging it and taking care of him. He remembered being bone-cold, which explained why she'd joined him on the pallet in nothing but her shift.

It had worked. He'd warmed up. Indeed, he was on fire. Particularly in the groin. On fire and getting hotter and harder every time she drew breath and her breasts pressed against his chest. The cotton of the shift was so thin it might as well not have been there at all. He could feel every contour of her body, the smooth skin of her bare thighs, the curve of waist and hip, the heat of her—

Christ. So much for not thinking about her.

He opened his eyes but that was equally futile because he found himself staring at her pretty face. She had long, sweeping lashes, fair like her hair, and creamy skin that begged to be nuzzled. She sighed and stretched her head back, exposing her throat. It looked so soft, so warm, he just wanted to bury himself there, kiss her, lick her...

So he did.

A voice in the back of his head told him to stop, to not touch, but it was small and easy to ignore. Besides, Lizzy tasted too good to stop. Like the first strawberries of summer.

No, better than that. Strawberries in midwinter. A delicious impossibility that he must devour because he was incapable of doing anything else.

His body ached with desire, burned with it. His mind had gone numb and he was only vaguely aware that he wasn't thinking straight, couldn't. She'd scrambled his wits and stolen every last sensible thought. All he knew for certain was that he wanted her. Wanted to keep tasting her, wanted to be as close to her as possible.

Wanted to be inside her.

She moaned sleepily and pushed herself against him, lifting her leg higher up his thigh so that his cock was nestled right where it wanted to be—almost. Somehow he managed not to slip into her and take her right there on the kitchen floor.

He pulled back, drew in a deep breath in an attempt to regain his mind, even as she rolled on top of him. He winced as the pain from his wound flared, but then she kissed him full on the mouth and it vanished. He was lost. Hopelessly lost.

And he didn't care.

Her eyes were closed but she could not have been asleep, not anymore. Yet she was a different woman. Not the fragile, timid creature he knew, but strong and willful and utterly without shame. God, she was beautiful.

He dug his hands through her hair and held her head gently in place. *Don't move. Don't leave.*

She stayed right there, her own long fingers holding him too. Her tongue teased and tasted his mouth and his cock rubbed between their bodies until he thought he would explode. The pressure built and he felt the first tingles down at his toes. It was both heaven and hell. Sweet, sweet torture. He groaned, a primal sound he hardly recognized as coming from himself.

"My angel," he murmured against her mouth. "I cannot bear it any longer. I must have you."

Her eyes flew open. She gasped and quick as lightning sprang off him and scrambled away. She took one of the blankets with her and covered her body. Her big eyes had grown even bigger, more than ever like the doe he'd first thought her.

Damn and bloody hell.

He rubbed a hand over his face and pressed his fingers into his eye sockets. He was a cur. A prick. He deserved a tongue-lashing for what he'd almost done. No, he deserved a real lashing. He'd never done that, never lost control with a woman, and certainly never taken a virgin. Not that he had taken Lizzy, but God he'd wanted to more than he'd wanted to breathe. He would have too if she hadn't stopped it, and that scared him more than Barker or Treece or the thug in James's cell.

James.

Fuck, fuck, *fuck*, FUCK!

~ ~ ~

"I…um…" Lizzy cleared her throat but still couldn't think of what to say to Rafe. Should she apologize? Should she demand an apology from him? No, that wasn't fair, it had been as much her fault as his. "Are you feeling better?"

Good lord, what a ridiculous way to start a conversation after what had just happened. Of course he was feeling better or he wouldn't have almost ravished her right there on the kitchen floor.

In fact, she would say he felt…wonderful. He tasted good too. Delicious, in fact.

Oh lord, what was she thinking?

"What?" he said, slowly, stupidly. He blinked, shook his head. "Oh. My wound. Yes, better. Thank you."

"You were in a state last night. There was blood everywhere and you were wet. What happened?"

He sat up and the blankets puddled low on his hips. Lizzy tried not to stare at his chest, she really did, but failed spectacularly. Fortunately he didn't seem to notice. He was looking at his hands resting in his lap. She gave up fighting her instincts and simply gazed. In the warmth of the daylight, his skin was beautifully golden and a light sprinkling of dark hair trailed down his chest and stomach and disappeared beneath the blanket. She very much wanted to tease it with her fingers. Or her tongue. All the way...

"Um..." Where were they? Oh yes. "You said last night that it wasn't Treece who hurt you." She checked the corner of her mouth for drool. "So who did? Vagabonds?"

"Barker," he said.

She gasped. "He caught you!"

"No, I caught him."

"Er...it doesn't seem that way. Or is he injured too?"

It was a moment before he said, "He has a sore jaw and a scratch on his thigh."

"Oh. So he got the better of you and escaped."

He cleared his throat but still didn't look at her. "It wasn't quite like that. I got distracted by Treece."

"I see. So it was the two of them against you. Difficult odds for any man."

He grunted. "You don't seem to have much faith in my abilities."

"Not at all! I have a lot of faith in you. I'm sure Treece came off far worse than both you and Barker. He doesn't have your mercenary training after all."

He plucked at the blanket and said nothing. The silence widened like a yawning chasm between them. Lizzy clutched her blanket tightly in her fingers and wished she'd woken earlier so she could dress.

But then she would have missed out on the kiss. No matter what happened next, she would always have it locked safely away in her memory—she could recall the softness of his lips against hers, the taste of him on her tongue, the strength of him beneath her. How she'd wanted his hands to touch and explore her body, find the points that made her sigh and moan and the ones that heightened the sensations swamping her. She'd felt like a boiling pot with the lid on, her body almost bursting with frustration and desire.

She had never felt that with James.

She closed her eyes and wished with all her might that she hadn't thought of him. But she had and it was likely that Rafe had too. Was that why he wasn't looking at her? They should discuss what to do about their desire, how to stop it.

But she couldn't face that conversation. Not yet.

"Why did you go looking for Barker and not tell me?" she asked. It was easier and less confusing to discuss the murder instead.

He finally looked up at her. His eyes were dark, swirling pools as he frowned back at her, puzzled. Had he heard the hurt and confusion in her voice? "I didn't go looking for him. He found me."

That made sense. Rafe wouldn't be taking food to Barker. "So who were you feeding?"

She might as well have struck him. He turned pale, although not as white as the previous night. "It was for me. In case I got hungry." He returned his attention to the blanket as if he couldn't bear to face her.

"You took more than half of our provisions with you! It was enough to feed an audience at the Rose."

He shrugged.

"Rafe! Tell me where all our food has gone. You cannot distract me from finding out."

He shook his head. "If I tell you, you'll stop."

"Stop what?" It was like having a conversation with a half-wit.

He sighed and stood, keeping the blanket wrapped around his waist. She focused on his face and did not look down at his chest or even his shoulders. Her eyes hurt with the effort.

"You'll stop speaking to me with the ease of an old friend," he said.

She chewed on the inside of her bottom lip and her gaze faltered. She couldn't look at him anymore. He was right of course. She had been speaking to him freely, the way she had when she wore the old crone's disguise. Except she'd shed that disguise and the one borrowed from Kate and somehow forgotten that she was scared of Rafe.

Perhaps it was because she'd seen him vulnerable and weak. Or perhaps it was all the fault of that kiss.

"See?" he said on a sigh. "I knew you'd stop." He fixed her with an intense stare and stepped closer.

She stepped back. She wasn't sure why. Habit? Or was the fear still there, lurking deeper now but nevertheless a part of her that could never be completely left behind?

She shook her head, unsure of what to say. So she changed the subject. "The food. You haven't answered my question about the food."

He picked up his damp clothing from the floor. It hung limp in his hands. "I told you. I was hungry. Leave it be, Lizzy."

And that ended *that* conversation. She didn't have the gumption to insist on an answer. Her fear of him had returned, sharp and piercing.

Rafe set the clothes out to dry on stools positioned near the fire and disappeared upstairs. Lizzy dressed in the bodice and skirt she'd borrowed from Kate while he was gone, then cooked bacon for breakfast. He returned wearing men's clothing. She served the bacon on trenchers and cut up cheese and bread and slices of beef. They sat opposite each other and ate in silence.

Awkward silence. She hated it. She wanted to speak to him, but it was like her tongue had forgotten how to work.

Why was she like this with him again? Why couldn't she get over her shyness around Rafe?

He did nothing to ease her anxiety. He didn't try to talk, didn't try to tease or cajole. His mood had darkened and he seemed as comfortable with the silence as she was uncomfortable with it.

They finished eating and after tidying up there seemed to be nothing to do but sit down again. They both sat. The silence endured. And endured. She tapped her finger on her thigh, on the bench beside her, on the tabletop. She looked at Rafe again, looked at the storeroom, the door, at her hands, back at Rafe. He was perfectly still, calm. How could he be so relaxed when the air around them crackled with tension?

Enough. She couldn't stand it any longer. She drew a deep breath. "Does your side pain you?" she asked. It was the only topic she felt comfortable enough to pursue.

He gave her that look again from beneath his lowered lashes, the one where the corner of his mouth lifted in a secret smile. "I was wondering when you'd speak," he said.

He'd been testing her?

"Go on, say something," he said. "I know you're mad at me—I can see steam rising from your ears."

She bit down on her retort and forced a smile. "I'm not mad. Not at all. I simply wanted to know about your injury. There's more of that Wound Heal in the jar if you need it." Or perhaps she could poke his cut and see how *he* liked being prodded.

He held up his hands in surrender but was still smiling. "A truce then."

"I wasn't aware we were at war."

He smiled again and she realized with surprise that she'd been sparring with him without a hint of her fear appearing. No doubt that had been his intention. She was too annoyed with him to let him know how much she appreciated it, however.

"My injury is fine," Rafe said. "It doesn't hurt as much, thanks to you. If you hadn't warmed me last night, I might still be a shaking, feverish mess this morning."

And with that, the previous night's events returned with a slam. The hard smoothness of his buttocks against her thighs, the feel of his member growing in her hand, the way he'd been cradling her when she awoke, and the kiss. Oh yes, the kiss. She would never forget it. Never.

But she must. There was James. She had to talk to him and sort out what lay between them before she deciphered her feelings for his brother. But who knew when she'd get to speak to James again with their current situation.

"Rafe," she said.

His face softened, grew concerned. "What is it, Lizzy?"

"What do we do now?"

He reached across the table. His fingers hesitated before they covered hers. "I'll take care of it," he said. "Do not be afraid."

She shook her head and although she wanted to keep her hand inside his, she withdrew it. "You will not take care of it alone, Rafe. You must tell me what you're going to do. This concerns me too and I must know." She lifted her gaze to his, almost too afraid to see if he was angry with her for her defiance.

But he was not. His eyes were soft and...sad? "Lizzy. I'm not telling you what I'm going to do because I don't think you want to know."

He was going to kill him. She shivered.

He frowned. "Are you cold?"

She shook her head. "Are you going to go in search of him today?"

His gaze shifted to the left, not meeting hers. "I am going out again."

"So soon? But you're not fully healed."

"The wound won't trouble me."

How could she make him stay? It was much too dangerous for him to be out. Treece and his men would be crawling
over the city and Southwark. It was madness. He would be
hurt again and she wasn't sure her nerves could cope with the
waiting.

She could tell him none of that, of course. It wasn't her
place and he wouldn't want to hear the silly ramblings of a
female. So she said, "You'll have to wait until the clothes are
dry."

He glanced at the skirt and bodice drying on the stools. "I
won't wear them today."

"Shall I prepare one of the other garments Shakespeare
lent us?"

"The beard, perhaps, but I want to be a man today." Why?
Did he want Treece to find him?

When she didn't rise, he got up and went into the storeroom. He came back out wearing the red beard and a broad-
brimmed hat to cover his hair. "How do I look?"

Like a man who should *not* be leaving. Her sight blurred
and she turned away. Didn't he know he might not make it
back at all?

"Lizzy," he said on a breath. He slid onto the seat beside
her, so close she could feel his warmth. "Please, don't worry. I
won't leave you to fend for yourself."

"I'm not worried for my sake!"

Her outburst seemed to take him by surprise. He stood
suddenly and lifted his chin in a nod. "I'll be back before
nightfall." He went into the storeroom and came out again
carrying a wrapped parcel. It had to be food.

Where was he taking it?

He left without saying good-bye. She hurried into the
storeroom and rummaged through the sack of disguises. She

found a long dark wig, a tall hat, and a cloak, which she threw around her shoulders to cover the low-cut bodice. She also grabbed the pouch of coins Blake had given them.

The wig and hat were firmly in place by the time she clambered over the fence after him.

CHAPTER 14

Rafe suspected he was being followed again, he just couldn't see who it was, or think who it might be. Barker, Treece, or one of the constables would confront him if they saw him and raise a hue and cry, not skulk in the shadows. Rafe kept walking, taking a circuitous route to the prison. He half-expected Barker to be there, but instead there was a man he'd never seen before. He was certainly one of Treece's. While he appeared to be lounging against a post without a care in the world, he was watching the passersby beneath the lowered brim of his hat. Despite this apparent vigilance, he didn't see Rafe. He wouldn't be looking for someone with a limp, a slow gait, and a red beard. Barker, on the other hand, wouldn't have been so easy to fool. Treece too perhaps.

Nevertheless, Rafe decided not to go into the Marshalsea. It was too much of a risk, particularly when Treece could be inside. James could wait another day without starving.

He turned around and went home again. At least Lizzy would be happy to see him.

~ ~ ~

At first Lizzy thought Rafe was going to the Rose but then he stopped on Borough High Street across from the Marshalsea. She watched him for a few minutes as he knelt and tended to his boot. He'd been walking with a limp, part of his disguise she guessed, and he was making a show of removing his boot, rubbing his foot, and putting the boot back on. Although she couldn't see his eyes beneath his hat, she suspected he was checking his surroundings the entire time. The one thing she did notice was a lingering final glance at the prison before he left. Very odd.

She ducked into an apothecary's shop and purchased a balm for healing wounds. While the assistant wrapped up the jars, she watched the comings and goings from the Marshalsea, across the road. The building was a wooden structure set back from the road, its turreted entrance lodge giving it a regal presence. She'd never really taken much notice of it before. She'd heard of people who'd been incarcerated there of course, including the playwright Ben Jonson, but she'd never visited anyone at the jail.

Rafe must know a prisoner or he wouldn't have taken an interest in the building. It also explained why he'd taken food from the storeroom. But who was in there? Whom did he know well enough that he would risk his life to feed them? One of his friends? Lord Oxley? But his friends weren't in London, so Rafe claimed, and Oxley surely had the means to keep himself out of debtor's prison. The Marshalsea held other sorts of prisoners too, but someone of Lord Oxley's standing would have been sent to the Tower if he'd committed a more villainous crime.

So if not Rafe's friends, then who? The only other person he cared about was James. It had to be him. Lizzy tried to think back to when he'd left London, but she couldn't recall his exact words. He'd claimed he was leaving the city for work. Although that was odd in itself, it had been even odder when her father had suggested James's employer was no longer in business. Rafe had suppressed that conversation before Lizzy could ask questions.

The apothecary cleared his throat and held out the package. She paid him and, with the package tucked under her arm, crossed the road to the Marshalsea.

The warden greeted her with lurid curiosity. Her immediate reaction was one of embarrassment. She wanted to leave, but she forced herself to remain.

"Do you have a prisoner named James Pritchard housed here?" she asked.

He pushed out his fat slug lips and eyed her up and down again. "Who are you?"

Had he been told to seize anyone who came to see James? She checked over her shoulder but she'd not been followed. Since she was already there, she might as well try to sway the warden not to arrest her. She fished a gold crown out of the pouch and laid it flat on her palm. She tilted her chin as she'd seen more confident women do and said, "Do not tell anyone James has a visitor and I'll give you more when I leave."

He took the coin. "Follow me." They crossed an open yard where several male and a few female prisoners watched her openly through bleak, hollow eyes. Many were dressed in little more than rags.

"Who you got there?" one of them called out.

"Got coin, pretty lady?" a woman asked. "Food?"

The warden ignored them. Lizzy quickened her pace to keep up with his long strides. They entered another building with a series of doors off a long corridor. He opened one and stepped inside. She peered around him and four sets of eyes immediately turned her way. One of them belonged to James.

His gaze skimmed her, looked away without recognition, then quickly snapped back. "Lizzy!" He rose and she was struck by how thin and pale he'd become. Small sores spotted his mouth and he had the same hollow-eyed look as the prisoners in the yard. A large bruise darkened his jaw.

"James." She ran to him and gripped his arms. She pulled him into a tight embrace and she felt him relax, but just for a moment. Then he pushed her away.

"Don't," he said. "I stink."

"I don't care." But she stepped back anyway. She didn't want to embarrass him. James was always so fastidious.

"Call me if they look like they'll eat you," the warden said with a snort and left the door open since the prisoners could go out to the courtyard whenever they wanted.

She was alone with James and the other inmates. Two were little more than a collection of bones covered in skin. Their hungry eyes followed her every move. One of them licked cracked lips and elbowed the other in the ribs. The third prisoner was bigger. He stood up and she swallowed a gasp. Big didn't begin to describe him. He was about as tall as Rafe but more massive in waist, legs, shoulders...everywhere! She'd seen ancient oaks with narrower trunks than him. He winked at her.

She edged closer to James.

"What have you done to your hair?" he asked her.

She touched the wig. "It's my disguise."

He grunted. "You and Rafe with your disguises. I don't like it."

"Our disguises or my wig?" She removed it and checked that her real hair was still bound on top of her head.

He lifted one shoulder and turned away. Four pallets lay end to end around the cell, but there was little else in the way of comfort for the prisoners. Some personal items, a pack of cards, and some dice. The room was rank with sweat and urine, and beneath that was an air of desperation and wretchedness ingrained in the very walls.

"Please sit," James said with a mocking bow. "Come share my flea-riddled pallet with me." He scratched his neck and plopped down on the pallet.

She knelt down next to him and offered a smile, which was wasted because he didn't look at her. "Rafe came here yesterday," she said, carefully not framing it as a question.

"I'm glad he came to his senses after he left."

She waited but he didn't elaborate. "What do you mean?"

He rubbed the back of his neck. "He didn't want to ask you to come here. When he told me about the murder and why he'd been in disguise, I told him he wasn't to come anymore. It was too dangerous. I suggested you could come in his stead, but he didn't like that idea." His gaze flicked to the other prisoners. All three of them watched avidly. The big one was picking dirt out of his nails, the other two pretending to be playing cards. "It appears he changed his mind."

"It would appear so." She'd been angry at him a few moments before. Angry that he hadn't told her about his predicament, that he hadn't trusted her enough to tell her. But upon seeing the horridness of the cell and the misery etched into every line on his face, her anger dissolved. Poor James. He looked so pathetic. Getting mad at him would only heap more misery on him, and she couldn't do that.

"You should have told me in the first place," she said gently. "I could have helped you."

He gave a brittle laugh. "Could you? Lizzy, I know you have little coin and your troupe's future is uncertain, and I know you would have tried to help anyway. That's why I didn't tell you."

She shook her head. "I don't understand. We're supposed to be betrothed. You should have trusted me."

"Of course I trust you." He looked at her like she was a fool.

"Then...why? Surely it's not really about me offering you money."

He sighed and leaned back against the wall, dark gray from centuries of grime. "Because...you're so...so...good."

"Pardon?"

"Perfect," he added.

"I most certainly am not." A perfect woman would not have kissed the brother of her intended. She felt her face heat and she glanced down at her hands to avoid his gaze.

"You are. You have a good job where everyone likes you. Your sisters and parents love you very much. You're nice to everyone, you've always abided by your father's wishes, and you've never done anything wrong in your life."

She pulled a face. "I sound perfectly dull."

The big prisoner grunted and said, "Aye."

James didn't tell him to be quiet. Rafe would have. "You're not dull, you're wonderful." James sighed heavily. Not quite the reaction that naturally followed upon declaring her to be wonderful. "I didn't want you to be ashamed of me," he said. "That's why I said nothing."

"Why would I be ashamed of you? Did you do something to lose your apprenticeship?"

"No. Cuxcomb went out of business." He waved a hand to encompass the small cell. "He was in here for a time, but his debt got paid by his sister's husband, so he's out now."

"Then it's not your fault and I don't think any less of you." She touched his shoulder. He shook her off. "James...please. How can I help?"

"Did you bring any food?" He eyed the apothecary's package with hope.

"No."

He sagged against the wall. "Money?"

She gave him the pouch, keeping a crown for herself to pay the warden on the way out. It was all the money she and Rafe had but at least Rafe was a good thief and could get more. James needed it far more than they did. He could use the funds to buy food, candles, and even water for bathing at the prison shop. "What is being done to pay off your debts?"

"What *can* be done?" He sighed again. "I'm in here, not earning a penny, and Rafe is hiding away because someone's blaming him for a murder. Hopefully it'll all be settled by the time he's supposed to start work for Lord Liddicoat, otherwise..." He shook his head.

"How much are your debts?"

"A little over three pounds."

"That much! That would take you six months to earn."

"If I was still working."

"Oh, James, I'm sorry. Father doesn't have that kind of money."

"I'm not asking him to pay it," he snapped.

She lifted her brows and he looked away. He rubbed his arms as if he couldn't get warm. "Blake might loan—"

"That only transfers the debt to a different creditor. I still wouldn't be able to pay it. I am out of luck until Rafe can sort out his problem and start his new job."

It seemed Rafe hadn't told James that she too was being pursued, only himself. It also seemed that James didn't understand how much trouble Rafe was in.

"You're not concerned about him?" she asked.

He frowned at her. "Rafe? No, of course not. He'll sort everything out. He always does. He's very capable."

"Very. But..."

"But what?"

She didn't want to say it, didn't want to think it, but she had to. For James's sake. "What if something happens to both Rafe and me?" She stroked the long dark tresses of the wig. "What if neither he nor I can come here?"

"Something happen to the both of you? That would be an unlucky coincidence."

"But still a possibility. James, no one will know you're even in here. Do you realize that? Not a soul. You'll be left to die in here alone. That money won't last forever." She nodded at the other prisoners. "Or do you think one of them will come to your aid?"

He watched the two smaller prisoners playing cards in the corner. Neither had spoken since she'd entered, not to each other or to the big prisoner. Odd. Surely they'd want to at least comment on their game.

"I think you're worrying unnecessarily," he said. When she protested, he held up his hand. "But to ease your mind, I'll allow you to inform your parents. Make sure your father understands I do *not* need anything from him. I am perfectly comfortable while you are visiting me."

"But if I am not here to visit—"

"Stop saying that, Lizzy!"

She rocked back and blinked at him. He never spoke harshly to her, never raised his voice, and yet he'd done it on more than one occasion since her arrival. He must be far more agitated than he was letting on.

"Very well," she said, stiffly.

He groaned and pulled his knees up. He put his head down and ran his hand through his greasy hair. Lizzy's heart ached for him. He was so vulnerable, so unlike the happy boy she'd grown up with. She wanted to wrap her arms around his shoulders and hug him but she couldn't be sure he'd let her.

"This is hopeless. I'm hopeless."

"Enough of this," she said. "Why not go into the yard? I saw some other prisoners outside on my way here and you could do with the fresh air and to stretch your legs. It doesn't do you any good to sit in your cell all day and wallow in your misfortune."

He lifted his head and screwed up his nose at her. "Wallow? You think I'm wallowing?"

"Yes," she said boldly. "You have your life and your health. That's more than many."

He stood suddenly and paced the room, back and forth, like a chained bear in the baiting pit. It was pitiful. Worse than pitiful, it was worrying. James might be alive, but she was beginning to suspect he was losing his mind.

"You're right, Lizzy," he said, abruptly stopping in front of her. He pulled her to her feet, depositing the things in her lap onto the floor. "You're always right, that's why I...I...love you."

Her heart plunged into her stomach. She suddenly felt heavy-limbed and sick. A strange reaction considering she loved him too. Of course she did. She always had. They were so perfect for each other.

So why couldn't she say it back?

Because of that kiss with Rafe. When she'd been kissing him, she'd not felt even a hint of confusion. She'd known exactly what she wanted. She wanted Rafe. She'd hardly thought of James at all.

He clasped her hands in his. "We *will* be wed when I have some money. I promise you. I'll not leave you waiting forever. A woman like you must be cherished. A man can go far with you as his wife. *I* can go far." He kissed her on the mouth. It was dry and chaste. "Don't forget me in here. You won't, will you? Lizzy?"

She squeezed his hands. "Of course not. But I have to leave. I've been gone too long." She called for the warden to escort her out and glanced over her shoulder. The three prisoners watched her as intently as they had upon her arrival. James waved. She waved back and hurried away.

~ ~ ~

Rafe returned to the house after his third search of the area to find Lizzy sitting at the kitchen table, a cup of ale in hand and an empty trencher in front of her. He paused in the doorway and gave her the sort of glare he reserved for someone who'd wronged him. She merely lifted her eyebrows, not at all concerned.

"Where have you been?" he growled. "I've looked everywhere for you! Why weren't you here waiting for me?" He sounded like a shrewish wife. So be it. Lizzy needed to know how dangerous it was to leave in the middle of the day without him.

"Not much fun, is it?" she said, rising.

"What?" He came inside and flung the beard on the table.

"Waiting for someone to come home when danger is everywhere outside." She dipped a cloth into a pot of water warming over the fire and wiped her trencher and cup. Didn't she notice how angry he was? Didn't she care that he'd felt sick when he returned to find her gone not once but three times?

His jaw hurt. He unclenched it. Tried to be calm. It didn't work. "This is not the same thing. I can take care of myself."

"It most certainly is the same thing."

He sighed, but it came out more like a long, frustrated grunt. "Lizzy. Do not do that again. Understand? Never leave here without my permission."

She turned to face him, her eyes narrowed as she fixed him with a glare that equaled his in ferocity. She was not the timid Lizzy he'd left behind. Something had changed. He was glad she was no longer afraid of him, but that didn't soothe his ire.

"I am not your woman, Rafe. Not your wife, sister, daughter, or niece, so do *not* speak to me in that manner. Ever." She stepped closer to him and shook the cloth in his face.

Right. So she was angry at him. He understood that. Interesting how anger made her body tremble and her breasts jiggle above the tight bodice.

He tore his gaze away and concentrated on her face. "Very well," he said. *Not his woman*. No, of course she wasn't. She was James's. "I can see that you were worried when I didn't return yesterday. Shall we call a truce?" He looked down at her breasts again despite his resolve not to and his cock stirred. She had a luscious body. All soft curves and—

"Look at my eyes, Rafe. I haven't finished yet."

His gaze swept up. *Not his woman.* Christ. "Haven't finished what?" Ah, yes, worry. She'd been worried about him too. He smiled. He couldn't help it.

"Stop smiling. This is important!"

He bit the inside of his cheek until he tasted blood. It stopped the smiling. He apologized and nodded for her to go on.

"I followed you to the Marshalsea."

"You did what!" he bellowed.

She gave him a defiant look. "You should have told me where you were going and I wouldn't have needed to follow. You should have told me about James."

He stared at her. His mouth fell open and he shut it again with a snap. "That was..." Resourceful. "...a foolish thing to do! Bloody hell, Lizzy, Treece's men are everywhere. What if one of them had seen you? What if something had happened to you?" He strode off, came back to her, shook his finger, and almost told her she was to remain in the house forever but stopped himself. Perhaps it was a little extreme, and perhaps he should have told her where he was going in the first place. Besides, shouting at her might snap her out of the new ease she'd developed around him.

She folded her arms beneath her breasts, which only pushed them up more. He groaned. Was she trying to deliberately distract him? He forced his gaze up. *Concentrate.*

"I was at the Marshalsea an hour ago at least," he said. "I came straight home. Where have you been since then?"

"Visiting James, of course."

He choked on his expletive. "You went *inside*? Alone? Lizzy!" He scrubbed a hand over his chin. He should have told her. Should have taken her himself so he could protect her.

"Did anything happen? There's a big prisoner in the cell with him. Did he...?" He swallowed. "Is he still there?"

"Rafe, don't worry. I am unhurt, see?" She held out her arms. Naturally his gaze slipped to her breasts. "But I'm so angry with you for not telling me."

"You're angry with me? *You're* angry with *me*? Ha!"

Her eyes darkened and he braced himself. He'd never seen her like this before, like a small intense storm ready to burst. "Yes, I am. You should have told me. James is alone in there and extremely vulnerable. What happens if you and I..." She gulped. "What happens to him if something happens to us? Have you told anyone where he is?"

"No. He didn't want me to."

"He is my friend," she went on. "My very dear friend." She looked away and he wondered if tears welled in her eyes but then she met his gaze once more and they were dry, but softer. The anger had disappeared, replaced by something else. Worry, yes, but other emotions too that he couldn't place. "Are you aware that he's going mad in there?"

"What do you mean? He seemed perfectly well when I saw him yesterday."

"He's not today. He's agitated and distressed. I think he's desperate to get out."

Rafe sat down on the bench and lowered his head into his hands. "I should have stayed in London to take care of him these past years."

She sat next to him and sighed. "He certainly needs a steadying influence in his life. I see that now." She spoke quietly, as if talking to herself, convincing herself of something. It unnerved him.

"What is it, Lizzy?"

She seemed to make up her mind about something and turned to him. Her eyes were clouded, her gaze unfocused. "He needs me," she said, her voice empty of emotion. "I hadn't realized how much until now. His mind is fragile. He's not like us."

Rafe wanted to touch her cheek and hold her face in his hands so he could look at her. Really look at her. Because he knew now that he'd been wrong too. Wrong about her. She wasn't delicate. She never had been. Shy, yes, but not weak. She was strong and capable. The fact she'd conquered her shyness in most situations was a testament to how capable.

But he could not touch her or hold her. She wasn't his.

"He certainly needs someone," he said carefully. "It doesn't have to be you." He hadn't known how much he meant it until he said it. The thought of Lizzy wedded to James wasn't right. His brother was a good man but he was no match for her in spirit. In many ways he was still a boy, whereas she was very much a woman. "I'll take care of him. Or we can do it together." *You don't have to marry him.*

She shook her head. "No, Rafe. He's my responsibility. We have an understanding. We always have."

"So?" He couldn't believe he was about to say this. James was his *brother*. But he had to. Needed to. "An understanding can be easily set aside."

She turned her face away. "I can't do that to him. He doesn't deserve it." Her voice was flat, devoid of feeling, and her shoulders stooped.

He wanted to hold them gently, hold her, tell her to forget about her obligation to James and think about herself for once. "Tell me, Lizzy." He came up behind her but didn't touch her. Her hair curled at the nape of her neck, around her ears, small swirls of fine silk against creamy skin. He touched one curl and released it, watched it spring back up. She drew in a sharp breath and her shoulders tensed as if bracing herself. "What do you feel?" he whispered. He reached around and laid one hand on her left breast. It filled his palm so perfectly. "What do you feel in here?"

Her breath released in jagged puffs. She tipped her head back and rested it against his chest. Beneath his palm, her heart fluttered quietly like a small caged bird seeking release. She sighed heavily and closed her eyes. He circled his arms around her and kept her close against him, her head tucked neatly under his chin. Everything felt right, perfect. They were exactly where they were meant to be—together. James would understand.

He had to.

He held her. Just held her. And she let him.

Then everything shattered.

The door smashed back on its hinges. Treece barreled through, sword raised and yelling, his men at his heels. More men banged on the front door, shouting for it to be unlocked.

Bloody hell.

CHAPTER 15

Rafe shoved Lizzy behind him and she stumbled. By the time she recovered, Rafe had drawn his sword and engaged Treece and two others in a duel. She scrambled to her feet, grabbed a knife, then backed out of the kitchen.

But another two men broke through the front door, shattering the wood and sending splinters onto the rushes. She glanced over her shoulder. Rafe had already dispensed with one attacker. He lay bleeding on the kitchen floor.

"Rafe!"

"I see them," he said, parrying Treece's blade. "Come close."

She did, one eye on the other men approaching from the front door.

"Up on the table," Rafe said.

She climbed up and kicked out as one of the constables lunged for her feet. He reeled back and swore.

Rafe jumped over a blade as it struck at his legs. He landed on one foot and kicked Treece on the side of the head with the other.

Treece fell back and slumped against the wall. The two remaining men hesitated when they saw their leader on the floor, his eyes rolling up into his head.

Rafe dropped and caught Lizzy around the waist. He helped her off the table and together they raced out the back door. Only one man followed, but when he glanced over his shoulder and saw his fellow constables hadn't joined in the chase, he gave up. Lizzy wasn't surprised. Only a fool would have hunted a man like Rafe on his own.

She ran as fast as her skirts allowed and followed Rafe through small, crowded alleys, behind houses, over fences. When they reached the river she had to slow down or her heart would have burst through her ribs.

"Where are we going?" she said between gasping breaths.

He shrugged as he scanned the area. She still held his hand and could feel the alertness rippling through him.

"I know where," she asked. "But it's best we wait until dark."

"Can you keep moving until then? It's too dangerous to stay in one place long."

She nodded. "It'll help if I change into men's clothing."

They set off along the river until the houses grew fewer and the streets became muddier. It had begun to rain lightly, so there was no washing out to dry. They peeped into windows and finally found an empty kitchen with hose and a jerkin drying near the fire. Rafe crept in, took them, and turned his back to keep watch while Lizzy dressed behind the milk house. They left her women's clothes behind and set off once again, circling back the way they'd come.

The urge to leave London entirely wasn't as strong as Lizzy thought it would be. They could do it but she entertained the thought for only a moment before dismissing it. She couldn't desert her parents, her friends, or James, and she did not want to be running away her entire life, never able to stay in one place long lest the authorities find them. They had to clear their names, once and for all. Rafe never suggested the idea to her.

Night finally came and she led him through darkness lit only by the occasional lamp outside the better taverns or brothels. Most folk had returned home but some revelers remained and the cool evening air was filled with bursts of their laughter and talk.

Soon the Rose loomed like a wide, squat castle tower. Lizzy and Rafe kept to the shadows as they circled the theatre and spotted two men watching each entrance.

"I'll remove them," Rafe said but Lizzy held him back.

"I have a better idea."

She led him to the Bankside, the street running along the south bank of the Thames, an area renowned for its brothels. She chose one with a clean stoop—as good a method of choosing a brothel as any—and hired a girl from the thick-necked, black-toothed man who greeted them. He glanced at Rafe, eyebrows raised, but Rafe merely shrugged and handed him the dagger he kept strapped to his forearm as payment.

"I want it back," Rafe said.

"Aye," the man nodded, running his hands over the carved bone handle. "When you pay me in coin." He filled a small leather pouch with money from a locked coffer and handed it to his whore.

Outside, Lizzy gave the woman her instructions and Rafe asked for her hairpin. She gave it to him and he sent her on her way. Lizzy and Rafe returned to the copse of trees near the theatre and watched as the constable stationed at the back door was led away by an amorous whore with enough money in her purse to get him drunk.

Lizzy and Rafe climbed the steps to the tiring house and Rafe used the hairpin to open the lock. They snuck inside and she led him through the darkness up to the storeroom, where she collapsed onto a stool. She put her head down on the central table and allowed a small sob of exhaustion to escape.

"My wig," she groaned. "I left it at the prison and Treece's man must have seen me leave. He must have followed me to the house then collected Treece and the others. I led him straight to us!" What a fool! Perhaps if she hadn't been so angry with Rafe or worried about James or distracted by Rafe's touch…No, there was no excuse. She buried her face in the crook of her arm.

"Hush, Lizzy." Rafe's cool, steady hand rested against the back of her neck. His fingers teased her hair and loosened it from the pins. It tumbled down her back and across her shoulders. "It's not your fault. None of this is."

"But—"

"Shh." His fingers massaged her scalp, the gentle rhythm lulling her. She was tired and everything ached but she wasn't ready to sleep. Not with his body pressing into her back, solid and comforting, and his heavenly fingers working like magic.

He knelt down beside her and kissed her shoulder. "Do not worry," he whispered. "I will end this."

He said it with such conviction that she would have believed him if the situation weren't so dire. She turned to face him and could just make out the swirl of desire in his eyes by the moonlight coming through the window. "Oh, Rafe," she murmured. "It's all so hopeless."

He rested his forehead against hers. "It will be all right. I will end this. Trust me."

She did. With her life, her fears…her heart.

She held his face gently in her hands and kissed him lightly on the lips. He responded with a harder, more urgent kiss that quickly warmed her all the way through to her bones. Her skin tingled with it, every part of her sang an exquisite tune as he dragged her to him and pressed against her. Hard. Fierce. Unashamed.

He kissed her chin, her throat, and that place beneath her ear that made her want to both giggle and sigh at the same time. Heat spiraled down her spine to her inner thighs as he unhooked the fastenings of her jerkin then unlaced her shift and freed her breasts. They ached with fullness. Her nipples tightened. She pushed herself into his hands and he massaged, his thumbs gently strumming the nubs until she could stand it no longer and had to have more of him. Had to see him. Touch him like he was touching her.

She removed his jerkin and snaked her hand inside his shirt. He sucked air between his teeth as she teased his nipple. He tipped his head back and she licked the skin at his throat because she wanted to know what he tasted like there.

Delicious. Spicy. All man.

He groaned low in his throat and his eyelids fluttered closed. "You will be the undoing of me," he murmured.

She didn't have the wits to understand what he meant. All she knew was that she had to see him, have him, possess him. She pulled his shirt over his head and drank in the sight of his bare chest. It was too dark to see him in detail, so she used her fingers to trace every sleek muscle, every hard contour, and commit them to memory. She would always have those.

But it wasn't enough. She had to taste him there too. She flicked a nipple with the tip of her tongue. His breath hitched. She grinned against his skin.

"Wicked wench," he growled and scooped her up and planted her on his lap. He nuzzled her breasts and her smile vanished, swallowed by her gasps.

Oh God, she was drowning in sensations. Beneath her, Rafe's length prodded her thigh. "I want to see you," she whispered. "All of you."

He gently placed her on the table and stepped out of the rest of his clothes. He stood before her, the moonlight polishing his right side to a soft glow and throwing his left into shadow. His bandaged wound didn't seem to bother him. He was a magnificent creature. Powerful and beautiful.

Then she looked down.

She congratulated herself on not gasping, not making a single sound, although she felt herself grow hotter. Thank goodness her face was in darkness and he couldn't see her.

It was on fire, like the rest of her. He was quite the sight to behold.

"You can touch it if you want," he said, amusement edging his voice. He put his hands on his hips and then his member did a very curious thing. It moved. On its own. Well, she hadn't expected it to do *that*.

"Are you laughing at me?" he asked.

"No! Not at all. I wouldn't. I mean, it's not a laughing matter. It's very...serious. Your...um..."

"Cock."

"Do I have to call it that?"

"You can call it whatever you like as long as it doesn't include the word *small*." His teeth flashed white in the darkness.

She grinned. "Very well. Your very large...rod just moved by itself. And when I held you last night, it grew. Does it always do that?"

He leaned closer and placed his hands flat on the table on either side of her. Trapping her. His lips brushed against hers. "Only for you," he said huskily.

She snorted. "A pretty sentiment."

"Trust me," he murmured with a deep, dark rumble, "there is nothing pretty about what I feel for you. It's primal. Basic. Fierce." He drew in a deep breath. "I've never felt anything like it." He spoke with wonder in his voice, as if the sentiment had taken him by surprise.

She cupped his cheek and caressed the curve of his lips with her thumb in a futile attempt to catch that tone, so unlike the sure one he always used. He turned his head and kissed the palm of her hand.

Then he stopped, straightened. "Lizzy." He released a sigh that seemed to come from the depths of his body. "We can't do this. I can't take you here like this. You're an innocent. You must wait until your wedding night."

He began to turn away before he'd even finished and she caught him by his arms. He didn't shrug her off but she felt him shudder.

"What if I don't have a wedding night, Rafe?" She hopped off the table and shook him until he looked at her again. "What if we're arrested first?"

"Don't."

"I don't want to die without knowing—"

"Stop, Lizzy, you're not going to die. I won't allow it."

"We all die sometime, Rafe, and I don't want to go to the afterlife without knowing *you* in that way."

"Me?"

She nodded and hoped he could see it in the moonlight because she suddenly wasn't capable of speaking. Her throat had squeezed shut. Tears stung her nose and burned her eyes.

"Me," he said again.

She reached one hand around his neck and pulled his head down for a kiss. It was sweet and tentative until she wrapped her other hand around his penis. He groaned against her mouth and deepened the kiss.

She stroked his length, so smooth despite the ridges, and rubbed the droplet seeping from the tip around the tight head. He gasped.

"Your fingers..." he mumbled, "...are sheer torture."

She grinned against his mouth.

"Lizzy, I won't be able to stop soon. Do you understand? If you don't want—"

"I do want. I want you, Rafe, only you." She wanted him inside her and *beside* her. Always. She reached around and grabbed his rear. "I've been wanting to do that ever since we met."

He chuckled. "I think, wench, that you are trying to take advantage of me. I feel vulnerable standing here without clothes on."

"Is that a subtle attempt to get me to disrobe?"

"Not subtle in the least." He undid her jerkin and tossed it aside. She removed her men's hose, then he took his time over her garters and stockings, drawing each one down her leg with frustrating slowness.

He kissed her foot, her knee, and trailed tiny kisses up her thigh to her…Oh my! He laughed. "Like that?" he asked.

"Yesssss." She braced her bottom against the table and dug her hands through his hair, holding him in place. "Do it again."

"Whatever my lady wishes." He licked.

She cried out.

He licked again and she bit back another cry. A few more licks and she turned into a quivering mess, her body no longer in her control. She burned all over, hot liquid swirling through her, swamping her, drowning her.

Then everything tightened. Her skin, her breasts, nipples, and especially her nether region all constricted. It was like she was being wound up by his tongue and might unravel at any moment.

Then she did unravel in an explosive way. And it was like a release she didn't know she needed, waves of pleasure flooding her inside and out, head to toe. Her heart thundered inside her, slamming against her ribs, its echoes pounding through her. She'd never felt so alive, so aware, her senses heightened to every touch, every breath on her sensitive skin.

He stood and cradled her gently against his chest. His heart beat loudly and erratically too, as if in sympathy with her own. He massaged the back of her neck and kissed her hair.

They stood like that for a long time until she caught her breath and her mind began working again. "Was that supposed to happen? I mean, were you supposed to do it like that?"

She felt him smile against the top of her head. "Did you like it?"

"Yes!"

"Then I was supposed to do it like that. And I will again. Every day, if you'll let me."

"Oh, I'll let you. But now it's your turn." She reached down between them and gripped him. "Am I doing it right?"

He sucked in air between his teeth. "I don't think you're capable of doing it wrong."

She tugged and teased and marveled at how big it grew in her hand. He dipped his head to hers for a kiss and gripped her hips. His breathing grew strained and sweat dampened his brow. Lizzy closed her eyes and listened to the thrum of his heart, the rhythm of pleasure through his body. It drove her to distraction, made her nerves jangle.

"I want you inside me."

He made a small sound in the back of his throat. A protest? "Are you sure?" he rasped.

"Very."

"I don't think that's a good idea."

"Then don't think."

His fingers dug into her hips. "God help me, I can't say no to you." He picked her up and lay her down on the table. He rose above her and pressed the tip of his length into her.

"Stop?" he whispered in her ear.

"No!" It was the last thing she wanted to do. She widened her legs and arched her back, pushing her breasts up.

He sucked one until she could stand it no longer. "Now," she whispered. "Take me now."

He groaned and pressed the tip of his hard length inside her again. He set a slow, steady rhythm that seemed to be designed to drive her mad. She rocked her hips and he slipped farther in with a moan of pleasure. He quickened his pace. She matched it with another thrust and a sharp pain pierced her.

He stopped and covered her cry with his mouth, kissing her until she relaxed again. Gently, gently, he pushed farther in, all the way until he was buried deep inside her. Some distant part of her was amazed that she could take him to the hilt, but that thought was quickly shattered by an intense pressure building inside her. Not like when he'd licked her, not explosive and liquefying, not as intense, but just as powerful in its own way.

Above her, Rafe grunted once, twice, then roared. A great shudder tore through his body and he tipped his head back. She wished they'd lit candles. She wanted to see him in that moment, see what pleasure looked like on his face.

When he finished, he rolled off to the side and lay next to her on the table. She nestled into him, wanting to keep him close. Being together felt so...right. So wonderful. He wrapped his arms around her and stroked her hair. Then his hand stilled. He groaned.

"What is it?" she asked, half-rising so she could look at him in the moonlight.

He pressed the heel of his hand into his eye. "I should have pulled out. I shouldn't have—"

"Shh," she said, stroking his cheek with her knuckle. "It doesn't matter if your seed is planted inside me now."

"You're not going to mention dying again, are you?"

"No. I thought we could get married after this is over." She felt shy again all of a sudden, awkward. She blushed heavily. Held her breath.

He linked his fingers through hers and kissed the tips. It was difficult to tell but he appeared to be blinking rapidly. "Yes," he said simply.

She breathed again. Smiled.

But he drew back. "James..." he choked out.

"I know," she whispered. "I know. We'll have to think of a way to tell him."

He rubbed her knuckles with his thumb and said nothing. She swallowed past the lump forming in her throat. Did Rafe's loyalty and responsibility toward his brother extend to forgoing his own happiness?

"He is wrong for me, Rafe," she said. "I know that now. He is my friend. My very dear friend. But it's you I love, in an entirely different way." Still he said nothing. Cold fingers curled around her heart. "Please. Do you understand? Even if nothing comes of this, of us...I will not wed James. Not now. It wouldn't be fair to him because I don't love him enough. I never will."

Rafe could hear the crack in her voice and his heart lurched into his throat. It felt full, heavy, like it would burst and shatter him into a thousand pieces. He never thought he'd ever feel like this. Never thought he'd hear any woman say those words to him. And never thought it would be Lizzy and that her quiet declaration had the power to break him apart.

It's you I love.

"I understand," he whispered because he wasn't capable of speaking louder. He traced his thumb across the ridge of her cheek, down to the point of her chin, the curve of her bottom lip, swollen with his kisses. So exquisite. Beautiful. Like a rare jewel. All his.

But James...

He groaned and shut his eyes against the image of his brother bruised and defeated in the Marshalsea. He had no money, no dignity, no pride left. How could Rafe take away the one thing of any value he still possessed?

But he couldn't give Lizzy up.

She sighed and rested her cheek on his chest. Her breasts pillowed against his ribs and her breath warmed his skin. She was lithe and soft and she fit perfectly, like her body was meant to be exactly there. He stroked her hair and felt her relax into him. All her inhibitions were gone around him now and he felt privileged that she'd allowed him to see the real Lizzy, the amazing, sensual woman with a strong mind. He wanted to tell her but her breathing had become steady and soft. She was asleep. It would have to wait until tomorrow.

He tried to sleep too but couldn't. His senses were too alert to sounds of intrusion and besides, who could sleep with such a woman as Lizzy naked beside him?

About an hour after dawn, as he thought of what to tell James, he heard it. A door opening then closing. He woke Lizzy with a hand over her mouth to silence her. Her eyes grew wide and he signaled for her to rise and dress quietly. He watched her out of the corner of his eye as she put on hose and stockings, shift and jerkin. She glanced at him, her gaze dipping to his nakedness. She blushed fiercely and he kissed her thoroughly, silently. Then he finished dressing and approached the door. Someone came up the stairs, their footsteps light and quick.

Rafe stepped back from the door and pushed his sleeves up. The door opened and the actor named Antony came inside. He took one look at Rafe then Lizzy and covered his gasp with both hands.

Lizzy threw her arms around him. "Oh, Antony," she said and buried her face in his shoulder. "It's so good to see you."

Rafe cleared his throat. Antony set her aside and looked at him, eyes narrowed. He glanced at Lizzy then back at Rafe again and smiled slyly. "Taking good care of her, I see."

Lizzy dipped her head. Rafe folded his arms and Antony held up his hands in surrender.

"Believe me, I'm glad that you are," he said. "Very glad. She needed...taking care of."

"Who does?" said another man entering the storeroom. He had the red-rimmed eyes of a drunk and the beginnings of a patchy beard clinging to his chin. "Lo, Liz, you murderess!" he said, sweeping past Rafe without a second glance and aiming straight for Lizzy.

"You're in early, Freddie," she said.

"Fucking Style's got me reading an extra fucking part today. Got to learn new fucking lines by this afternoon."

Rafe snatched his arm and dragged Freddie around to face him. "Think you can speak without using the bad language?"

"Fuck no." Freddie snorted a laugh. "So they haven't caught you yet?"

"Not through lack of trying," Lizzy said with a heavy sigh and a glance at Rafe. She blushed again. His fingers relaxed and he let go of the little turd.

"We've seen the constables outside every day," Antony said. "How did you get in with them watching all night?"

"We distracted one long enough to sneak inside," Lizzy said.

"That would explain why he was propped up against a stile, his eyes barely open." Antony laughed and drew Lizzy into another hug. "So now what, pet?"

"Now, I finish it," Rafe said.

"How?" came another voice from the door. Lizzy greeted the newcomer as Edward. Rafe remembered him as Roger Style's brother. Behind him stood the manager himself, a tall peacock feather sprouting from his black hat.

He pushed past his brother and stood in the center of the room, feet apart, hands on hips. "What are you doing here?" he said to Lizzy. "You'll put us all in jeopardy."

"Roger," Edward snapped. "Have a care."

"Lizzy needs us," said Antony. He squared his shoulders and thrust out his chest, as masculine as any man defending the honor of a lady. He ruined the effect by tossing his long golden hair over his shoulder. "She's only in this mess because of you."

"Me?" Style spluttered.

"Aye," came another voice at the door. It was Shakespeare. He nodded at Rafe. Rafe nodded back and wondered how many more would join them. "And you know it, Style, or you wouldn't have offered the reward for the real villain's capture."

"Reward? I don't recall—"

"I do," chimed four voices, including the brother's.

Style deflated somewhat. "What are you doing here?" he growled at Shakespeare. "You deserted us to work for that cheating, scheming Burbage, remember?"

"If I were you," Shakespeare said, "I'd try not to make any more enemies."

"I don't make enemies of *them*, they make enemies of *me*."

Antony and Edward rolled their eyes. Freddie laughed loudly.

"I came to ask if I could borrow a beard," Shakespeare went on. "Red if you have it. I was storing ours, but...it's gone missing." His gaze didn't once switch to either Rafe or Lizzy. He was a good liar, or actor, or both.

"No, you can't," Roger said. "And go away."

"Should be in that trunk over there," Edward said.

Shakespeare thanked him and opened the trunk lid. "So what happens now?" he asked Rafe as he rummaged through wigs and costumes. "I see the constables are still outside, although one looks like he's been in a drinking contest with a shipful of sailors and lost. He just threw up in the bushes."

"Rafe's going to finish it," Antony said. "You missed that part."

"Finish it how?" Edward asked.

"A sword rammed through their guts?" Freddie said, hopeful. "Can I watch?"

"Can you ram *him* through the guts?" Antony said, screwing his nose up in distaste as Freddie belched.

"Fuck you," Freddie said and belched again.

"Lizzy," Rafe said quietly. "Stay here but keep away from the windows."

Her eyes widened. "No! Rafe, you can't go out now. It's too dangerous. Wait until nightfall at least."

Nightfall was too long to wait. Besides, he *wanted* to be seen. He needed to draw Barker to *him* and end his life then hope his written witness account would be dismissed. If not, he could always steal it. Without it, the authorities had no proof that he murdered Gripp. All he needed to do was avoid Treece and his men. He went to get his boots. She got there before him and snatched them away. She folded them against her chest and glared at him.

"I'll go out barefoot," he said.

She regarded him fiercely for one moment, then her face suddenly crumbled. He closed her in his arms, boots and all, and held her. He heard Freddie's snort behind him and then they all shuffled out leaving him alone with Lizzy.

"I don't want you to do this," she mumbled.

"I have to."

"I know."

"Don't be afraid. I'm good at taking care of myself."

She looked up at him through watery eyes. "When this is over, *I'm* going to take care of you."

He kissed the top of her head and reluctantly let her go. Walking away was the hardest thing he'd ever done.

CHAPTER 16

The constable stationed at the back door of the playhouse was propped up against a stile, fast asleep and snoring loudly. Rafe easily avoided him and headed straight to the Marshalsea, taking a long, circuitous route so that his path couldn't be retraced to the Rose. Once inside the prison, he walked fast to James's cell. There was so much to say and so little time in which to say it.

~~~

Rafe had only just left the theatre when Antony and Will Shakespeare returned to the tiring house's storeroom in a panic.

"You have to go!" Antony cried, hustling Lizzy toward the door.

"Why?" she asked, glancing from one to the other. They were flustered, not at all like their usual carefree selves. "Rafe! Is he—?"

Footsteps thundered up the stairs and Edward barreled through the door. "A disguise!" he said. "Now!" He rummaged through a coffer and found a beard and short black wig. She put both on, tucking away her own hair.

"Rafe left," Will explained as he helped her. "But one of the constables must have seen him go. He roused the other and is coming this way."

"Henry overheard them as he passed by on his way here just now," Edward said. "One went to follow Rafe and the other is coming to see if you're within. So move!" He rushed her down the stairs and toward the back door.

But it was too late.

A man entered, tall and square-set with a thick brow over bloodshot eyes. He wiped a drooping mouth with the back of his hand and looked into the faces of each member of the troupe. His gaze whisked past Lizzy and settled on Antony.

"Take off that wig," he snapped.

Antony flicked his hair. "But, sir," he said in the high voice he used for the stage, "this is my real hair, sir."

Edward gave Lizzy a little shove toward the door. She slipped past the constable, who ignored her. "Take it off or I'll take it off for you."

Outside, Lizzy ran. She had to find Rafe, had to warn him the other constable was on his way. She would be safe, disguised as she was. Besides, if need be, she could blend into the crowd at the Marshalsea, where she guessed Rafe had gone.

~ ~ ~

"Rafe!" James leapt up and clasped him by the shoulders. The three other prisoners watched with undisguised interest. "Thank God you're still alive. And..." He swallowed. "And Lizzy?"

"Well enough when I left her."

James muttered a prayer to the celing. "But...where's your disguise? If someone's watching the prison, you would have just been recognized."

"I know. That's the point."

James stared at him. Then he punched Rafe in the shoulder. "You fool! You damned ox-headed fool!" He shoved Rafe back toward the turreted entrance. "Get out. Now! Go or they'll catch you!"

Rafe gripped his brother's wrists and James winced. "I will in a moment. But first, I need to speak to you. I need to know...do you love her?"

"What? Lizzy? Of course."

The big prisoner snorted. Rafe didn't care. He felt like his heart was falling through him to the ground.

"What's this about?" James asked.

"It doesn't matter," Rafe whispered.

"He fucked her," Briggs said.

Rafe slammed his fist into the ox's face. Briggs reeled back into the wall.

James's jaw dropped open. "You did what?"

Rafe should have denied it but he couldn't and James wouldn't believe him anyway.

"We didn't mean for it to happen."

James plopped down on the pallet and bent over double like he was in pain. Beside him, Briggs groaned. Rafe touched his brother's shoulder but James shook it off.

"I'm sorry," Rafe said. "I couldn't help it."

"Of course you couldn't," James sneered. He fixed Rafe with a glare so fierce it burned. "You had to do it, didn't you? Had to ruin the best thing in my life."

Rafe felt heavy, like he was weighted down with a thousand boulders. "I'm sorry. But I love her and she—"

"Love her! Love her! You don't know what love is, *brother*. How could you when you take away lives without a thought—"

Rafe rocked back on his heels. James knew. He knew Rafe was an assassin and he loathed him for it.

"Do you know if any of the people you killed for money had loved ones?" James spat. "Do you care?"

"They deserved it," Rafe said.

"Did they? Like I deserve to be in here? Or you deserve to be hunted for killing Gripp? *Did* you kill him, Rafe?"

"Of course not."

James's face twisted into an ugly grimace. "Why did you have to come back to London? Why did you have to drag her into your vicious world? She's an innocent, Rafe. Or she was until she met you." Every word dripped with venom and hatred, stinging and biting Rafe until he could stand it no longer.

"Enough," he said.

But James shook his head. "I don't hate you, Rafe. I can't. You're my brother and you looked out for me back then. But I never want to see you again. Understand? I want you to leave London. With you gone, Lizzy will be safe."

"No. She won't."

"She *will*!"

Rafe blew out a breath. Christ, this was the hardest thing he'd ever done. His first kill hadn't been this gut-wrenching. "How did you find out about my work? Who told you?"

The change of pace seemed to catch James by surprise. "A man came here and gave me a message for you."

"Who?"

"He said his name was Barker."

Rafe felt himself drain away, felt his body empty of his life's essence. It was replaced with cold, dark hatred. "And what did he say?" he asked quietly, calmly.

James's nose dripped and he wiped it with his dirty sleeve. "He said you no longer have a position with Lord Liddicoat. He said Liddicoat has been informed of your prior employment as an assassin. He told Liddicoat that you'd even killed one of his cousins or nephews or something."

"That's not true."

James shrugged and wiped his nose again. "It doesn't matter. The point is, you don't have a job to go to and Lord Liddicoat now wants your head on a pike." He scrubbed both hands through his hair and let out a low moan that echoed around the cell. "This is all a bloody mess and I'm never going to get out of here."

"I don't need Liddicoat's money to get you out." Hughe's payment for killing Barker would be sufficient.

Rafe put his arm around his brother's shoulders, but James shoved it off. Beside him, Briggs staggered to his feet. He rubbed the back of his head.

"Try that again, cockhead, and I'll break every bone in your body," he said.

Rafe ignored him. "I have to go," he said to James.

Briggs spat on the floor. "Go on, run back to your little wench and fuck her brains out. You can think of me in here, fucking the brains out of your br—"

Rafe punched the sneer off his face. The oaf's head snapped back. Rafe hit him again and again and again until his knuckles bled. But he didn't feel any pain. He didn't feel anything at all, not even rage, not anymore. He'd reached the place beyond that, a place where nothing could touch him.

He watched, detached, as the big man collapsed to the ground and lay there without moving. The two small prisoners tucked their legs up and stared at Rafe through frightened eyes. James said something too, but he wasn't looking at Rafe. He was looking past him to the door. His face was white.

"Lizzy," he said.

Rafe turned. Saw her standing there in a short black wig. She stared slack-jawed at Briggs. Her wide eyes swept up to Rafe and she stepped back, recoiled. She shook her head over and over, blinking those big doe eyes at him. Her wig slipped off and fell to the floor near her feet.

The world returned to Rafe with a slam that made him stagger. His head pounded and his fist ached, but his heart hurt most of all.

No, no, no! "Lizzy! Please, you don't understand." He heard the way his voice sounded stretched, thin, and didn't care.

"You didn't stop," she whispered. "He was unconscious and you kept hitting him."

"You didn't hear what he said," James said.

"Just words," she mumbled. "Only words."

Rafe reached for her. "Lizzy, I—" The look of pure terror in her eyes made him drop his hand.

She spun on her heel and ran. Right into the arms of Barker.

Lizzy reeled back. Or tried to. Someone held her and she couldn't move. Someone tall like Rafe, but not Rafe. He was behind her, yelling at the newcomer, telling him to let go of her. She could hear the worry in his voice but also the hatred, cold and sharp. So like the Rafe of old, the one who'd terrified her seven years ago when he'd beaten his stepfather to a bloody pulp.

He had not changed. He was the same brutal, angry man. What had they done or said to turn him into such a fierce beast?

What if one day she did something to upset him too? Would he turn on her?

"Let her go, Barker," Rafe said again. "I'll go with you instead."

Lizzy closed her eyes. So this was Barker, Rafe's enemy. Did that make him her enemy too? Or an ally? She couldn't be sure anymore. One thing she did know, she'd seen the man she thought she loved turn into a vicious animal and almost kill someone with his bare hands. And he'd done it all without a hint of emotion.

The man who held her, Barker, laughed drily. His fingers tightened their hold. "Come and get her." He spun her around so she faced Rafe and James.

The look of horror and fear in James's eyes matched how she felt. But Rafe looked composed, emotionless. He stood very still. Not even his eyes strayed from Barker.

Barker let go of one of her arms, very briefly, then something cool and hard pressed against her throat. A blade.

"No!" James screamed. "What are you doing?"

Rafe still didn't move but his face went white. His gaze sharpened. "Let her go," he said, voice ominously low, "or I will kill you."

Barker's chuckle rippled through the air above her. "Not before I kill her first."

A tremor racked her. She tried to hold herself together, make herself smaller. Barker reached an arm around her waist and held her hard against him. The blade bit into her skin and burning pain ripped across her neck. She cried out and struggled against him but he held her tighter.

"Stop!" James screamed again. "You'll kill her!"

Rafe's fingers twitched but he didn't move. It was like he was frozen, except that his eyes grew darker. Blanker.

"That is the whole point," Barker said lazily. "To make your brother suffer. He loves her, you know. He'll want to die without her. You'll have your revenge."

"What?" James spluttered. "No! I don't—"

"Yes, you do. He stole your woman. Admit it, you want him to suffer like you're suffering now."

"You're mad!" James screamed. He ran at Barker and Lizzy but Rafe caught him by the jerkin and held him back.

Barker laughed again and switched the blade to the other side of her neck. Warm, sticky blood trickled from the cut he'd already made and she closed her eyes again as the blade pierced her skin once more. She couldn't watch the horror in James's eyes and the emptiness in Rafe's. It was difficult enough trying to hold herself back from crying out in pain. She would not give the monster the pleasure of knowing he'd hurt her.

Behind her, the door opened and Barker's hand slackened. The warden must have—

Before she'd even finished the thought or opened her eyes, she was knocked to one side. The blade didn't touch her. She was free. James knelt at her side and bundled her into his arms.

"Are you all right?" he gasped.

She nodded and peered past him at the chaotic scene beyond. Rafe and Barker struggled like two ancient gods, their blows landing with bruising *thuds*. Sweat poured from their temples and mixed with blood dripping from cuts. Neither man seemed to have the upper hand.

But Rafe couldn't possibly win. Treece and several constables and wardens crowded near the door. They couldn't get to Rafe past Barker, so they stood back, watched.

Then Barker did something odd. He ducked under Rafe's blow but didn't rise. Instead, he lunged for the knife he'd dropped near Lizzy, and plunged toward her.

She screamed.

"Lizzy!" Rafe shouted and leapt at them. Something metallic flashed in his hand.

Barker's knife kept coming. And then it didn't. It fell to the floor with a *clank*. He clutched his chest where a small dagger protruded.

Rafe knelt on one knee and let go of the dagger's handle. He was breathing hard. For a long moment, no one spoke or moved. Then Rafe reached down and closed Barker's sightless eyes. He whispered something she couldn't hear to the body then glanced up at Lizzy. Slowly, slowly, the blankness in his eyes dissolved, but it was replaced with something she'd never seen in him before. Something like the horror she felt, but a deep sadness too. Like he'd lost something very dear.

She shivered and curled into James, wanting to be as far away from Rafe as possible. But James was staring at his brother.

"Thank you," he whispered. He was shaking, crying. "Don't worry. I'll take care of her for you."

Rafe looked up at the ceiling and the veins in his neck throbbed. He swallowed hard and closed his eyes as if in prayer and didn't fight Treece's men when they hauled him to his feet.

"Her too," Treece ordered. Two men took her between them.

"I'll find some way to get you out," James called after them. "Both of you."

She was marched out of the cell behind Rafe. He didn't once look back at her. His head remained bowed, his shoulders stooped. Meek and submissive. So very deceptive.

CHAPTER 17

Rafe didn't know if it was a blessing or a curse that he was put in a small cell with Lizzy. Treece told them it was a temporary measure until they could be moved to a prison more suited to their heinous crimes.

When Treece closed the door and slid the bolt home, Rafe remained standing. Lizzy trembled in the corner. Her hair fell over her face, hiding her eyes. He didn't need to see them to know she was terrified.

"Lizzy." He moved toward her and she scampered back into the corner. He retreated. "Lizzy, it's still me. Nothing has changed. *I* haven't changed."

She drew her knees up to her chest and wrapped her arms around them. "I know," she whispered.

He hadn't expected her to speak. That alone must have taken courage. His surprise meant it took longer for him to register what she'd said. But when he did, his heart lurched in his chest. Then it cracked. "I don't understand," he hedged.

She shook her head and hid her face behind her knees.

"You have to explain it to me!"

She shivered again. "You told James you're an…an assassin."

So she'd heard that. "Was. I *was* an assassin."

"And you hit that man, again and again. He couldn't defend himself yet you kept hitting him. Then you killed Barker."

"He was going to hurt you!"

"A change came over you." She sniffed and glanced up through her hair then quickly looked away as if she couldn't bear to look at him. "I don't know you when you're like that, Rafe. I'm beginning to think I never truly did."

He wanted to be sick. This wasn't happening, was all wrong. "Lizzy. Don't." It was barely audible in the heavy silence of the cell.

"I was a fool to think I could tame you," she said.

She spoke as if he were a wild animal. He *was* an animal. Something had shifted inside him when Barker had threatened her, something he couldn't control. It had been the same with Briggs the big prisoner, and with his stepfather too. It was as if part of his mind shut down, the part where reason resided. It had been swallowed up by anger so dense he couldn't see through it.

"I knew what you were like," she went on, her voice a whisper. "And yet I thought you'd changed. I thought..." She shook her head and buried her face in her arms.

"You saw me that day," he muttered. Blood pounded between his ears, and his legs felt weak. He sat down. He rested his head back against the wall and closed his eyes.

The scene came to him easily. He hadn't thought of that day in such detail for many years. His stepfather had stormed out of the house after killing his mother. Her husband had never hit her before, never shouted so loud that the neighbors heard, but he'd ground her down a little bit every day for years with barbed words aimed at undermining her. Slowly he sucked the life out of her, a piece at a time, until she lost all her strength and will. She'd only hung on to life for the sake of her sons, especially for Rafe, the son by her first husband, who bore the brunt of his stepfather's insidious wrath. He tried to thwart Rafe at every turn, spreading rumors and lies so that Rafe could not find work or keep friends.

Then on that fateful day, his mother *had* found the courage to confront her husband. But she'd paid the price. He shoved her into the wall and her weakened heart had given out in fright. Rafe had seen it too late to stop it, but the change had come over him for the first time that day.

He'd been in fights before but this had been different. Something flashed before his eyes, blinding at first then clearing so that his mind was empty of everything except hatred and anger so bright it hurt. The result was inevitable. He couldn't have stopped himself beating his stepfather any more than he could have stopped a boulder rolling down a mountain.

Could he?

Perhaps the youth of only twenty-two couldn't, but the man of almost thirty *should* be able to. He thought he'd left that rash anger behind him, thought working with Hughe had taught him to control it. But it had not. The events of the day proved that.

Lizzy had every right to be afraid of him. He couldn't be trusted not to turn violent.

He pulled his knees up in a pose that mirrored Lizzy's and rested his forehead on them. "I'm sorry," he muttered. "I'm so sorry."

She said nothing and he didn't look up to see what effect his words had. He couldn't face seeing her disappointment, her fear, her sorrow.

Nor did he look up when the bolt slid back and the door opened.

"Don't push," snapped a familiar voice.

"Lizzy!" cried another.

Someone belched.

Rafe raised his head. The cell had suddenly become crowded with the players of Lord Hawkesbury's Men. Antony crouched beside Lizzy, his arms around her shoulders while the others settled themselves on the floor. Only Roger Style pounded on the door with his fist, protesting loudly at his incarceration.

"Enough, brother," Edward said. "There is nothing we can do."

"We'll be out in a day or two," Freddie said, wiping his nose with the back of his hand. "Lord Hawkesbury will see to it." He stretched out his legs, yawned, and closed his eyes. "Wake me when it's over."

"He's right for once," the man named Henry Wells said. "We've done nothing wrong."

"We aided fugitives! Murderers!" Roger pulled his hat off his head and pointed the long peacock feather at Rafe. "This is all your fault. If you hadn't killed Gripp—"

"Roger!" Edward warned. "Stop worrying everyone. Our crimes are not bad. We'll be released soon enough, perhaps with a fine—"

"And who will pay the fine for each of you? Who will pay *me* for the lost revenue from the performances we must cancel? While we're stuck in here, Burbage is stealing my audience."

Rafe watched Lizzy talking quietly with Antony in the corner. They didn't once look his way.

The players argued, gossiped, and sometimes sang as the sun tracked across the patch of sky visible outside the cell's high window. Rafe guessed it to be midafternoon when Sir Robert Blakewell arrived. Rafe couldn't deny that he was glad to see him. Blake had influence at court. Perhaps he could get Lizzy and the others freed.

Blake greeted Lizzy affectionately and handed over money and two sacks, one with fresh clothes and one with food. They all thanked him profusely. The players sat down on the floor to eat.

"Shakespeare told us as soon as he heard you'd been arrested," he said.

"Thank you for coming," Lizzy said. She offered Blake a weak smile.

He returned it. "Min is terribly worried, but I persuaded her not to come. A place like this is not safe for unborn babes. Nevertheless, it wasn't easy to convince her to stay away." Blake glanced from Lizzy to Rafe then back again. He forked a brow. "Something wrong?"

Roger snorted. "We've been arrested for harboring murderers and bloody Burbage is going to reap the profits of our canceled shows. Of course something's wrong!"

"I don't think that's what he meant," Antony said.

Style ignored him and bit into a pie.

"You have to petition the queen," Rafe said to Blake. "If Lord Oxley were here, I'd have him aid you, but he's not in London. What about Lord Hawkesbury?"

"On his way to the palace as we speak. He's not as favored by Her Majesty as he once was, but he still has influence."

"As do you," Rafe said.

"Rest assured, I'll do what I can for you all."

Lizzy placed a hand on Blake's arm. "Thank you," she said quietly. "You are a true friend."

"I keep telling you, we're family," he said. "Now that the witness is dead..." He glanced at Rafe. "...I think we can have you released easily enough. The players too." Another glance at Rafe. "But..."

"But not me," Rafe finished for him.

"Not as easily," Blake said quietly. "I believe the witness wrote down what he saw and was very specific about you, less so about Lizzy."

Rafe dragged his hands through his hair and shut his eyes against the flood of relief that almost undid him in front of everyone. *Lizzy could go free. Thank God.*

Composed once more, he opened his eyes. The players and Blake watched him. Lizzy did not. She was once more sitting on the floor, knees up, face buried in her arms.

Rafe nodded. "Very well."

"You accept it?" Blake sounded outraged. "You accept your fate without a fight? I expected more from you, Fletcher, not this resignation."

Rafe shrugged one shoulder.

"You are innocent of the murder, are you not?"

"Of Gripp's murder, yes. But consider this fitting punishment for other crimes."

"I knew it!" shouted Freddie, triumphant.

"Hush," said Antony. "That was a rumor."

"More than a rumor. The constables claimed the man Rafe killed today called him an assassin."

"He might have made it up," Henry Wells said.

"Certainly could have," Edward said. "Can you really imagine Rafe as an assassin?"

No one answered. All heads bent to avoid looking at Rafe. Lizzy seemed to shrink farther into the corner.

Blake was the only one to meet his gaze. "I heard what he said to Lord Liddicoat. Everyone has."

No mention that he thought the claim false, a fabrication of Barker's. It seemed no one considered that an option. "So all of London knows," Rafe said. All his potential employers. If he ever got released—and that was a large *if*—then he would have to leave the city to find work.

So much for turning over a new leaf and staying for James. Staying for Lizzy.

"Liddicoat is not very good at keeping his mouth shut," Blake said. "That's why he needs someone like you to protect him. The fool may be a privy councillor, but he has a lot of enemies. Having you in his employ would enhance his personal guard considerably. They need training. As do the ones protecting Her Majesty. Undisciplined ruffians, most of them."

Rafe stopped listening as Blake kept talking. It didn't matter now. Nothing did except that Lizzy might be free very soon. And Rafe was going to leave her, either in a coffin or by leaving London.

Blake left with assurances he would do what he could to free them. The warden returned and said they could mingle with the other prisoners in the courtyard so long as they didn't cause trouble. The troupe filed out one by one in search of conversation or to stretch their legs and Antony convinced Lizzy to go with him. In truth, she didn't need much convincing. Indeed, she took one look at Rafe and the emptying cell and agreed to accompany him.

Rafe watched her go with a bone-aching weariness. It pressed heavily on his shoulders, weighed him down, and squeezed his heart until he thought it would burst from the pressure. Perhaps he should go after her. He could try to convince her he wasn't the monster she thought him.

If she looked back at him, he would follow her out and speak to her. It would be a sign of her lingering affection. Even a small glance would mean she still cared for him.

Look back. Look back at me.

She didn't.

~~~

"You're a fool, Elizabeth Croft," James said. Lizzy sat with him on a bench in the prison courtyard as the afternoon light faded. "I never thought I'd say that, but there you are. You're a fool, which makes me an even bigger fool but I can live with that. I have been one for quite some time."

"Have you finished?" she asked. "Because that's no way to speak to your future wife."

He blinked. "You still want to marry me?"

"Yes. When I'm released—"

"Wait." He held up his hands. "I don't recall asking you."

"Is that important? We had an understanding."

He gave her a withering glare then sighed. He leaned forward and rested an elbow on one knee and his chin on his palm. "Lizzy, stop this foolishness. I can't wed you now. You know that."

Tears burned the back of her eyes. "Of course you can. It'll be a perfect arrangement. You're a tailor and I'm a seamstress. My wages can support us both until your apprenticeship is complete. We'll live next door to my parents, or perhaps with them, and we'll all sew and be happy. We *will* be happy, James."

He put a finger to her lips. "You cannot talk yourself into happiness with me, Lizzy. You don't love me. You love him."

She shivered and couldn't stop. It felt like her whole body rattled with cold. "He's not the man I love. He's violent and dangerous. You're nothing like that, James. You're kind and tender. *That's* what I want in a husband."

"No, Lizzy," he said again. It wasn't until he pried her fingers from the front of his jerkin that she realized she'd been clutching it. "What you want in a husband is Rafe."

"Aren't you listening to me? Your brother scares me half to death! I will not marry him. I can't bear to be in the same room as him."

He gripped her shoulders and she expected him to shake her until her teeth loosened, but he did not. He looked at her with all the kindness and tenderness he possessed and she knew she would never love him. Not like she wanted to. Not like she loved Rafe.

She burst into tears. "Why couldn't you have just shaken me?"

"What?" he said, drawing her into a hug.

She let her tears flow and when they finally eased, she felt better. Empty on the inside, swollen in the face, but better.

"Now listen to me," he said, dipping his head to meet her gaze. "I know I haven't been the sensible one of late. I've been selfish and stubborn and not seeing things clearly."

"Do not blame yourself. You've been going through some difficult times."

"I am seeing things clearly now, however," he went on as if she hadn't spoken. "And I have some things I want to say to you. Firstly, I don't love you and I don't want to marry you."

She wiped her nose. "Oh." She should be devastated by that revelation, but she wasn't. What she felt for James wasn't the sort of love between a husband and wife. She knew that now. Knew how that sort of love was supposed to feel.

"Secondly, there's something you need to know about Rafe."

"Something else? Something aside from the fact he's an..." She couldn't say it. It was too awful.

"Assassin," he finished. "I found that difficult to swallow too when I heard. But it makes sense."

"Makes sense? How can it make sense? Your brother cannot go about taking lives. No one can. It's wrong."

"Is it? Lizzy, it's possible that the people he killed were villains themselves."

"You don't know that."

"No, but I'd wager it's true. I know my brother and he is not a bad person. In fact, he's the best of people. He's everything you think I am. Caring, thoughtful, and utterly selfless."

"With a violent streak the size of England."

James said nothing for a long time. He stared off into the distance to where Freddie sat on the packed earth and played cards with the two small men from James's cell. James seemed to stare right through them. "Do you remember my father?" he asked.

Odd question. "Yes."

"Do you remember how he used to make me redo my stitching time and again until it was perfect?"

"My father used to do that too."

"But do you remember how he would tell me I was hopeless if I failed? Or that I was letting him down when the stitches weren't straight or were too big? When I was twelve and old enough to be an apprentice, he told me no master tailor would take me on. I was too lazy, too greedy, too slow, too careless."

"Oh, James, I didn't know." Why was he digging such awful memories up now? His father was long gone and good riddance it seemed. Lizzy truly had no idea what he'd been like. She thought he'd been a good neighbor, father, and husband.

"I had calluses on my fingers by the time I was thirteen. They split and bled all over the fabric once. He made me clean it but it took all night and I was exhausted the next day and couldn't perform my duties. Rafe did all my chores, but I still had to do the mending. I did a terrible job. My eyes stung and my fingers hurt and I just couldn't do it right. Father called me all sorts of things. I believed him. I thought he was right and that I *was* useless. Rafe tried to tell me otherwise. He tried telling Father I needed to rest, but Father turned on him and told him he too was lazy, just like his father had been. I thought Rafe would hit him. He was big enough by then, a grown man almost. But he didn't. He just walked away."

He gave a short, brittle laugh. "Rafe is the least lazy person I know."

Lizzy nodded, her heart lodged in her throat.

"After that, Father set about destroying Rafe. There was something in the defiant way that Rafe *didn't* hit him that irked Father. It was like he wanted to goad Rafe into losing that iron self-control. He told the most awful things about Rafe—at church, the taverns, to our friends. Ask your parents, they probably heard most of it. How Rafe was angry all the time, called our mother awful names, or how he used to hit me. None of it was true. Poor Mother could do nothing. She tried to talk to Father, but it was too late. By then he hated Rafe to the point where that hatred consumed him. Father could think of nothing else except ruining his prospects, his life. His campaign of lies worked. Rafe could not find work, but he never showed that it bothered him. Not one complaint passed his lips. It annoyed Father immensely."

"But why? Why did he hate Rafe so much?"

James shrugged. "Mother loved Rafe's father. She spoke of him often, and always with glowing words. Apparently Rafe was like his father in looks and manner, and I suppose my father wanted to punish the son from the union out of jealousy or spite."

"So what changed?" she asked.

"My father is what changed. He tried a different tack, beginning with Mother. He had always been miserly, never giving her enough for the marketing so that she had to make hearty meals with very little, and never making new clothes for her even with the off-cuts from his commissions. But then he started calling her names too. He said she was weak and ugly, a pathetic wife. He told her she'd raised two useless sons and that she'd killed her first husband out of boredom." He drew in a deep breath. "It worked. Rafe stood up to him. He told Father to stop, but Father kept going." James frowned and tears filled his eyes. "He just kept on. And Rafe was powerless to stop him. I could see him seething with barely contained fury. It must have cost him a great deal to control his anger.

"Until one day Mother found the courage to tell Father to stop. She was ill by then, her heart weak. Father ordered her to be silent but she wouldn't. It was like a dam had burst and she was letting out years of frustration and anger on him. So Father pushed her. She fell back and...died." He sniffed and wiped his nose. "I saw it. Rafe did too. He ran after Father, chased him into the street. I didn't see what happened next, I remained with Mother, but I saw Rafe return. There was blood all over him and he was...blank. It was like watching someone else walk through the house, not my brother. I shouted at him but I don't think he heard. He simply went to his room, packed some things, and left." James stopped talking and sat without moving. He simply stared straight ahead.

Lizzy touched his hand and finally he turned to her. His fingers curled around hers and he blinked.

"Why didn't you tell me any of this before?"

"Father made me promise not to tell a soul. I was so afraid of him, I didn't dare break that promise. Not even for Rafe. By the time Father died, I was so ashamed of my own weakness that I...I said nothing. I'm sorry for that now. Rafe deserved better from me."

"Do not be hard on yourself. I'm sure he understands. And you're not weak, James. You were a child and your father was a beast."

"Perhaps." He lifted one shoulder. "Do you see now that the violent streak you've seen in Rafe takes a lot of provocation to surface? And it's not random." He placed his other hand on top of hers. "But it does exist, I won't deny it. The question is, can you accept that flaw and love him anyway?"

Her mouth felt dry, her throat tight and achy. She swallowed but it didn't help. "I was there. I saw Rafe hit your father from my window. Afterward, Rafe looked straight at me." She shook her head. "But he didn't see me. As you said, it was like he wasn't really there."

"Is that why you were afraid of him at first? I thought you were acting odd."

She nodded. "I'd almost forgotten about it, but when he returned, it all came back to me. The blood, your father's cries for mercy, my terror. I was so afraid of being near Rafe. But then a strange thing happened. When I was in disguise, I could be myself around him. I wasn't afraid anymore. Before long I realized I didn't need the disguise either. I think it was after I visited you here that my fear finally vanished. I was so angry with him for not telling me that I got mad and just... forgot to be afraid."

He smiled. "And then?"

"And then...I fell in love with him." She lifted her gaze to meet his. "That's what terrifies me now. I cannot fear the man I love. I should not."

James held her chin gently. "Listen to me. Rafe will never hurt you or me or..." He waved a hand at Freddie. "Or even him. He's not like that. He attacked Briggs because he'd been goading him for some time and hurting me too. Rafe killed Barker because he was going to kill you."

"And the others? The ones he killed for his job?"

"You'll have to ask him about those. I'm sure what he will tell you will ease your mind."

Her heart swelled like it had just been released from tight bindings. She needed to breathe and cry and laugh all at once, but it came out a strangled sob. She loved Rafe. And he loved her.

"Go and find out what those reasons are," James said. "Then put those two clever heads together and find a way to set you both free."

She hugged him fiercely and blinked through her tears. "Thank you, James. I adore you."

She ran across the courtyard, down the corridor to the cell she shared with the rest of Lord Hawkesbury's Players and Rafe. But it was empty.

"Where is he?" she asked a passing guard. "Where's Rafe Fletcher from this cell?"

"Gone," he said without stopping. "Taken to Newgate just now. That's where the murderers go."

CHAPTER 18

Lizzy sat on her pallet on the cell floor, too numb to rejoin the others in the yard. Too numb to cry or think beyond the fact that Rafe was gone and didn't know that she still loved him. She didn't stir until Antony burst in, an enormous smile on his face.

"We're free!" he said. "Lizzy, get up, we can go."

She blinked at him. "What?"

The rest of the troupe crowded in around him, all beaming, even Roger. Antony pulled her to her feet. "The warden came to us in the yard just now. The queen has shown mercy and released us," he said. "Come on. Let's get out of this filthy hole."

The queen? Mercy? Why? "Blake," she said on a breath. "Bless him."

"And Lord Hawkesbury himself," Henry said. "The warden told us that both of them petitioned the queen relentlessly on our behalf."

"That and the fact the queen adores me," Antony said, doing a twirl and flipping his hair back to finish off the little dance. "How could she chop off this head? She once said I had the face of an angel."

"A fallen one," Freddie said but he too was grinning madly. Lizzy was the only one not smiling.

"What of Rafe?" she asked. "Has he been released too?"

"Forget about him," Roger said. "We're to perform for Her Majesty! She commands it in this personal letter to me." He flapped a piece of paper in front of her nose.

"It's a condition of our release," Edward said. "We'll perform a new play for a select audience at the palace. It'll be written by Min, of course, but Her Majesty has suggested what it should be about."

Roger left the cell, beckoning them to follow by waving the letter in the air. "She wants it to feature a fairy queen of great beauty and wit who delivers her kingdom from many evils, is much loved by her advisors and subjects, and becomes immortal at the end."

"Sounds as dull as dog shit to me," Freddie said.

"And what would a baseborn idiot like you know?" Roger called back over his shoulder.

Lizzy shut out their quibbling as she brought up the rear of the troupe alongside Antony. He wasn't smiling anymore but watching her with a troubled expression. They passed James out in the yard. He gave her a sad smile.

"I'm so glad you're going home," he said.

"Rafe," she murmured.

"I know."

She hugged him and he held her for a long time. "I'll bring news and provisions soon," she whispered, wiping away her tears.

The soft glow of dusk had all but been swallowed by the night by the time her parents folded her into their arms in the familiar surroundings of their parlor. Blake was there too, looking weary and unhappy. A terrible foreboding engulfed her.

"He's not free," he said before she could ask.

Her heart plunged and she sank onto a chair before her weakened legs gave way. "I have to visit him! I need to speak to him."

"Visitors aren't allowed in Newgate after dark."

"Why wasn't he freed when I was?"

Blake and her father exchanged worried glances. "You were not mentioned by name in the witness's account, but Fletcher was," Blake said. "It stands, despite Barker's death."

"But he was lying! How can they believe a dead man's story?"

"I tried, Lizzy." He shook his head and looked down at his feet. "I'm so sorry."

He left with a promise that he would do all he could for Rafe but Lizzy could hear the hopelessness in his voice. It made her feel ill. She couldn't even stomach her mother's hearty soup despite not eating well since going to prison.

Afterward, her mother cried as she helped wash the prison grime from Lizzy's hair and skin, then she cried more as she listened to her daughter's story. Lizzy told her parents everything that had transpired since her flight. Almost everything. She left out the part where she'd given herself to Rafe and the part where he'd beaten up the prisoner, but she did tell them he'd killed Barker.

"So you love him?" her mother asked in her blunt way. The tears had abated but she seemed to have aged in that short time. Exhaustion imprinted itself into every deepened wrinkle. "Rafe Fletcher, not James?"

"I do."

"No," her father said. "He's no good. Best forget him, Lizzy."

"I can't, Papa. And he's not bad. Not in the least." She told them everything James had told her about Rafe's past. When she finished, her father still frowned, but her mother's face had softened. She even shed a tear.

"I can't believe we didn't see Pritchard for the man he truly was," she said. "He wasn't the most amiable neighbor, but he was polite enough. We had no reason to think he treated his wife and sons so ill."

"It's a sad business," Croft said with a shake of his head. "But Lizzy, listen to me. Rafe Fletcher may not be as bad as we thought, but James Pritchard is, well, an ideal match for you."

"Hush, John," his wife said. "Love doesn't choose."

He gave her a blank look and shrugged. "I don't understand."

"Of course you don't." She tucked a strand of Lizzy's damp hair behind her ear. "If our daughter tells me she loves Rafe and he loves her then I know it's true. She's the most sensible of all our girls and knows the difference between love and infatuation."

"Aye," he said, nodding. "She is the sensible one. Very well then, I consent to the union."

It was Lizzy's turn to cry. She couldn't stop the tears. She felt like her heart would crumble if she didn't let them out. It was crumbling anyway. Rafe thought she didn't love him. He was incarcerated in the miserable hell of Newgate thinking she was terrified of him. Did he still hope she would come to her senses?

Oh, Rafe, I'm sorry.

She hugged each of her parents in turn then wiped away her tears. Crying would not get Rafe released. "I need to ask something of you," she said to her father. "I need to borrow some money to hire a lawyer."

Her father stood, rubbed his hip, and limped out of the kitchen. He returned several minutes later with a bulging purse. He held it out for Lizzy but her mother took it.

"Are you sure hiring a lawyer is the best way to have Rafe released?" she asked.

"What do you mean?" Lizzy said.

"A lawyer can do little for a man the Crown claims committed murder. Few would take on the case and they'd be unlikely to win anyway. The Crown—the queen—is always right. Always," she said with a pointed raise of an eyebrow.

"Oh. Yes. I suppose so. Should we petition Her Majesty again? Perhaps Rafe's friend Lord Oxley will have more success. But I don't know when he'll return. It may be too late."

"My dear daughter. You've always been a good girl."

"Ye-es."

"I think it's time you were a little less good. For the sake of your beloved."

Croft groaned. "I'm going to pretend I'm not hearing this."

"How is being less good going to get Rafe released?" Lizzy asked.

Her mother eyed her husband. "The only thing working against Rafe is Barker's written account. I do believe those sorts of things are kept under lock and key. If you could get your hands on it, you could destroy it."

"Wife! Has your mind curdled?" Croft sat heavily on the bench seat and threw up his hands. "Do you know what you're suggesting?"

"I am suggesting our daughter save the man she loves. Now, you are either going to help her or not. The choice is yours."

He folded his arms over his chest and glared at her. "I forbid Lizzy to do it."

"Bah."

He threw up his hands again. "Women! Why couldn't I have had sons? Men are much less devious."

"It is a man who got Rafe into this trouble in the first place," she said reasonably.

"And you think our Lizzy is capable of doing such a thing? She's never so much as stolen a pin in her life."

"Of course she's capable. Aren't you, Lizzy? This is a little more important than a pin."

Lizzy swallowed hard. Could she do it? Dare she? It was certainly an intriguing possibility. Without the document,

Rafe could not be held accountable for the murder of Gripp, and the death of Barker would be attributed to self-defense, which carried no punishment.

"I still forbid it," Croft grumbled. "I don't want her to get into any more trouble."

"Very well. Whatever you wish, husband." She plopped the purse of money on the table. "Lizzy, take this and engage a lawyer. Then wait and hope and pray." She poked the purse closer to Lizzy. "Take it." She winked.

Lizzy stared at her mother, who winked again. She was right. Lizzy had to do something to save Rafe. There was no other way. A lawyer could do nothing, even if there was one willing to work for them. If Barker's account was evidence enough to arrest Rafe, then it would be evidence enough to convict him. Legally, the court required no more. It was up to Lizzy to free him, and her alone. She would not drag any of her friends down with her if it all went wrong.

Later, as her mother sat on her bed with Lizzy, she said, "The crime was committed outside the city walls, I believe."

Lizzy nodded. "At the Revels office at the old Priory of St. John. Why?"

"Because the sessions house on the street known as Old Bailey is where they hear those trials. I expect the sheriff would have the document locked safely until then. If I was the sort of person to take wagers, I'd say the sheriff and perhaps undersheriff would be the only ones with a key." Lizzy's mother smiled and patted her hand. "Old Bailey is very near Newgate."

Lizzy kissed her. "Thank you, Mama."

~ ~ ~

"I want to look desirable," Lizzy told Antony as he applied kohl to her eyelids the next morning. "Not like a whore."

"You won't," he said.

It had taken Lizzy half the night to come up with a plan to steal the document and the other half to think through the details. It was taking Antony half the morning to implement his part of it.

"Nor do I want to look like an actor." The heavy paint he used with his costumes was appropriate for the stage but not up close.

"Don't worry," he said, "I know what I'm doing."

When she looked in the mirror, she had to agree that he did. The makeup was subtle, enhancing her cheeks, lips, and eyes instead of overpowering them.

He left her in the tiring house storeroom so that she could change into the low-cut bodice Will Shakespeare had delivered earlier. It belonged to Kate and fit Lizzy well enough, although it was tight across the chest, something that would serve her purpose well. Perhaps too well if the gasps from the players as she descended the stairs were any indication.

"Well," said Henry, his eyes wide. "Look at you."

"Aye," muttered Freddie, staring at her breasts. "Look at those."

Edward thumped him without taking his gaze off Lizzy. Even Roger looked up from the script he was reading and nodded his approval. Lizzy had not told them of her plan. They thought she was going to see Rafe in prison and give him a memory to take to his grave. They didn't know she was about to break the law.

"You're shaking," Antony said as he tucked Lizzy's hair under a long red-gold wig. "Stop fretting so. He'll love this disguise."

Lizzy left the Rose and made her way back across the river by wherry, alighting at the Blackfriars' stairs. She had decided not to visit Rafe first even though he was housed nearby in the massive stone gate that doubled as a prison. Visiting him before she'd accomplished her task served neither of them, and her nerves were frayed enough. She felt sick to her stomach and terribly exposed, as if everyone was looking at her and seeing straight through her disguise. She wanted to run home and hide in her room.

But she did not. Rafe needed her to have courage.

The sessions house was attached to Newgate prison like a wart on a big toe. It was gray and stern, much like the prison, and without cheer both inside and out. A man greeted her at his desk, peering down his sharp nose at her. She removed her coat, leaned over his desk, and was pleased to see his gaze soften. He moistened his lips with his tongue. The change was quite remarkable, not only in him but her too. She felt powerful, as if she could get this man to do almost anything given the right words and amount of cleavage.

"Kind sir, are you the sheriff?"

"Undersheriff Ward at your service," he said without lifting his gaze.

"Oh. I wanted to speak to the sheriff." She glanced at the adjoining door. "Is he here?"

"Not at present, but I am the next in charge. Perhaps I can help."

She sighed. "I think it's more a matter for the sheriff." She began to walk off.

He rushed out from behind his desk and stepped in her way. He was tall and stood close, which meant he could see straight down her bodice. She fought back a blush but her neck warmed despite her efforts.

He smirked. "I'm sure I *can* help. I'm well versed in all matters of the law. It is a legal question, isn't it?"

"Why yes. What luck that you're an expert!" She tried a simpering pout.

"Come sit down." He took her by the elbow and steered her toward a chair. She sat. He remained standing. "Now, tell me, what is the matter on which I can advise you?"

She coughed. "It's quite detailed." She coughed again. "Do you mind if I have something to drink first?"

"Of course."

"You will join me, won't you?" she asked.

He hesitated.

"Only if you want to," she added. "My mother told me never to drink when a man in my company is not. She said it wasn't a woman's place to be drinking or eating when her man might be starving or dying of thirst." She put a slight inflection on *her man* and it didn't go unnoticed. Undersheriff Ward's eyes dipped to her breasts again and he pressed his lips together.

"We cannot disappoint your mother."

She put a hand to his arm to stop him walking off. "Allow me to pour. A man should not have to serve his own wine when a woman is present, surely."

He laughed. "Another of your mother's directions?"

"She was very wise." She approached a small dresser where a wine bottle and three cups stood on a tray. With her back turned to Ward, she removed a small phial attached to her girdle. It was easy to slip the sleeping herbs and aqua vitae into his cup.

She handed it to him and sipped her own. He sipped too and pulled a face. "This tastes different."

"I like a little aqua vitae with wine," she said and drank the contents of her cup. "It balances your humors."

"Did your mother tell you that too?" He laughed and drank it all. "Now, what was your legal question?"

"Well. My sister is in love with the man accused of murdering the Master of Revels."

Ward's gaze flicked to a small coffer sitting on his desk. Lizzy's heart leapt but she dampened any outward show of her excitement. "And?" he pressed.

"And she's heard of the existence of documents that put him at the scene of the crime."

"Document. Only the one." He shrugged and sipped. "We don't usually use written evidence in our trials. Verbal witness testimony only. But this is different. The witness was murdered by the accused man in plain view of everyone. Must have been to silence him, something the witness suspected might happen, hence the document."

"I believe he was killed in self-defense."

He shrugged again. "That may be so, but we cannot discount his original witness testimony while we have his written account."

But if they couldn't find it, they would have to discount it.

"Tell your sister to forget him and find herself a better man. Now, what about you?" He licked his bottom lip, leaving a distinct shine behind. "Is there someone *you* love?"

Lizzy happily launched into a long story that began with her being left all alone after her husband died and her parents too, and ended with a very dull story of her childhood, which went on for an age. By the end of it, he was asleep.

She crept to his desk and tried the small coffer he'd glanced at. Locked. She rummaged through other unlocked coffers to find the key but they contained only papers. She checked under the desk, in the dresser, everywhere. Nothing. She would have to break open the lock. Unless...

She poked Ward's shoulder. He snored loudly but didn't wake. She checked his clothing for a hidden key but found none. She tentatively felt behind his ruff and cringed when she touched his cool, clammy skin. But it was worth it. She found a key attached to a leather strip hanging around his neck.

She untied it and inserted the key into the coffer's lock. It clicked open and she lifted the lid. Inside were papers. Lots of papers, but it didn't take long to find Barker's. It identified Rafe Fletcher as the murderer of Gripp with an unnamed female accomplice. She threw the paper into the fireplace and blew on the glowing coals. The edges blackened and curled, then flames gobbled it up until all that was left was a pile of ashes.

Lizzy wanted to whoop and kiss the sleeping Ward's forehead. There was nothing keeping Rafe in Newgate now. Barker was dead and his evidence gone. There were enough witnesses to Barker's death to confirm that Rafe acted only to save Lizzy's life—they could not arrest him for that. And if the sheriff was the good, honest man Blake claimed, he would not falsify a new document to replace this one.

With a head and heart so light she felt giddy, Lizzy got up to leave. She stopped when the door opened and a tall, willowy man walked in. Treece.

CHAPTER 19

Treece's gaze met hers. Narrowed. Faster than she could react, he was standing before her, his fingers wrapped around her wrist. They flexed, twisted. She swallowed a cry.

"What are *you* doing here?" His voice might be cool but his grip burned. He glanced at Ward, slumped in the chair.

It was useless to pretend she was someone else. Treece knew it was Lizzy, despite the wig and face paint. "I came to discuss a legal matter with the undersheriff," she said. "But he fell asleep."

His grip tightened. She winced as red-hot pain shot up her arm. "Don't talk to me as if I am a fool. You may be free, but doing something ill-conceived now to release your lover will see you back in prison. It'll be Newgate for you next time, then the gallows."

She bit the inside of her cheek and warm, bitter blood filled her mouth. "Let me go. If you harm me, I will report you to the sheriff. I am related to Lord Warhurst and through him to Sir Robert Blakewell and Lord Hawkesbury. They will not like to hear that I have been mistreated while on an innocent visit to the sessions house."

The words simply rolled off her tongue as if someone else were saying them. Not the terrified, shy Lizzy Croft but the confident one with the steady voice and direct gaze.

Treece's grip loosened then he let go but did not move away. "Why wear the wig if you are here on an *innocent* errand?"

"I like to wear wigs. Is that against the city's laws? If so, I believe you would have to arrest half the ladies at court." Not to mention Her Majesty herself. "Move aside, sir, I am busy."

He did not. His gaze skipped to Ward again then to the fireplace. He sniffed the air. "You burned it, didn't you?"

"I'm not sure what you're suggesting." She fixed him with a hard, unwavering glare. A simpering one wouldn't work on a fox like Treece. She doubted he saw her as a woman at all, merely a criminal who'd escaped his clutches.

"Then let me put it this way." He grabbed her wrist again. She tried to snatch free but his fingers screwed down and she cried out. "Elizabeth Croft, I am arresting you for destroying an official city document with the objective of hindering a legal process." His lips flattened and he shook his head. "You should have left well enough alone. You were free. Is he worth so much to you that you would risk your life?"

Instinct screamed at her to plead for mercy, to throw herself at his feet and let the tears that stung the backs of her eyes flow. But she did not. She forced herself to stand tall, to look him in the eye and use the wits God gave her to untangle herself from the mess. Rafe needed her to be stronger than she'd ever been.

"I don't expect you to understand. Rafe is worth more to me than—" Worth! Money! She possessed something better than mere words to convince Treece to let her go. He may not be the sort of man whose morals swayed when faced with a pair of breasts or big eyes, but he might be the sort who liked coin in his hand. She brought out the purse filled with her father's money.

His grip slackened and his flat eyes flared.

"Shall I tell you again who I'm related to?"

His mouth lifted on one side like it was caught on a hook. "That won't be necessary."

She shook the purse and the coins inside made a solid, full clanking sound. "I'm not the type of woman who does anything wrong. Ask anyone. I've always done the right thing, the sensible thing." She locked her gaze with his. A few short days ago she could never have battled wills and glares with a stranger, especially one as formidable as Treece. She was different now. So very different. "And I'm extremely shy. No one would believe me, a seamstress, capable of stealing a document from right under the sheriff's nose. It's simply not something I would do. Many, many people will vouch for that."

"Including your important relations?"

"Especially them."

He grunted or laughed, it was difficult to tell which, and let go of her wrist altogether. She untied the purse hanging from her girdle and dropped it into his outstretched palm.

"In that case, I never saw you here," he said.

"What will you tell the sheriff about the document?" she hedged. "And Ward?"

This time he gave a definite smirk. "I do not know what happened to the document and Ward will be reported to the sheriff for falling asleep while on duty. It may prompt him to finally promote a better man to the position of undersheriff." His lips stretched into a smile. No doubt he wanted the job himself.

Suppressing a shiver, she hurried out of the sessions house and didn't look back.

~ ~ ~

There was dried blood on the walls of Rafe's cell and scratches in the old stone—some deep, others not so. The prisoners must have gouged them with buckles or fingernails, perhaps yesterday or perhaps four hundred years ago. Rafe wondered if the air smelled as stale and putrid then as it did now.

He'd been in much worse prisons but never had he felt like this. Like his heart was being squeezed between a clamp, building up an excruciating pressure. Maybe it would burst. He wanted it to. Wanted everything to end so he could forget and not feel. Not think of Lizzy's big eyes filled with fear, not see her shrink from him.

Soon. It would end soon. She would get her wish and be rid of him. Would she be sad? Would she remember how they'd made love—

Christ. He didn't need to add *that* memory to the others.

One of the prisoners locked in the cell with him said something. Rafe closed his eyes, shook his head. It must have been the right response because the prisoner left him alone. They all left him alone. He didn't know how many there were but the cell seemed to be teeming with them.

Somehow time passed. It felt interminable, and yet much too fast. How could that be right? It didn't make sense. None of it did. Perhaps he was mad.

"He hasn't moved since he came in yesterday," said a voice. "Been sitting against that wall the whole time."

Rafe had the vague sense that the man was speaking about him. He didn't bother cracking his eyes open to see. Let him talk.

"Hasn't ate nothing neither," the man went on.

"Thank you," came a soft voice. A woman's voice. A voice that screwed the clamp surrounding his heart harder. He couldn't breathe. Couldn't move lest he shatter.

She came closer, a gentle *swish* of skirts on the floor. He could sense her next to him, smell the freshness of her skin, her hair.

What was she doing in Newgate? They told him she'd been released but perhaps they'd changed their minds. Another screw of the clamp.

"Rafe," she murmured. He didn't need to see her to know she knelt beside him; he just knew. "Rafe, are you awake?"

And then she touched him. A whisper of fingers across his jaw. Light. So achingly good. "Rafe." More desperate now. "Rafe, please."

"Don't," he whispered. "Unless you've come to tell me you feel differently...don't. I can't..." He should pull away from her but he couldn't. Her touch was a balm and he needed to smother himself with it.

"I don't feel differently at all," she said.

His heart wrenched from his chest. His stomach twisted painfully. He shook with the effort needed to hold himself together, to gather the frayed fragments of his dignity.

"I feel the same as I did that night at the Rose," she said. "The same as I have all along. If only I had admitted it to myself..."

Everything went still.

And then his heart did finally burst. Despite his efforts, he was breaking apart. He drew in a sharp breath and opened his eyes. Blinked. God, she was beautiful.

"You're free, Rafe." She smiled and the cell instantly brightened.

She wasn't afraid anymore. Not of him. "Lizzy." His voice shook. He rubbed his hands through his hair. He must be mad, because his mind wasn't working. He didn't know what to say next.

Fortunately he didn't have to think or talk because she kissed him. Hard and fierce at first, like she couldn't get enough of him, then softer, with all her heart and soul. He could have gone on like that forever but through the mist shrouding his head, an insidious thought crept in.

"Lizzy." He pulled away and met her gaze. She didn't dip her head, didn't look away or even blush. "Have you been arrested again?"

"No. Didn't you hear what I said?"

"I heard you say you feel the same about me now as you did at the Rose." He grinned. He couldn't help it. "I remember that night."

She laughed. "It will forever be etched in our memories, I agree. But I also said you are free. The document with Barker's written evidence is gone. It seems the sheriff can't find it."

He paused. "Gone? How is it gone?"

She shrugged and kept smiling. He did not.

"Lizzy, did you..."

Her smile turned impish. "Ask me later."

"Oh, I will." He should be angry with her for putting herself at risk but he couldn't be. Not ever.

Her smile faded and she turned serious. "Rafe, I'm sorry I abandoned you at the Marshalsea."

"You didn't—" She put a finger to his lips. He kissed it.

"I did," she said. "And I regret it deeply. I thought you hadn't changed from that young man I saw many years ago, the day you left London. And I suppose you haven't changed. It's the information that has." She brushed a thumb across his cheek and smiled wistfully at him. "I love you, Rafe Fletcher, and I want to be your wife."

He stared. And stared. He found he couldn't speak—his throat was too tight—so he kissed her instead. Eventually he pulled away and managed to whisper, "I love you too. I always will with every piece of my heart. It belongs to you alone, Elizabeth Croft, so please treat it with care."

She smiled. "I will." She stood and held out her hand to him. "Come. There's much to do. Oh, I almost forgot. Blake informed me just now that the queen's Captain of the Guard wants to see you. Despite your imprisonment, Blake never gave up petitioning the queen. She wouldn't release you, but did advise her captain to employ you if you were ever found not guilty. Her guards have a reputation for ineptitude, you see, and it seems you have a reputation for being formidable. Can't think why, you're much too gentle natured." She sighed theatrically and knocked on the locked door. "But it seems the rumor of your past employment has served you well. Blake assures me he and Lord Hawkesbury didn't need to try very hard to convince her."

The guard opened the door and stepped back to let them past. Rafe and Lizzy walked out of the cell side by side, their arms wrapped around each other's waists.

"It seems my future here is set," Rafe said, smiling down at her. "Shall we go and tell the troupe the good news first, or your parents?"

"My parents and then James, then the troupe."

He stopped. "James," he groaned. Christ, how could he forget his own brother? "He'll be heartbroken."

"Piddle. He won't. He doesn't love me. We've already had that discussion." She looped her arm through his and pulled him toward the stairs. "Let's hurry. I can't wait to see Roger Style's face when we come to collect the reward money."

~ ~ ~

"No," said Roger Style, brandishing a scepter decorated with fake leaves and topped with a lily made from starched linen. "I promised a reward only if the true killer was arrested. It seems that no one has been arrested for Walter Gripp's murder. So I owe no money to no person." He ended his speech with a flourish that caused the wings attached to his sleeve to knock a tankard of ale off the table in the tiring house.

Freddie leapt off his stool and caught it before a single drop spilled. Lizzy had never seen him move so fast.

"Actually, you remember incorrectly," Edward said.

Roger narrowed his gaze. "Is that so, *little* brother?"

"It is, *big* brother. You said the reward will be given to anyone who can name the true killer. A vital difference in my opinion."

"Aye," Henry Wells and Antony agreed.

"And the true killer has been named," Will Shakespeare said from where he stood by the rear door that led directly to the street. "Just this morning it was attributed posthumously to that nasty cur."

"John Barker," Rafe said. He pulled Lizzy tighter into his side and smiled lazily down at her. She melted into him, so happy she thought she might burst.

"What are you doing here, Shakespeare?" Roger growled. "Haven't you got your own company to pester?"

"I do, but I wanted to see Lizzy and give her my best wishes." He came up to her and forked a brow at Rafe. Rafe paused, shrugged, and nodded. Will kissed her on both cheeks and squeezed her hand. "Congratulations, dear lady. You've caught yourself a fine husband." He glanced at Rafe. "I suppose it would be redundant to tell you to take good care of her."

Rafe's laugh rumbled around the tiring house. "I don't need reminding, but thanks anyway."

"If you don't, you'll have all of us to answer to," Freddie said.

"I'm quaking at the thought."

Lizzy let go of his hand and kissed Freddie on the cheek. "Thank you. You're quite sweet when you try."

He blushed, lowered his head, and belched into his chest. Lizzy quickly stepped back to Rafe and relished the strength of the arm he wrapped around her. She smiled up at him. He kissed the tip of her nose.

Roger groaned and stalked off to the stairs. "*You* are the ones who remember incorrectly," he said, taking up the threads of their conversation. "I will not be giving anyone a reward."

"You will," Antony said, one hand on his out-thrust hip above his voluminous velvet skirt. "Or no one performs today. Agreed?"

"Aye," chorused the rest of the troupe.

Roger's jaw worked furiously. "This is outrageous! I am your manager. You cannot threaten me like this."

"We can," Edward said, "and we are."

Roger stared at him. "You too, brother?"

"Aye. And don't forget, I have our sister's ear. I can make your life troublesome if I wish."

Roger wrinkled his nose and sighed. "Very well," he grumbled. "I have some coin upstairs." He trod heavily up the staircase as if every step was an effort to climb.

"Thank you," Lizzy said once he was out of earshot. "All of you. When James's debts are paid off we'll have a feast at the Two Ducks and everyone is invited."

"Our wedding feast," Rafe said.

"In that case, a hearty congratulations to you both," said Freddie and raised the tankard in salute before drinking deeply.

"I must go," Will said. He kissed Lizzy's hand and clapped Rafe on the arm. "See you at the feast."

"Bring Kate," Lizzy said.

He nodded and left through the back door. He passed Lord Oxley coming in.

"There you are!" Lord Oxley cried. "I've been looking everywhere for you, Fletcher. I hear you've had some adventures in my absence."

"Just a few," Rafe said.

"I miss all the fun." He kissed Lizzy's hand and eyed Rafe's arm around her waist. "A lot of fun, it seems. Does this mean this beautiful young lady is off the marriage market?"

"Back off, Hughe," Rafe growled.

Lizzy grinned. Hughe winked at her and bowed. "I will concede this victory to the better man, but I am allowed to regret the loss."

Antony sighed loudly and Lord Oxley glanced at him. He bowed elaborately. "It seems my sorrow will be short-lived. What a fair maid you are. Are you married?"

Freddie snorted into his tankard.

Antony smiled and held out his hand. "Not yet," he said, using his normal voice. It wasn't very deep yet still masculine enough to identify his sex. Antony might like to play games sometimes, but he never outright deceived people.

Lord Oxley paused then kissed the back of his hand. "A situation sure to be remedied when the right…person comes along."

Antony blushed beneath his face paint. Quite a feat since it was very thick and white.

Roger came downstairs carrying a pouch. He grudgingly handed it to Rafe. "I expect this to be spent wisely. Treat your new wife well." He shifted from foot to foot and swallowed heavily. "Or I will, er, be very angry." He *humphed* and shuffled back up the stairs. Everyone stared after him.

"Well," said Edward. "My brother might actually have a heart after all."

"Small and shriveled as it is," Henry said.

Lizzy and Rafe said their farewells and left with Lord Oxley. They had barely gotten to the street when Rafe asked him if his friends were well.

"Of course," Lord Oxley said. He handed over a pouch filled with coin. "Your payment."

"Thank you, my lord," Lizzy said. Between Style's money and Oxley's, they could pay off James's debts *and* pay back her father the money she used to bribe Treece.

Oxley bowed. "My pleasure, dear lady." To Rafe, he said, "So, what now, old friend?"

Rafe glanced down at Lizzy. The tenderness in his eyes made her want to weep for joy. "Now I free my brother, then I wed my beloved. After that I begin working for the queen to train her guards. And then…who knows. Whatever I do, it will be with Lizzy. Forever."

He kissed her, right there in front of his friend and the world, and she didn't care. Rafe was hers. All hers.

DON'T MISS MORE SPARKLING HISTORICAL ROMANCE FROM C. J. ARCHER!

In Shakespearean London, love and romance are just around the corner for the members of Lord Hawkesbury's spirited theatre troupe!

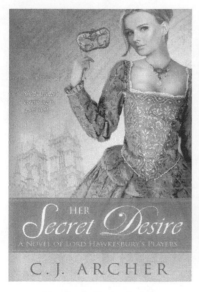

Her Secret Desire features
Min the playwright

Scandal's Mistress stars
Alice the seamstress

Available now on Amazon.com

ACKNOWLEDGMENTS

Heartfelt thanks to my writing friends: Chris Weston, Freya Croft, Keri Arthur, Mel Scott, and Robyn Enlund. Your wise advice, laughter, friendship, and endless supplies of chocolate kept me going when all seemed lost.

ABOUT THE AUTHOR

A native of Australia, C. J. Archer has loved history and books for as long as she can remember. She worked as a librarian and technical writer until she was able to channel her twin loves by writing historical fiction. She has won and placed in numerous romance writing contests, including taking home RWAustralia's Emerald Award in 2008 for the manuscript that would become her novel *Honor Bound*. Under the name Carolyn Scott, she has published contemporary short stories in several women's magazines, including *Take a Break*, *Woman's Day*, and *That's Life*. After spending her early childhood surrounded by the dramatic beauty of outback Queensland, she lives today in suburban Melbourne with her husband and their two children.